Falling Apart

Falling Apart

Jane Lovering

Published 2014 by Choc Lit Limited
Penrose House, Crawley Drive, Camberley, Surrey GU15 2AB, UK
www.choc-lit.com

A CIP catalogue record for this book is available
from the British Library

ISBN 978-1-78189-113-1

Printed and bound by CPI Group (UK) Ltd, Croydon, CR0 4YY

This book is dedicated to the memory of Aslam – he was very much loved and is very much missed.

Acknowledgements

For the people of York, who never complain about the liberties I take with their lovely city, even when I drop vampires on it; my friends at work, the RNA and Choc Lit, who all creak under the effort of keeping me sane; and my children, whose life's work is to drive me the other way ...

And to TMMQ, for the owls.

TOP SECRET – FOR YOUR EYES ONLY

From: Government Department for the Suppression of the Otherworld
To: Members of Parliament (HUMAN ONLY)
Date: 20 July 2012

This document is covered by the Official Secrets Act and should be destroyed after reading.

Gentlemen,

To summarise the situation: there are increasing rumours regarding a possible uprising by those termed Otherworlders, despite the apparent peace in which we currently live. (For the purposes of this document 'Otherworlders' comprise vampires, werewolves, zombies, wights and Shadows, with whom we are forced to share this planet as a result of a magnetic flux fracturing the barrier between our universes.) These rumours are from a reliable source and we fear that this uprising may generate a renewal of the violence that followed the Otherworlders' original incursion into our world, just over a century ago. For those unfamiliar with recent history, please advise this department and we can provide you with the documentation regarding the Troubles, the seventy-year period prior to our Treaty with the Others.

You may have been made aware that we have not been idle in our attempts to ensure the safety of the human race, vis-à-vis a possible vampire uprising. We consider the vampires to be the leaders, and therefore the most dangerous, among the Others, since they wield most power, and offer a degree of control over other species.

After the commencement of the Troubles our department established a small enclave of humans who seemed naturally immune to all vampire magick and glamours. These people were reserved by us and a process of selection was undertaken in order to produce a sub-species of human who could be used, if necessary, to fight and overcome the vampires without risk of their being infected with a vampire demon (communicated through the vampire's bite – for further information please refer to this department). This enclave was somewhat divisive in terms of government approval and was largely disbanded prior to the signing of the Treaty for Peace. The whereabouts of the engineered humans is currently unknown.

It is the opinion of this department that moves should be made to reconvene these individuals, or as many as remain alive. We are aware that it is some thirty-five years since the termination of the genetic experimentation, and many of these persons may have found adjusting to life away from the compound to have been beyond their capabilities.

Sirs, your urgent attention is required on this matter.

Yours,
Deputy Minister for the Department.

Chapter One

Blood. Blood on my hands, dripping onto the carpet, staining my sleeves, staining everything I touch ...

'Jessie?'

I jerked awake at the touch on my shoulder to see Liam, my co-worker, his face upside down in my field of vision.

'What the hell are you doing in my bedroom?' Life began to pull together in front of me, bleary shapes gradually resolving into boxes, weird noises into computer beeps and hums. 'And why does my bedroom smell weird?'

'I can only suggest that's because you collect mould.' Liam moved away and I heard the rattling of mugs being collected. 'But this is the office. Such as it is.'

I sat up slowly. My head had been resting on a sheaf of A4 paper and my left cheek had a seam running down it from the edge of the package. 'Oh, bollocks.' I stretched my arms and yawned. 'How long have I been asleep?'

'Fourteen e-mails, two phone calls and a cup of coffee with doughnuts. I thought the doughnuts might wake you, but you just dribbled a bit in your sleep.'

'I am going to open your next pay packet and do something spectacularly horrible inside it.' I yawned again and scratched at my head.

'Oh, York Council do that already. It's called my pay slip.' Liam went out to the kitchen, fist full of mugs. Working, as we did, in the Otherworld Liaison office of York Council meant lots of contact with the Otherworlders, acting as their PA (which, in my opinion, stood for Professional Apologiser) and tranquillising them for Enforcement to deal with when they got out of line. It also meant a hefty dose of standing on school stages explaining to hyperactive teenagers what being a vampire *really* meant. However, it did not mean earning very much money. They'd have paid us in book tokens if they thought we could read. Endless cups of coffee were our coping mechanism.

'Why so tired?' Liam went on. 'You and Sil having wild, rampant sex all night every night?' He sounded slightly wistful, but then he and his girlfriend had a small baby to keep them up at night rather than anything rampant. 'And please say yes, because anyone who lives with two gorgeous vampires had better not be watching late-night telly and crocheting into the small hours.'

A small burst of pain erupted, as though someone had detonated a bomb just under my navel, but I contained it. Walled it in. 'I don't!'

'Live with gorgeous vampires or watch late-night telly? Because being the girlfriend of the City Vamp and sharing a house with him and his sidekick qualifies you on the first count. Your lack of knowledge of *Dexter* would seem to rule out the second.' More clanking and the sound of kettle-filling. 'And I already know you can't crochet. Or knit, but Sarah says thanks for trying. She's going to use that cardi you knitted for Charlotte to cover the sofa. On account of our baby not being ten feet long and everything.'

'Yeah, well, at least I tried.' I worked my shoulders to try to lose the Quasimodo sensation and fiddled my mouse to wake up my computer. There was an odd feeling somewhere around my middle, as though someone had opened a window in my lower intestine. Not the same as the anxious pain that was pretty much permanently clenching my gut but something different.

'Jessie, what's up? You look weird. And considering I'm comparing you to zombies, werewolves, vampires and wights, that's really weird. Here's your coffee, but if you're going to throw up, don't drink it.' He swept a few papers aside to make room on my desk for my mug, then sat at his own and placed his mug squarely on the coaster which sat amid absolutely nothing at all. 'I am really tired of mopping.' He adjusted the picture of his baby daughter, Charlotte; framed, dust-free and the only thing on his wall-shelf apart from a calendar and a pot of paper clips. 'Love her to bits, truly, but there is one hell of a lot of mopping involved in fatherhood.'

'I ... don't know,' I said, rather faintly. 'I think lack of sleep might be making me hallucinate. And, before you drop the inevitable innuendo, no, it isn't nights of passion that are keeping me awake. I haven't *seen* Sil for ten days.' And here the anxiety came crowding in again, released from the tether that usually kept it away from conscious thought, and accompanied by the image of my lover – slender, with hair darker than a slate quarry at midnight and eyes like a storm at sea. Sensitive, sexy, overhung with guilt about what he was and what he'd done, but living with that pain for the sake of letting himself feel love for me. *Where was he?* 'He said he had something he needed to do, and then he was gone.'

Liam raised his eyebrows. 'What, leaving York to run itself?'

Liam didn't know what Sil had told me in confidence, that Sil's apparent Liam-equivalent co-worker Zan was the one who really ran the city; Sil was the figurehead, the apparent chief, *the target*. 'I think Zan has got it covered,' I said, rather weakly. The image of Sil kept repeating on the back of my eyeballs like cucumber-burps after a large salad. 'Everything seems to be quite calm at the moment; no mental demons trying to raise an army like a few weeks back.'

'So, where's Sil gone? Setting up Gretna Green for the wedding of the decade? He hasn't asked you about your preference in ring design lately, has he?'

I gave him a conversation-killer face. 'Liam, exactly what

were you thinking, bringing me this cup of coffee without so much as a Rich Tea to dunk? You know that we've got a whole new biscuit allowance since I managed to save the world, and if you're trying to siphon it off so that you can renew your *Doctor Who* Fan Club membership then you're going to find yourself at the Job Centre with no reference and a 'cyberman fetishist' label against your name. Good luck getting another job for the council with *that* kind of stigma.'

It worked. Complaining but distracted Liam got up and headed back into the kitchen, leaving me to worry about where Sil had gone. And, more importantly, *why*. Vampires are bad enough when you can keep your eye on them, when they start disappearing, it's time to worry.

Chapter Two

I am vampire. I am top of the food chain, a mover-in-shadow; desired by women, envied by men. I have the grace of a cat, the sight of an eagle and the speed of a greyhound – so why can't I find a bloody biro when I want one?

Sil sighed and rested his elbows on the table. His demon, driven to action by the conflicting emotions scything through his body, scrabbled for attention within him, but he ignored it and rubbed his forehead with a finger, trying to ease the deep ache that he knew wasn't strictly physical.

I am vampire. So why do I feel guilty?

He tried to distract himself by squinting around the tabletop in an attempt to locate the missing ballpoint, closing one eye and then the other and finally running his hands across the surface, riffling the papers that lay there. The girl sitting opposite, eyes fixed on his face with the intensity of a hawk scanning a hedgerow, pushed a pen in his direction. 'Here.'

I shouldn't be here, with this woman whose desire is thrusting from her in waves that make a tsunami look like a slight swell. It is unfair to let her believe that she and I could share more than a smile and a notepad, when I have a heart engaged elsewhere. And not just a heart, my whole body burns with what I feel for Jessica, and cannot wait to close the distance between us, yet here is where I must be. Only here can I find the answers to those questions she carries so silently, with such strength that it weakens me to see it. Answers that may give her the gift she doesn't know she wants.

'Thank you.' He picked up the proffered biro but instead of writing twisted it between his fingers. 'I'm just going to ...

there's something over here I want to look at.' He stood up and the girl's head moved to keep him in the centre of her vision, as though she was afraid he'd vanish if she took her eyes off him.

'I'll be here … if you need me,' she spoke in what was obviously her best 'seductive' voice, and Sil's demon gave an unwanted internal shiver of anticipation which made his fangs lengthen in his mouth and the blood-hunger writhe through his body like snakes dancing in his veins.

He didn't smile at her. She wasn't one of the five per cent of humans who could tell he was vampire, she just thought she'd got lucky with a good-looking man – he knew that much by her flirtatious glances and the way she constantly stroked her hair back off her face. *I wonder why women do that?* He wandered off, further back into the stacks of books. *Makes them look as though they're constantly checking for lice.*

And then he saw it, the book he'd come looking for. Not hidden at all, just jumbled with a bunch of identical others, the only difference being the detailing along the spine – a date. Sil pulled the book free, with a little puff of dust, from its fellows and flipped the pages. *I can't remember what it was to read at human speed.* The thought buzzed into his head. *So many human things I didn't remember, until Jess … She makes me remember, the times before I was this creature of blood and high drama, before the demon that makes me live on the edge so it may feed on the thrills. The time when I was a man, a husband and a father.* A flicker of memory, followed by a flare of pain that he extinguished by depriving it of attention. *Not now. I will not remember now. Only when she is here can I allow those memories that call forth the tears and the regret – the loss of my family, of my humanity. Jess eases the pain simply by being. And for that reason, I am here. Because she deserves payment in the only coin I know how to deal.*

A hesitation, and then a momentary astonishment made him frown. He started to turn, book in hand, to draw the attention of his companion to the peculiarity, but she was too far away, still sitting at the table behind the manifold shelves, hidden from sight by the ranks of dusty books. 'This ...' he began to say, before he heard the dull telltale thump of a gun firing and a sharp pinch of pain in the flesh of his shoulder. A hand came out, preventing him from falling, another caught his other arm. He was moving, semi-conscious, books streaming past him like dreams. And then, nothing.

Chapter Three

Zan lounged in front of his pristine state-of-the-art computer in the middle of his immaculate office. The sight of so much bare floor made me agoraphobic.

'Do come in, Jessica.' He spoke without looking away from the screen. 'But please don't touch anything.'

'There isn't anything *to* touch. It's OCD Central in here.' I went inside, careful not to accidentally knock any piles of books over, even though there weren't any. Liam's and my office was a testimony to the power of faith over filing; I kept most things on the floor. Liam was almost as tidy as Zan, but Zan had staff and cleaners and Liam dragged the weight of my incredible loathing for order and had, on occasion, debated the benefits of being demon-infected just to get to work in a tidy office. 'Don't you ever just ... you know, put something down?'

'Only humans.'

I *thought* Zan had a sense of humour, although it was almost undetectable underneath his obsessions, social-phobia and general old-womanness, but it was often hard to tell when he was employing it and when he was just being nasty. 'Okay.' I wiggled from foot to foot as I waited for him to stop looking at the screen and look at me. 'Anything exciting going on out there?' I saw his reflection freeze for a second, one dark eyebrow rising. Zan was one of the oldest of the vampires, still harbouring a longing for his ages-past world of class structure, impeccable manners and top hats. Despite this, he looked about thirty, with demon-enhanced bone-structure and pale skin counterpointed beautifully by a pair of green eyes and dark hair. Women fell in their droves at his feet, where he stepped over them. We had yet to determine whether Zan actually *had* a sex-drive, and Liam and I quietly speculated that, if he did, it was directed at something a lot more exotic than the vampire-groupies and casual flirts who tested their wiles on him on a daily basis.

'Have you heard from Sil?' Zan answered my question with his own, but he didn't swivel his leather office chair (another source of friction between our council-funded department and the vampires' – we had to make do with nasty plastic that smelled of wee) towards me. His tone was level, but Zan's tone was always level. I thought he probably practised.

'No. That's why I'm here.' I moved a bit closer. 'He's not been in touch and it's not like him. He ... he says he can feel me ... inside him.' I left the obligatory pause that Liam had trained me into after five years of office sharing but, of course, with Zan no innuendo dropped into the gap. 'So he knows when I'm thinking about him. If he ... feels me ...'—another tiny unentendre-filled space, just to make sure—'he usually phones, or texts or something. But this time'—my throat tightened—'he just went.'

Zan finally turned to face me, cross-legged in his chair, like a male model turned Bond villain. 'And you think ...?' He slotted his fingers together and held them under his chin, eyes interrogating me.

But I'm immune to the vamp-glamour. In fact, to blow my own trumpet just a bit, I'm better than the five per-centers who can tell a vampire just by looking at them, I can not only spot them, I can react almost as fast as they can to a situation. It means that I'm really good at my job: when an out-of-area vamp shows on our system I tranq them and send them back. I've also got blood that's pure vampire-heroin, but we keep quiet about that. If York Council find out about it they'll think of a way of using me for something else. And *still* not paying a proper salary. 'I've thought lots of things,

Zan, but now I'd really like some actual answers. So, come on. Where is he?'

Zan spun the chair back around to face the screen. 'Sil is a free agent. With the fiction we uphold of his being the City Vampire in charge of Otherworld York, he is perfectly at liberty to move around without being subject to the permits and paperwork that the Others would normally require.'

'You don't know where he is.' Sudden panic buzzed behind my eyes. 'Even *you*?'

In reflection, his eyes met mine. 'Now, what gives you that idea, Jessica?'

'Because you *love* to know more than I do. If you had so much as a whisper about where he was, this place would be more full of hints than'—I glanced around for a really good metaphor—'than it is of anything else,' I finished, rather feebly.

A shrug. 'He told me he would be away from the office for a few days. That there was some work he wished to do that necessitated his travelling. I have perpetuated this story for the sake of the press and all public agencies; we wouldn't wish to spread the rumour that we cannot keep an eye on our City Vamp, now, would we?'

'Okay, so what's "a few days" in vampire-speak? Is it "I might not be back for breakfast" or "don't expect to see me for six months"?' My voice was a bit high-pitched and the words came out rushed and jerky, like sheep herded by a collie on amphetamines.

'I am ... concerned.' Zan pushed his chair away from the desk and stood with the smooth speed of the vampire. 'Not that he has gone, but because he has been gone for so long without word.' He came towards me, his tall, slender figure crossing the beech laminate flooring silently. It was like being crept up on by an egret. 'And that it may be something to do with you, Jessica.'

'Oh, now, wait, you're not pinning this one on me! Okay, fair enough, things are a bit … well … awkward between me and some other people'—like just about every human who'd found out that my father wasn't really a retired English teacher but a semi-immortal demon—'but Sil and I are good. We're strong together, Zan, we …' No, I really wasn't going to go into detail about our relationship, particularly with someone who regarded sitting on a seat previously occupied by another as being too much physical contact. 'He wouldn't run out on me. He *wouldn't.*'

'I agree.'

'You do?'

'Yes. He could just wait for you to die. And, as ninety per cent of the world seems to have a grudge against you, Jessica, he probably would not have to wait long.'

'Bitch.'

'I beg your pardon?'

'Nothing, just … clearing my throat.'

'What do you wish me to do?'

I hated it when Zan talked to me as though I were an equal. It was downright scary. Here he was, actual vampire in charge of the Otherworld occupants of York, possessor of a demon that gave him enhanced strength, speed, hearing and all the other *Buffy* stuff plus a ridiculously long lifespan, asking me, York Council Human/Otherworld Liaison employee, possessor of millions of pairs of laddered tights and a store card for Gap on which I owed a fortune, for advice. It made me even more resentful of my undersized pay packet than I already was. 'Let's give it another couple of days. He might just have got really absorbed in something.' As long as the 'something' wasn't an acid bath – there was a human faction that opposed the Others and would gladly seize the opportunity to remove one of its more high-profile members. And vampires weren't that hard to kill, a stake or a bullet would do it, as long as you could move faster than a rattlesnake on military-strength drugs. 'Sil can look after himself. And anyway, if anything *had* happened to him, we would have heard about it – I can't believe that if someone took out a vampire as powerful as Sil it wouldn't be splashed all over the *Ten O'Clock News*, can you?'

Zan dipped his head in a slight bow. 'Very well.'

I *really* wished he wouldn't do that whole 'humble servant' thing. I knew that he could tear my throat out in a second if he wanted to. Actually, he probably *did* want to, but the vampires owed their entire success to sublimated urges and artificial blood, and Zan was extremely successful. Only in the wary depths of his eyes could I find any trace of anything other than an obsessively tidy beta-male geek with nice eyes and a *very* understanding dentist.

'Just ... you know, if you hear anything ...'

Zan turned back to his computer. 'You will, of course, be among the first to know.'

Gee, thanks.

'So, where did you get to?'

After Vamp Central our office looked like something out of a Dickens novel. 'I went to see Zan. I know it sounds weird but ... when Sil went, he didn't tell me where he was going or anything, and I thought Zan might have some kind of insight. But since "Zan" and "insight" are words that cancel each other out and leave a kind of verbal white noise ...'

'Nope, not weird at all.' Liam swung around to face me. 'What do you mean Sil's gone and you don't know where?'

Even the words were painful. *Gone*. 'If you think about that question, does it not answer itself?'

'Oh. Yeah, suppose it does, really.' He stood up, scrubbed both hands down his thighs and then patted me on the shoulder. 'But you don't need to worry about Sil, Jess, let's face it. He's a hundred and thirty years old, give or take a candle, and he hasn't got to that age without learning how to handle himself and if you so much as snigger at that last statement then you've had the last sympathy from me you're ever going to get.' Another pat. 'Coffee?'

'Mmmm. But why would he do that? Go off? Okay, I can imagine that he might ...' I swallowed down the personal fear of abandonment and faced the practicalities, 'but not to tell *Zan*? That would be like me emigrating and not telling you ... Oh, no, wait a minute, that's not odd, that's sensible.' I finally let the spiralling doubt move from where it had been hiding low down in my belly and auger its way up to my heart. 'Do *you* think Sil has run out on me?'

Liam stared. 'What, you mean like "it's not you, it's me, no forwarding address" time? Jeez, is *that* what Zan said, that Sil's buggered off? I know vampires sometimes have all the subtlety of an *American Pie* film but ... seriously? I'm supposed to be Sil's friend – wouldn't he do the whole bloke thing, you know, late night calls from bars, turning up to sleep on my sofa and all that? Just to *go*?' Liam rubbed his hands over his face. 'No. No, sorry, Jess, I don't see that at all. He loves you.'

'As much as a vampire can. Come on, Liam, I wrote the pamphlets – they don't really *do* affection. It's like keeping a cat; they love you right up until someone rattles a spoon in a bigger tin, they *have* to, they need the thrills to keep their demons happy.' I was astounded by the calmness of my tone – *what, care, me?* 'Maybe his demon just got the better of him.'

'Jessie ...' Liam reached over as though to touch me, but I reared back. Human contact right now would have cracked my careful facade wide open. 'Is that what you want to believe? Of *Sil*, of all people? That you mean so little to him that he'd just take off?'

'Maybe it's not what I want'—my voice choked down the scale—'but maybe it's what I *have* to believe. He's normally a stickler for keeping at least Zan in the loop. To do this he must have ... Something must have happened and it wouldn't be the first time a vampire has upped and run out on a human ...' I tailed off; then cleared my throat. 'Look, it's nearly six. Let's shut up shop for today. I need some sleep and isn't it Sarah's yoga night? You go home and put Charlotte to bed and I'll see you tomorrow.'

I got up and started getting my things together. Liam didn't move. 'That has to be the longest self-justification sentence I've ever heard,' he said.

'Do you want me to throw something at you?'

'It might help.'

I threw the nearest thing to hand; it was the electric pencil sharpener, which trailed through the air like the world's least aerodynamic weapon ever, hit the side of the bookshelf and took a chunk out of the MDF before crashing to the floor.

Liam didn't even duck. 'Go home, Jess,' he said gently. 'It's going to be all right.'

It was at *that* point I should have realised it really, really wasn't.

Chapter Four

Sil opened his eyes, which made no difference at all to his ability to see, and groped forward in the darkness. His fingers brushed against rock on all sides, beneath his feet was a gritty loose surface and above his head ... He stretched up, waving his arms until a fingertip touched something ... More rock. *What in the seven hells has happened to me? The last thing I remember is ... being with Jess, talking, and then ... I wake up in what feels like a tomb. Please don't let this be a tomb ... that's just so clichéd and embarrassing.* He could see the headlines now: 'York's Vampire Chief in Accidental Dracula Duplication'.

Deep inside him the demon that had made him vampire nearly a century ago danced and dived, feeding on the adrenaline of Sil's rising panic. It quietened for a moment as it felt the drag deep in his solar plexus that told him Jess was thinking of him. His heart ached for a second. *Jess.* The dragging sensation came again, as though he were attached to a tugboat, pulling him to harbour. *She's worried.* He shuffled a half-step forward and banged his head against the sloping rock ceiling. *And I'm beginning to feel a trifle perturbed myself. Where am I? How did I get here? And why?*

A faint tickle of hunger caught his throat. *So I've been here long enough to need some blood.* He lowered his head, as though gravity would assist the memory process, his hair dropping to tickle at his cheeks; the swipe which cleared it from his face caused him to scrape his knuckles against the rock and swear into the darkness. 'Bugger!'

His voice echoed more than he would have thought it could in such a confined space. The sound of it made him feel, paradoxically, lonely. A quick shake of his head prevented the longing getting out of control. *Come now, Sil, think. You were ... where?* A vague not-even-memory of ... books? Some kind of paper? Another headshake. Then, nothing. Not even a memory of darkness descending; his body bore no pains that might have indicated battle had been joined. Although that really didn't mean much – if he'd been down here for more than a day any physical hurts would have healed, courtesy of his demon.

But you still have the memories of the time before, said a little voice in the back of his mind, that little conscience-devil that competed with his demon in fights that made the Troubles look like Rocky Balboa versus a small kitten. *The memories of your wife, your children. The loss of all that you knew, the stealing away of your humanity as you gave life to the demon inside. The things that you did to stay alive; power over humans exercised to the maximum, death dealt, pain apportioned. Is all this something to do with those memories? Has keeping the thoughts of pain and loss so suppressed somehow damaged my short-term memory? Is this some kind of vampiric Alzheimer's?*

Sil took a deep breath and deliberately scraped the knuckles of his other hand down the wall. The instant flood of pain and anger pushed the guilt and memory back where it belonged, tucked somewhere in the space between love and rage, and blanketed by the knowledge that this was how it must always be. Letting everything out meant letting out the hate, the fury at what he had become, at what he had lost. It meant that any emotion, even his love for Jessica, must be handled carefully, managed in small parcels to prevent anger detonating from the fuse which burned deep within.

Maybe that is why I am here, he thought. *Maybe this is some kind of vampire isolation tank, somewhere to think without distraction, to face what is happening to my life. The knowledge that I have fallen in love; that I must let myself feel love without giving power to the other emotions. And it is a very different love to that I knew with my wife, all those years ago – a love that winds through me, is a part of every strand of my being. This exclusion is exactly the sort of thing that Zan would come up with, for my own good. He's probably up there now, watching the clock until he judges that I've come to my senses.*

His stomach growled at him. *I do hope he's realised that it is very hard to look into one's soul without sustenance.*

Chapter Five

I headed out of the office and along by the river and wondered if I was looking for trouble. Right now I needed distraction, anything to stop this awful, evil daisy-petal cycle of 'he loves me, he wants me dead'. Something that would halt my relentless analysis of every second we'd spent together, dissecting it for any trace of resentment or restlessness.

I could see a knot of people clustering around a bench on the embankment. At first I thought they were just the normal crowd of evening sightseers, hell-bent on eating their own weight in ice cream and waiting for the pubs to get going, but these seemed to be different. They were all men for a start, and I might not know a lot about men but one of the things I *do* know is that when they form a tight group like this, something's going on in the middle. One or two of their faces were familiar, and I was pretty sure they were Britain for Humans' supporters, or some free-agents in the market for a loud fight and beer afterwards.

A little further down the river, on a bench, I saw a zombie filling his arms with the mixture of Araldite and bath sealant that a lot of them used to keep up and, if not running, then certainly lurching quite quickly. When I looked back at the group of men I realised what was going on.

I strolled down towards the bench, my stomach settling at the prospect of movement, of action. 'Hello.'

'Er, hi.' The zombie was young. He must have been good-looking once; his face bore a trace of chiselled bone structure and his eyes were still good, but he had the over-taut skin and general gloss of the PVA wash that they all used, like a cheap Californian facelift. 'Jess, right?'

I riffled my memory banks. 'And you're Ryan, yes?'

‘I’m just patching-up, that’s okay, isn’t it? Only I’m a bit …’ Almost apologetically he held out an arm and I saw the bagging skin. ‘You know.’

‘No, *you’re* fine. I’m just a bit worried about those guys over there.’ I nodded towards the men gathered around the railings, shouting to one another and raising fists. ‘They look like they’re spoiling for a fight. Might be a good idea if you get out of here fast.’

‘Er, yeah, sure. I can still do fast.’ He stood up, with a creaking sound I pretended not to have heard. ‘I’ve just got this face looking right – I don’t want to have it rearranged any more than nature is going to anyway.’

Ryan began to move away in a kind of rolling lope and I watched him carefully, refusing to turn around even when I heard the catcalls and whistles, then the single set of running footsteps that was some chancer setting out after him. As the runner drew level with me, I turned suddenly and grabbed hold of his shirt; his forward momentum wheeled him around me with his eyes bulging and his top button straining like an undersized gusset during ballet practice.

‘What the fu—’

‘Ah, now I’m glad you asked me that.’ I bunched his shirt under my hands, trapping him inside his designer label. He couldn’t whip around and punch me without garrotting himself with his hand-stitching. ‘What is it with you and the zombies?’

‘They’re just dead guys, yeah?’ came the slightly breathless answer. ‘Taking our jobs and our women.’

‘Yeah!’ A Greek chorus of approval, albeit at a distance they apparently considered safe, waved their arms. ‘Should have the decency to stay dead, right?’

I sighed and released my hold, giving him a small shove as I did so. ‘Look, you lot. The only jobs the zombies take are the ones where the main qualification is Already Being

Dead, and I think most girls would rather go out even with you lot than with people who are largely held together with Araldite.' I eyed the unprepossessing faces in front of me. 'Probably. So leave the zombies alone, all right?'

A rising tide of muttering made my palms sweat for a moment, but the collective brain obviously decided that discretion was the better part of not getting thumped and arrested by a girl, and the group started a kind of trickling retreat back along the embankment.

I waited for them to disappear behind the bridge, sighed again, and carried on walking. After a couple of minutes I found myself outside the flat I'd shared with Rachel until a couple of months ago. I'd walked that way without considering that this wasn't home any more. No, home was now the house that Sil and Zan shared in central York: three storeys of Georgian brickwork, decor that looked as though a French palace had collided with IKEA and the kind of sterile atmosphere you get when one member of the household sits around waiting for dust with a rolled-up newspaper and a can of Pledge.

But it was also the place where Sil and I could be together. Zan might lurk like a disapproving mother-in-law, but at least he didn't interrupt our quiet moments with trial-runs from the Vegan Cook Book and Holby City plot lines. Plus, Rachel and I were still a bit fragile in the friendship department. I'd had to pretend to kill her to lure the demon Malfaire into trusting me and, for a while, she'd behaved as if I really *had* killed her – only with more 'sending to Coventry' than your average corpse could manage. We'd resumed a tentative text-based conversation, but it still didn't feel as though I could turn up on the doorstep with my washbag and a year's supply of unhealthy foodstuffs, even if I'd wanted to.

Loneliness jabbed me in the heart and I threw a stone rather viciously into the water. Okay, I wasn't about to shriek and rend my garments – I wasn't paid enough to rend anything, could barely even afford to ladder my tights – but even so, I considered that I was entitled to a small moment of self-pity. For a second I imagined Sil standing beside me, not touching me but close enough that I could feel his soft coat brush the skin on my arms, smell that dark, bottom-of-a-wooden-chocolate-box scent that came from him, see the absolute blackness of his hair blowing in the breeze. I squeezed my eyes shut, felt that emptiness inside as though my soul had been removed with a blunt instrument. Tried to conjure him through imagination. *Sil, what happened? To you, to us … You said I was enough for you, that what you felt for me was enough to keep your demon happy, that feeling for me was worth letting all the bad feelings through – was it all a lie? Were you just biding your time, using me, until one day you just woke up and decided it wasn't enough any more?*

Another stone bounced savagely off a small boat and I felt the longing like a second skin drawn tight around my own. When someone tapped me on the shoulder it was a wonder I didn't turn around and bite them.

'Hello.' It was Harry; lovely, square-jawed Harry, the most *human* human it was possible to be without having it printed on a T-shirt. He was an Enforcement Officer, and he and his co-worker Eleanor had been part of the horror that night I'd had to kill the demon. 'If you're trying to sink one, I recommend dynamite.' He nodded towards the boats. 'Less accuracy required.' He watched as, determined not to be told what to do by someone who worked for the opposition, I flicked another set of pebbles riverwards. 'How are you, Jess?'

How do you think I am? 'Still walking, talking and keeping Liam off the streets. How about you?'

He rolled his shoulders. 'Ellie and I are back at work now,

after … well, they made us take some personal leave.' He blew a breath. 'It was a bit crazy, wasn't it? Did you get counselling, or …'

'I work for the council: I didn't even get "there there" and a pat. Well, tell a lie, Liam bought me a pound of toffee bonbons and in our office that's pretty much the same as three calls to the Samaritans and six months' therapy.'

There was a bit of an awkward silence. Harry and I were friendly, but work-friendly rather than hanging-out-friendly. In the end Harry, with a remarkable lack of male evasion, said, 'What happened with you and that demon – we, I mean Ellie and I, we didn't say anything, Jess. That was all pretty bad, and you pulled us out, you saved all of us that night. Pretty much the whole world too, from what I can figure. So. Yeah. Lips sealed and all that.'

'About what?' I frowned. I hadn't done anything *technically* illegal, apart from killing Malfaire, the demon who'd declared that I was his daughter, which was obviously not strictly a good thing, but he wanted to take over the world so I reckoned I'd be cut some criminal slack on that one.

'About …' Harry lowered his voice and looked around dramatically. He was in uniform, which gave the effect that we were passing official secrets. 'About *Malfaire being your father.* Ellie and I talked about it, well, we haven't stopped talking about it really, but we … well, I know you and she don't really get on.'

'Only because she shot Cameron.' I clenched my teeth and tried not to think about the loss of my friend to a misunderstanding and a hail of silver bullets.

'The court declared it accidental,' Harry said, slightly heavily. 'But even so, we know that there could be *implications* and everything so … like I said, lips sealed.'

Okay, Jess, time for a deep breath and to pull your big-girl panties up. So, your vampire boyfriend has buggered off, well, tough boots, sweetie, you've still got a job to do. 'Thank you, Harry. And pass on my thanks to Eleanor too, although if you can wrap them in explosives I'd appreciate it.'

We stood and looked around. Apart from a hen party being raucous on the opposite bank, there were no conspicuous signs of bad behaviour. The group of men had dispersed as completely as a fart in a breeze and the summer sunshine was doing a good job of making everything look newly scrubbed and innocent.

'Well.' Harry swiped his hands along the sides of his jacket as though his palms were sweating. 'I suppose I ought to ...'

'Have you got time for a drink?' I surprised myself with my desire not to go back to an evening in an over-furnished room with no company but terrible television and a vampire who relaxed by reading Greek texts and tutting. I wanted distraction, I wanted company.

'Sorry, Jess, on duty.' He held out his hands. 'Was on my way back to HQ when I saw you walking down here.' He raised his head and looked out, over the river, down towards the bridge, two spans of butter-coloured stone. 'I just wanted to make sure you were all right. How's Sil, by the way? Not seen him out and about lately.'

'He's ... busy. You know. Busy. We're both ... busy.' *Just don't ask what he's busy doing. I've been imagining since he went ...* 'Busy,' I said again, in a conversation-killing way.

'Great. Well. I'll see you around then.' With a nod he shoved both hands into his pockets and set off up the cobbled wharf back towards the middle of town.

Steeling myself for an evening spent listening to Zan cataloguing Greek pronouns by size and complaining about how much better they'd been 'in the Old Days', I headed home.

Chapter Six

Sil raged, almost beyond conscious thought now. The hunger was all. All he could feel, all he could see, all he could smell in this tight space, not enough room to stretch, to let his demon uncoil and move within him, the two beings pressed together, even for creatures that occupied the same body this level of confinement was unnatural. *Blood.* The imagined taste made his demon jerk uncomfortably in his chest. *We must have ... blood.* The hunger had become a third creature here in the darkness, a predator that circled and wouldn't let him sit or stand without showing its teeth. It gnawed and bit and sliced into his belly, raked through the air with wings like knives.

He groaned and wrapped arms around his stomach, trying to comfort it out of the feeling he was trying to digest himself. His demon flicked and twisted inside him, torn between the protection his body afforded and the knowledge that, alone, it could possibly escape. *No chance. I've investigated every inch of this place: there's not so much as a crack. Wherever we are, we are trapped. Trapped and starving.*

A brief shot of adrenaline and a sudden sharp tug along the invisible wire that connected him to Jessica relaxed him just a fraction. He shook his head and allowed the briefest of smiles – Jessica was the least of his worries right now. Her ability to look after herself so outweighed his that it was laughable. *Vampire. Top of the food chain. Strong, fleet. Staggeringly good-looking. And here I am, starving to death in a dark hole, while Jess is probably wrestling a werewolf to the ground and reading it the riot act. Messy hair and mismatched clothes ...* Another burst of emotion, but this time it came from the region of his heart. *She's random and uncalculating and completely chaotic and she can cope with anything. Can she cope with me?*

Forgetting the hunger, the impatience of his demon, the nature of his current state, he unwrapped his arms from his stomach and stretched them as wide as he could, as though to encompass her distant frame. Throwing his head back, he opened his eyes into the darkness and let out a scream of rage, of utter impotent fury. At his inability to be with her. At wanting her at all. *Didn't I know this would happen? That loving means trapping yourself in thrall to someone else's whims and fancies? She could destroy me with a simple look, a word … and I gave her that power …*

His cries echoed on, into the dark.

'Better get out there, Jess.' Liam looked up from his screen. 'Might be nothing, but there's a werewolf showing out of area, down near the train station. No permit, so …'

I didn't bother to look. 'It'll just be a mistake. No werewolf is going to do anything stupid in broad daylight on a Wednesday afternoon; he knows he'll get tranqued and end up missing *Silent Witness*.'

'Or she, you sexist pig.'

I sighed and rolled the gun between my fingers. 'If you're going to be like that about it …'

'I wasn't being like anything!'

'I'm going! Look, this is me, going.'

Liam swivelled the chair, making a grinding noise. 'Look, Jessie, I'm sure Sil is going to turn up safe and sound and we'll find out he's been doing something innocently somewhere and just lost track of the time. Zan … well, you know what Zan is like – he worries. About everything. I'm sure he double-checks the blood type on the Synth bottles just so he doesn't get any nasty surprises. You get out there, sort things out, and I'll see you back here in time for the *Jeremy Kyle* omnibus, okay?'

I gave him a grin, pocketed the gun and headed out, where the sunshine hit my senses like a dash of sherbet and I stood for a second, feeling an ache somewhere in my soul. *Sil is somewhere out there. Somewhere, standing under this same sun, watching this day carry on around him. Without me.* There was a chafe of tears at the base of my throat, a lump of words that I couldn't say to anyone.

My phone rang. I ignored it. It would only be Liam asking me to pick up some more milk on my way back or something. *Focus. This is what you do, Jess; this is who you are. Okay, you're upset, I get that. But, seriously? What did you expect?* Out of the office, turn left, over the bridge and towards the station. *You wanted to think of the vampire as yours – the key word there is* vampire. *Loyalty, trust, fidelity ... all concepts a demon wipes away, along with concern for anyone else. Their moral compasses spin like a* Dancing on Ice *contestant trying to master the pirouette. Your job is yours and no-one can take that away.*

The werewolf was sitting on the wall. I mentally stuck my tongue out at Liam – he was just watching the world go by. I even recognised him; he was the guy I'd danced with when Sil and I had ended up at one of the vampire clubs a while back. 'Hey, Tobe.'

A sudden jerk of his head; then a lazy smile. 'Oh, hi. How're you doing?'

I pushed the gun back into my pocket. 'I'm good but you're out of area, mate.' The phone rang again and I stabbed at it until it stopped. 'Just doing my job, you understand that.'

His smile died slowly. 'Bugger. I'm meeting my girlfriend from the train; thought the paperwork was all dealt with. There must have been some kind of hold-up or something. Can't you cut me some slack here, Jess? It's only another couple of minutes 'til the train gets in. And I did promise.'

I sat down next to him. 'I can wait with you, I guess. Keep an eye until you go back over the river.'

'Cheers.'

We sat and watched the crowds walking through the streets. 'Saw your picture in the paper this morning,' Tobe said eventually, eyes and meaning hidden behind dark glasses.

I snorted a mirthless laugh. 'Tell me about it. Ever since I started seeing Sil I've become some kind of D-list celebrity. And they don't even have the decency to use a good photo. Honestly, if anyone finds reading about me going about my daily business *that* fascinating, then I fear for the future of the human race.'

Tobe patted my hand. 'Jealousy,' he said. 'Reckon there isn't a woman in that newsroom who wouldn't jump into your shoes in a heartbeat, and probably plenty of guys too. They're just stirring.' The phone started ringing again. At least I'd managed to program it back from Liam's 'witty' attempts to get it to say something about my personality. 'Maybe you should get it,' Tobe said. 'Might be important, they seem pretty persistent.'

I pulled the phone out. 'No, it'll be Liam. Probably wants me to pop to Smiths for him again.' I glanced down at the screen. 'It's my sister.' My heart did a weird jumping thing. Abbie was ringing me? What could she have to say that couldn't be said face-to-face? But she'd stayed away since that awful night when I'd killed the demon. It had driven a wedge between us, when she'd seen me – maybe for the first time – as something more than a little sister. Something *other*.

I punched the button to answer. 'Abbie?' We'd not even spoken much since then. I suppose finding out that your sister is really the child of a demon and a girl from the streets will rather put a crimp in family get-togethers 'What's up?' And then, because we'd been brought up as sisters, despite the fourteen-year age gap, and I *still* held her telling Mum that I'd been seen at a party I wasn't supposed to have gone to against her, I said, 'I thought you weren't speaking to me ever again?'

A breathy pause. 'It's Dad. He's in the hospital. Heart attack, they think, but they're doing tests.'

My mouth dried and the phone slipped between my fingers. 'What? *When* ... I mean ... he ... is he ...?' It felt as though my heart had stopped in sympathy and my blood settled in my ears, muffling the sounds of life around me.

'We're in the hospital. They're doing an ECG ...' Her voice broke and there was a crackle of background noise for a second; then she came back, still tired but stronger. 'You need to come, Jess.'

'I'm coming now.' I disconnected and turned to Tobe, who was watching me over the top of his glasses. 'Look, you. Don't do anything, all right? Meet your girlfriend and then get back to Strensall, understand?'

'More trouble, girl?'

'Yes.' Although the air was warm, my skin pricked with the shock chill and it was an effort to get my legs to move. Abbie was a nurse – if she thought the situation warranted summoning me, then things must be pretty bad. *He needs me.* I forced myself to action, drove my weight forward until I almost fell and then took off. Running through the streets, people jumping out of my way as I went. A lot would recognise me as Liaison, probably thought I was rushing to a call-out; those who didn't move in time I shoulder-barged, no politeness now, just a single focus, like a laser cutting through the crowds – I had to get to the hospital. To my father, the man who'd brought me up as his child. The man who'd read to me at night, stroked my forehead when I was ill, taught me the difference between 'who' and 'whom' and the correct definition of 'decimate'. The man who'd scolded me when I was late back from dates and outings – I'd just thought he was being petty and mean, but now I understood he'd been terrified. He and Mum must have lived on a knife edge for my entire thirty-one years and yet they'd brought me up as just a normal girl with a big sister. Things had been a little awkward between us since my real parentage came out: none of us really knew quite what to say to one another. I'd wanted to tell them that I understood but … I didn't know how. And I'd made myself distant, retreated into life with Sil rather than face The Conversation. But he was still Dad, just waiting for me to come to terms with the way my life had changed. Come to terms, get over myself, and get back to being the slightly wayward younger daughter that I'd always been to them.

I skidded around the corner at the traffic lights, headed down Lord Mayor's walk, battering tourists out of my way as I went, knocking one man's camera from his hands but not even slowing down to apologise. Two vampires neatly sidestepped as I came through, and, even focused as I was, I saw a raised eyebrow and a mirthless half-smile but I didn't waste time slowing down to eyeball them. I put my head down and powered the final mile, arriving in the reception area panting, sweaty and red-faced.

Luckily the hospital wasn't huge. The magnetic flux that brought the Otherworlders into this dimension also brought advances in science and medicine, so there was no longer the pre-Troubles need for vast spaces dedicated to the treatment of illness. The Cardiac Unit was tucked at the back behind reception.

My mother was sitting on a plastic chair in the corridor. She'd always been small and delicately boned, which should, of course, have given me the heads-up that I couldn't possibly have been her natural daughter, but now she looked tiny, as though the heat of worry had shrunk her down. 'Jessica! You came!'

'Of course I did! Where's Abbie?'

'She had to go on duty.' A quick hug. 'Come on in and see your father.'

He lay attached to a machine, looking rather better than my mother did. We hugged, a long hug, despite the tubes and drips and constant bleeps, and I nearly cried again. 'So. How's work?' he asked eventually, and his voice was a bit thin, lacking some of the volume built up over years of shouting at students and then more years telling sheep to 'give over, you buggers.'

'Um. It's fine. Work, you know. A bit of bother with zombies – looks like the "tough guys" have decided to move on from baiting vampires to a target that doesn't come after them teeth-first.' From my father's expression it seemed that he wanted this normality, just a father and daughter chatting, rather than questions about his health. 'I really should warn them that when zombies throw their hands in the air it's not metaphorical. And it looks as though Liam has decided to cut my biscuit ration.'

A sudden hand groped up over the hospital blanket and caught mine. 'Take care, Jessie.' His words were whispered, and not, I thought, because he was feeling poorly. His eyes raked the room and settled on my mother's back as she fumbled in her handbag for something. He gave a strained, upward nod, as though he was trying to tell me something without attracting her attention. 'Please.'

As opposed to what? I wanted to ask. *Running around yelling 'bite me, bite me'?* But given the grey tint to his skin and the clammy feel of his hand, this didn't seem the moment, so I just nodded.

'And how are you getting on with Sil?' My mother fished some knitting out of a bag and began, rather inexpertly, to jab needles at wool. She wasn't a natural knitter, but the frustrated grandmother in her came out to play sometimes.

'I suppose you're working for them now, are you? I hope the pay is better than you were getting from Liaison. Well, it must be, I can't see those vampires going around in off-the-peg suits and amateur haircuts.'

'Not exactly working *for* them, more ... not actively against. And Sil and I are ...' I looked down at Dad again; he looked even more shrunken than Mum did. Nope – now was not the time. 'How are you feeling? I'm sorry, if I'd thought I'd have brought some magazines ... or ... something.'

'Your mother doesn't like me reading magazines. Says they give me "ideas".' My father stopped speaking and gasped quickly a couple of times. The rims of his lips were blueish and a machine made an alarming stuttering sound.

'Now, Brian, let the medication do its work.' My mother dropped her needles and began fussing with his bedcover, straightening the sheets and fiddling with the height adjuster. 'And you know perfectly well I don't mean *those* sorts of ideas.' She spoke over her shoulder. 'He tried to build a chicken shed from a magazine once. Put his back out for weeks.'

'Don't talk for me, Jen.' There was a wonderful note of annoyance in Dad's voice. 'I've had a heart attack, not a lobotomy.'

'I know, Brian, I'm only saying ... He had some kind of fit, you know, Jess.'

My father looked between my mother and me, and I couldn't read his expression. 'It wasn't a fit. It was a heart attack.'

'He was thrashing about on the floor when I found him. Looked like a fit to me.'

'Come back tomorrow, love. The doctors say they'll know more by then, and I might be a bit more capable of holding a conversation without your mother interfering. Fit! Next you'll be telling everyone I had chickenpox as well.'

'I am *not* interfering! And it was definitely a fit.'

I gave them both a quick kiss and left them to their bickering. My clothes, clammy with sweat after my run, were sticking to my back and a huge boulder of worry was pulling my heart and stomach together as though my internal organs were made of rubber. Halfway back to the office I realised that none of this was going to be fixable with the packet of Baby Wipes I kept in my drawer, and phoned in. 'Liam, I'm going to pop home for a shower and to change. I'll be back in the office in an hour, okay?'

'Wow. Werewolf put up a fight? I'm picturing you dripping with entrails.'

'No. It was just Tobe, I had to ... there was something else I had to do. I'll tell you later, okay?'

'It's nearly six, I was going to switch the Tracker over for HQ to ignore and then go home. It's Sarah's French conversation night and I get to read Charlotte a bedtime story; we're half way through *Unseen Academicals*.'

'You're reading Terry Pratchett to her? She's six months old!'

'Yeah? So? She won't understand *Goodnight Little Bear* either; one of us might as well enjoy the story. See you tomorrow.' Liam hung up, leaving me with that lingering loneliness I often felt when the office closed.

Great. Another sleepless night reading the classics and listening to Zan stalking the hallways.

Chapter Seven

I slept, but my dreams were disturbing. In one, I lay in the huge four-poster that Zan had allocated to me when I'd moved into Vamp Central for safety reasons. Sil was standing near the window, a silhouette, while I reclined naked, my skin tingling with the expectation of his touch.

'Where have you been?' I stretched out to try to touch him, but then realised I was tied, hand and foot, to the bed frame. 'I was worried.'

'Oh, there's no need to worry about me.' Sil's voice was low, sounded a long way off. 'You never need to worry about me, Jessica. I can look after myself.'

I looked down at my body, spread-eagled over the covers, hands restrained above my head and my feet tied, one to each post. The pleasant tingle of anticipation was turning to a sweat of fear. 'Are you coming to bed?'

Sil moved from the window, crossed the room at vampire-speed until he stood by the door. He was wearing his gorgeous black Armani suit; his hair was loose and his wonderful cheekbones were lightly highlighted by dark stubble. His eyes were black too, the full dark they went when he was glamouring someone, putting them under. 'No.'

I wriggled, feeling the pull and tug of the ropes that bound me. 'So why did you tie me up?' I'd felt relieved at his presence, but now my heart was cantering. 'Sil?' Trying to reach out, to touch his cool skin, to make contact with him … hold him.

'Because I'm going to kill you.' As he leaned in, I could see the fangs sliding down, locking into place, his face drawing up into the cold, tight-focused expression of a vampire not biting for fun, not for the high his demon would get, not for the carefully controlled blood feed from a willing donor, but for a death-strike that would tear out my throat.

I screamed, but the sound was muffled, a poor little thing in my throat. I managed to twist my head to one side and closed my eyes, waiting for a sensation like a punch in the veins; then the dream let me go and I sat up, sweating.

'Sil!' I let his name out into the darkness, an involuntary cry of longing and pain and anger, directed towards the space where he wasn't. I could almost feel him, as though his body was only just out of reach – if I stretched my fingers far enough I'd be able to brush them along those edgy cheekbones, down to his lips.

There was a commotion at the door, possibly the briefest of taps and Zan came in. 'Jessica? I heard you shout ... I thought ...' He whipped his head back and forth, taking in the whole room. 'Is he here?'

I was still caught between sleep and reality, the dregs of the dream falling from me and leaving me with a sense of loss that made my stomach ache. 'No. Just ... dreaming.' I clutched the duvet to my chest and blinked hard. Having any kind of conversation with Zan required full use of the faculties; I needed to be awake and alert, not sliding around in a liminal half-state. 'Just a dream,' I repeated. But Zan was still there, lurking in the middle of the room and, evidently, trying to stare behind the curtains. 'It's all right; I'm awake now. Sorry I disturbed you.'

The vampire turned slowly to face me. A small amount of light seeped in through the curtains, not enough for me to see his expression, only the outline of his face, the set of his shoulders and the way his hands were cupped together at groin level. Zan looked like a carved stone angel, if angels wore Versace and had the kind of supercilious attitude that automatically made most people feel inferior. 'I also apologise.' He gave me a bow that a nineteenth-century

Russian would have been proud of. 'I was ... startled by your calling out.'

'No, it's fine.' I waited for him to leave the room. When he didn't, I hugged the duvet a little closer to me. While I neither flattered myself that Zan had any feelings for me other than the mild contempt he held for all humans, nor feared that he would suddenly attack me, there was something about his behaviour that was making me uneasy.

'Jessica.' He stopped speaking and shuffled his hands. 'You and Sil, you have a ... connection, yes?'

'Well, he says so. I can't feel anything.'

'Nevertheless. You dreamed he was in trouble?'

'I dreamed he was going to kill me, actually.' Tattered remnants of the dream flickered in my mind, like small flags of memory. 'He ...' I rubbed at my forehead to try to eradicate those last traces. 'It was scary.'

'Then this may be very bad. I fear your connection has somehow created a link to his current emotional state.'

'You seem to think he's gone somewhere to ... do vampire things.'

Zan inclined his head. 'It is a logical assumption. He would not confess such to me; he knows my opinion of such practices.' He managed to get such a degree of disgust into his tone that I almost had sympathy for Sil wanting to indulge himself. 'He would not want you to know because he would not wish to hurt you. I have no idea why, since you seem to lack emotional sensibilities of any kind, but that is beside the point.'

I almost retorted at this point, but bit down the words. If Zan really wanted to think of me as unemotional, then that was probably for the best.

'I can only hope that he has not let his desires get too much the better of him,' Zan went on. 'If, as your dream would suggest, he is killing, then we must hope he has had the sense to keep the expression of his desires to the lower classes. These "clean-up campaigns", as they are so regrettably called, can be so demanding of one's time and energies.'

'You really are horrible, aren't you?' I muttered.

Zan turned away from me and moved towards the door. 'I am vampire, Jessica,' he said. 'And you …' He sighed. 'We must work to maintain the fiction of your being purely human.'

Liam and Harry's faces floated around in the back of my mind. Seven people know I'm not completely human. Nine, if you count my parents – the nine people I am closest to in all the world. Well, not Eleanor from Enforcement, obviously. I wouldn't be close to her if you stuffed both of us into a bucket. 'What do you mean?'

Zan sighed again. 'Don't be obtuse, Jessica. We have had this conversation before.' He put his hand on the doorknob and turned it.

'Can we, just for a second and for the sake of argument, pretend that I've forgotten?'

'Fine.' He let his hand drop and turned around. Now the streetlight positively glistened on his alabaster skin. There were no imperfections, not even a trace of stubble marking his perfect face – he looked a bit like Prince Caspian, if Prince Caspian had hated dirt and had a series of obsessional behaviours. 'Then let me clarify matters for you, *for the sake of argument*.' He did that slow, stalky stride thing that made him look like he had heron in his ancestry. 'Jessica. Other factions, by which I mean the weres, wights, ghouls, Shadows and others, may decide to stage an uprising to attempt to overthrow vampire control. If this is achieved, and vampires are no longer able to keep Otherworlders in check, then anarchy may break out as various groups struggle for control. Now, taking this as a posit, and further speculating on the desire of those who know of your ancestry to bargain for the safety of themselves and their families, we may extrapolate a future where *you*, as the surviving offspring of an incredibly powerful and semi-immortal demon, may become a figurehead and rallying point for those who wish to overthrow humans altogether.' He sighed again. '*Now* do you understand?'

All trace of sleep had fled. 'You mean they might want me to lead some kind of fight? Against you lot ... I mean, against the vampires? But I work for the *council*!' I wailed. 'You can't be a figurehead if you work for the council! Dickhead, yes; figurehead, no.' I wriggled right up the bed, chastity-duvet still clutched tight. 'I file, for God's sake! I have a screensaver picture of kittens and I believe chocolate to be a major food group. Those are *not* the marks of a figurehead.'

Zan cocked an eyebrow. 'I believe the City Vampire in charge of Edinburgh has an elderly spaniel called Batzo. This neither makes him less vampire nor less dangerous if challenged.' He opened the door and stood for a moment, haloed by the dim light from the passageway. 'Sleep well, Jessica.'

He closed the door just in time to avoid being hit by the shoe I flung in his direction.

I lay back against the pillows, all thoughts of sleep replaced with a weapons-grade sense of horror.

Chapter Eight

Anger. Pain and anger, both so deep and so intense that I hardly know where they begin and I end. This should not be. This should not be.

Sil was aware of little now, other than the black, rising up from behind his eyes and into his brain. He knew that there was a woman, out there, a woman who lived in his soul, a woman whose existence meant everything, who was waiting for him to … to … But he knew this with the part of his brain that didn't think, because that part was only aware of the huge, beating pulse of the world outside this prison. The air pressure in his ears throbbed with it; his demon slavered and twisted for it, like a dog on a chain. His whole body ached with the knowledge of its presence. *Out there. Out where there is sun and wind, there is heat that walks and talks, sweet and juicy and just waiting to be burst like an overripe fruit.* But his mouth didn't water now at the thought of blood, it ached with the need to bite and tear and feed.

His screams were no longer frustration at being kept away from his love. Now they were animal, the hoarse-throated shrieks of a dangerous beast kept penned. His connection to Jess was a dull tension in the very core of him but it was feeble in comparison to the sheer agony of the blood-hunger, an easily disregarded thing that only served to emphasise his isolation.

Feed. Me.

His demon rattled around like a penny in a box; there was little of him left now. Just the shell. The shell and the ache, and the terrible, wicked thoughts that had taken the place of feelings; thoughts of the blood that whispered through so many veins, so easy to liberate, so hard to stop flowing …

Voices. Sil held what little breath he still had and strained his ears. Before the demon he'd always had trouble hearing anything that hadn't had his name in it somewhere – it was one of the things his wife had complained about all those years ago, his inability to actually *listen* to anything she said. But now. *Listen ...*

Beneath the paddle of madness that was beating his brain, he could make out words. Distant fuzzy words, but sounds that meant he was not alone. The world hadn't ended and left him trapped in rock. His demon stilled, alert now, and he could hear broken conversation filtering through with the air.

'... puzzle ... what to do.'

'But he ... saw nothing.'

'Nothing to see ... all dealt with years ago. However, he cannot be allowed ... or questions may be asked ... *must not* be raised. But if ... kill ... even a disappearance ... investigated.'

A sigh, strangely portentous through the rock. 'Then ... let them kill him ... Simple, clean ... no longer our problem.'

The first voice came again, slightly slower, as though the speaker was thinking as he spoke. 'There's still ... what he was doing ... How he knew where ... what to look for. What is going on in York?'

Another sigh. 'Are we paid ... I don't believe so. *This* ... under our purview ... time to deal ...'

And now, Sil was sure, there was light. The very faintest, merest tickle of light, like a hallucination but growing. His demon surged, alert to something beyond the light, giving him the strength to move, to stretch his body up against the darkness, feeling the space around him growing. His knuckles didn't graze the rock this time, and as his prison flexed and extended he rose up within it, driven by the hunger and the anger and the sheer madness that came from the impotence of imprisonment. By the time it was light enough to see, he was beyond seeing. Beyond caring, beyond the law. Beyond anything which might touch him. All he knew was the blood he could feel moving only a few feet distant from him.

And the walls dropped.

By seven I was up, showered and heading for the hospital with a copy of *Top Gear* magazine in my bag for Dad and a book of Sudoku puzzles for Mum. They were pleased to see me, of course, but my father was having some tests run and my mother had to go back to their smallholding to make arrangements for the animals, so I only stayed a few minutes. Then I headed off towards the office, where, to my surprise, Liam was already waiting for me.

His expression told me that the Happy Bunny had not been by that morning.

'I do hope you being in already isn't a sign that you're going to start taking your job seriously.' I hung my jacket up on the back of the door and sat down at my desk.

'No. It's actually a sign that I'm taking *your* job seriously.' Liam pushed the *York Herald* under my nose. 'What happened yesterday, Jess?'

After the dream and my heart-to-demon talk with Zan, yesterday seemed so long ago that I had to struggle to remember. 'I … what do you mean?'

'*This.*' He shook the paper out to the relevant page. ' "We can report that Miss Grant, pictured below"—and they used that horrible picture of you on your own at that party—"was called to a rogue werewolf yesterday afternoon, but chose instead to go visiting family. Perhaps it is time that questions were asked about the necessity of the Liaison office, given that council costs are escalating and two departments are under threat of closure." The lovely, friendly York press again. So, what happened?'

I took a deep breath, told him and watched his eyes cloud

over when I explained how my Dad was hooked up to the machines. 'I went in again this morning but they're preparing him for some tests or something.' My voice ran down an octave as I struggled to keep it going. 'And he's the nicest man in the world, Liam. He doesn't deserve this.'

Liam made a face and screwed the newspaper up into a fist-sized ball; then he flung it into the corner of the office with surprising savagery. 'Why didn't you tell me?'

'I didn't want to disturb you. You said you were reading to Charlotte and that's more important than having to listen to me whinge.'

He shook his head. 'No. No, Jess. You've gone through enough this last couple of days and you're my *friend* – of course I would listen to you. Your poor dad. And this poisonous rubbish ...' He waved at the paper, which was uncoiling under the shelving unit like a shy snake. 'You could have Facebooked me, at least.'

'You know what I'm like, I'm not good at ...' I dropped my face into my cupped hands. 'I wish Sil was here,' I said in a small voice. 'I want him back, Liam.'

There was a short, quiet moment, which I let go without feeling that I had to make some snappy remark. I just felt the loss of Sil in my heart and my head.

'Coffee?' Liam eventually asked.

'There is no other reason on earth for your existence.' My hands fell away from my face and I took a deep breath. 'Okay. Well, no-one said this job was going to be easy.'

'No, but they did say it was going to be regular hours and paid at a rate beyond that of a sixteenth-century peasant.' He picked up the mugs. 'So I don't think we can believe a word they say, quite honestly.'

'I'd better drop an e-mail to head office, let them know what happened. Just in case they get shirty about our journalist friend.'

'Blimey, they've never started reading the newspapers over at Town Hall, have they? Doubt they read the *York Herald* anyway, there's never a sniff of a page three girl, and they only have the football in once a week.'

'Nevertheless.' I logged in and began drafting something succinct and pithy. 'Even though they'll have to go to Personnel to find out who I am. I swear they think Liaison is a place in Belgium.'

'That's Liege.'

'Go tell them.' I typed another line and Liam went out to the kitchen, but then came back in at a run when a strange, high-pitched pinging noise started coming from his computer. 'What the hell is that?'

'News alert.' Forgetting coffee, he sat down and started scrolling. 'It's coming down the feed from Vamp Central.' He clicked on a flashing icon and a recorded image flickered into action on the screen. 'Oh, shit.'

I stared at the pictures coming down the line and my mind fell into the little black hole that shock had reserved for it. 'I don't ... Liam ... please, tell me this isn't real.'

Chapter Nine

Like shooting one-winged birds. They panic so, rushing hither and yon as though it might save them. He bit and drank, feasting on the blood as his demon feasted on the terror. *They've got soft, these humans, since the Treaty. They used to fight back, some of them, their attempts to free themselves from the onslaught was rather endearing, but these ... these just stand and take it, or blunder about with no idea of packing tight, running with the herd and making me pick them off one at a time. No, they make it too easy.*

Sil ran. Each mouthful of blood gave him more strength; with the strength came the joy, the sheer singing of the heart that freedom and the rapture of attack brought. He wheeled and spun through the London crowd, sometimes holding and sipping, sometimes tearing and indulging the darker side of his demon's demands, his brain barely capable of thought and his mind empty of everything except the need to feed. *Power. Power to make fear and horror my friends, the power to take over and over and to feel the earth dance beneath my feet with the speed of passing.*

Vision was nothing but a blur of movement and light, the smudges of faces darkening as the blood sprayed them, and then turning ashen white, hearing so sharpened by the need to hunt that loud noises battered his ears. But the quiet, shocked cry of a child needled through the chaos direct to his senses. *Child. Crying.*

Another heavy body against his, another deep bite that sent his demon skittering inside him, almost sickened with the surfeit. The child cried again, 'Mum!' Sil let the weight drop from his arms to the pavement, and stood amid the ruin that had, only a few moments ago, been a crowded street. *Child.*

He turned, saw the boy, crouching half inside a shop doorway. Inside, the staff, who had closed and bolted the door against the blood-hungry beast, huddled behind their stationery display, screaming, a noise which intensified as he took one, two steps towards their windows. The child crouched lower, but raised his head as Sil approached and, to his astonishment, jumped up and began swinging juvenile punches at the vampire.

'That's my mum!' he was crying, tears preventing his punches from being anything other than perfunctory. 'You bit my *mum*!'

And Sil stopped. Fangs down, lips drawn back, ready to attack, he considered the child now attempting to kick him in the leg. His mother was, presumably, one of the many littering the paved way, some sitting up and groaning while others lay tumbled as they'd fallen. *Child. Not much older than Joseph when the influenza struck.* His fangs retracted. Strength – that superhuman, all-encompassing strength that had made him so fast, so invincible – left his arms, his legs, and he staggered. Turned.

And ran.

Chapter Ten

'Oh *shit*.' It was all I could say. Liam and I held on to each other and watched the film Zan was sending from a security camera in central London. When it came to the end, we watched it again, slo-mo; even through the blood and the terror, I couldn't look away.

Finally Liam turned the video off and we just stood and stared at one another. 'Shit,' I said again.

'Definitely him?' Liam looked pale and his eyes were huge.

'I ... yes. Only Sil and Sherlock Holmes wear a coat like that.' The shock had kicked in, leaving my brain driving uselessly forwards, like a clock with no hands, trying to force me into action. I had no idea what action I could usefully take right now. 'And, yes. It was him. I suppose ... we should call Zan ...?'

At that moment the phone rang and we both stared at it. 'That will be him,' I said, still distant with shock. 'You'd better speak to him. I don't think I ...' I waved at the handset and Liam, green-faced and shaking slightly, picked it up. There was a static buzz of words and Liam took a deep breath.

'No, Jess has no idea either, he ... no, we've not heard anything from him.' I was glad Liam had taken the call; I had the feeling that I was going to come over all hysterical any moment now, and Zan's phobia-list had 'crying women' right up there. 'Yes. As soon as we hear anything.' He lowered the phone and looked across the office at me, his eyes wide with panic now. 'Shit, Jessie. What has he done?'

'We know what he's done. We saw him doing it.'

'Zan found the footage in a live feed – he must be sitting there running all the cameras in the country, Jess.'

I remembered Zan sitting there in front of his huge screen, alone with all those images, searching for ... what? *This?* Was this what he'd expected? 'Yeah,' I said, almost inaudibly. *Blood, fear ... a vampire in a feeding frenzy.*

'Zan reckons'—Liam's professionalism slid into a hoarse baritone of disbelief for a second—'that nobody died. He didn't kill anyone, Jess. There's a lot of injuries, blood loss, shock, that kind of thing, but he stopped himself from killing.' Liam flicked the screen back on; it was silently showing the attack on a loop. 'That's a good thing, isn't it?'

'Is it? We both know what happens to a vampire that attacks, Liam. We know what *has to* happen. It's not like a dog, where we can sometimes give the benefit of the doubt ... I really don't think anyone's teased Sil with a stick recently.' I swallowed down an encroaching sob and kept my eyes facing front. Pretending an interest in what we were watching, while my brain refused to believe it. The screen now showed a still-shot of the aftermath, people strewn around the street, some unconscious, others sitting up and holding gaping wounds. 'The Hunters have to take him down.' A whisper was all I could manage past the huge swelling in my throat. 'And if the Hunters can't find him, then it's a Liaison job, hush hush, behind the scenes.'

Liam blinked at me. 'And how are we supposed to do it? We're not allowed anything more powerful than a tranq gun, and that's like asking someone to take down a charging elephant with a straw and spit-pellets.'

I took a deep breath and tried to push everything away, even the knowledge of what must be done. 'You are disgusting. No, the clue is in the name: we liaise. Use our knowledge, the knowledge that's on the streets, to track him down, tranq him and then bring Enforcement in. Or the Hunters, depending on how "immediate" we're feeling.' My hands were shaking, I put them either side of the monitor to try to warm the shock out of them. 'There's no "due process of law" for a vampire that's gone rogue; we put them down like a charging elephant. Only with less spit.'

'Wow.' Liam sat down so heavily that his chair rocked and creaked. 'We've never … not since I've been here. I'm not sure we covered it in training.'

'I keep telling you, you did *not* have training! York Council don't *do* training; what you had was half an hour in an office with a man who kept trying to touch your leg. A vamp went rogue once, just after I started. They sent me out, but the Hunters picked him up before I got any further than asking around – he wasn't the brightest saw-blade in the toolbox, that one.'

'Wow,' Liam said again. 'What happened?'

I swallowed hard. *This isn't happening.* My brain was running the images on my own internal screen, over and over, to a frozen soundtrack of tears. *This can't be happening.* 'They chased him down to Rowntree Park and shot him in the bandstand.'

Liam shook his head slowly. 'So, this really *is* a real job? Liaison? We're not just getting paid for you to do the PR in schools and chat up werewolves? There is actually a *point* to all this?'

'Liaison. We liaise. To gain information or to give it, with a view to helping Human/Other relations run smoothly. I think that's on some headed paper somewhere.'

And inside my head, on another running loop, a voice was yelling at me, trying to break through the professional detachment. *This can't be it. This can't be how it ends. A love like yours doesn't end in a chase through the streets and a bullet through the head – that's not in any script I've ever read, or anything other than the most hardboiled of novels. It's not meant to go like this.*

'So.' Liam blew out a deep breath. 'What happens now?'

'Now, the London Hunters have the call. If he's really vanished, the entire Hunter community is on watch, everyone in any branch of Otherworld comms is on standby. I have to go out and try to get information from York Otherworlders; see if anyone, anywhere, knows anything. But first, you make me a really sturdy cup of coffee.'

As though he was happy just to have something to do, Liam leaped up. 'Yes. Well, obviously.'

'And before that, I think I just have to go and be a little bit sick.'

'Jess?'

I dashed down the flight of stairs and locked myself into the toilet. Disbelief. That was all there was, at first, a frantic denial of everything we'd just seen. *Not him. Of course not, of course it's not him.* I leaned against the back of the door and let the doubt wash through me, followed by the little trickle of hope at our misapprehension. *Of course.* And then, finally, a hot flood of acceptance and grief, which pulled my head to my chest and filled it with the images again. My love shattered and I tried to grasp pieces of it and stick them back into order, to make sense of the betrayal. I rested my forehead against the mirror and wrapped my arms around my ribcage, trying to hold my breaking heart together, trying to stop my body from flying into a million fragments. I flushed the loo repeatedly to cover the noise of the guttural sobs that sounded as though bits of my throat were coming away, while my body shook. *Sil. Four years of loving you. A few weeks of actually having you, and it was like all my dreams coming true together. And now, this.*

The ache in my soul wouldn't go away.

Finally I went back up to the office. Liam was on the phone and carefully averted his eyes from my face; he'd only once dared to ask me if I'd been crying and his computer still made a funny creaking noise, so he knew better than to repeat his mistake. Without looking at me, he pointed, dramatically, to a mug of coffee, now bearing a slight wrinkled skin, sitting on my desk.

'Thanks,' I mouthed across the room. Even cool, the coffee was warmer than I was, so I chugged it down and it soothed the chill in my psyche, made me feel a bit better. The caffeine hit my system and jerked it from numb horror into alertness. Liam put the phone down.

'Head Office. They want to see you re your flagrant dereliction of duty. Oh, and they want you out on the streets as soon as.'

'Because?' I put my mug down and wiped my clammy hands down my jeans.

'They reckon the word will be out among the general populace that our vamp went psycho down in London and that things might be a bit ... uneasy out there. They think, and God alone knows why, because I know you, that having you out there patrolling might calm things down a bit. You're to go in to the offices this afternoon. Three-ish.' He put his hands flat on the desk and leaned forward, like a TV detective mid-interrogation. 'Are you sure you're up to it?'

'Call my professionalism into question once more, Liam Prentiss, and you are going to be explaining away the scars for years to come.' I fetched the tranq gun out of its cabinet and pocketed a handful of cartridges. 'I need to do something. I might as well make myself useful.'

'I'll keep an eye on the channels. If any more info comes down, I'll ring you, all right?'

'Please.' I slid the gun into my other pocket and the weight was instantly reassuring. 'Even ... even if it's bad, Liam. I need to know. Whatever it is.'

A pause. 'Okay, if you're sure.'

Keep moving. It doesn't hurt so much if you're moving. 'I'm going to fly by Vamp High Command, check in with Zan too. He might have some inside information that I can use.' Assuming an air of perkiness, I patted my pockets down once more and bounced out of the office. As soon as I stepped out of the door three reporters from the local paper bundled into me, cameras flashing in my face and devices poised to record anything I might say. 'How do you feel about your boyfriend breaking the Treaty?' A tiny blonde woman, who looked as though all her knowledge about vampires came from the teenage end of the popular fiction market, simpered at me. 'Anything to say about that?'

'No comment,' I said firmly, and dodged through WH Smith, like a cut-price spy with a stationery fetish, popping out at the far side, away from the furiously inventive scribbling, and into the main shopping area, where I managed to reassure myself that the crowds would hide me from the spitefully inclined newshounds.

The streets seemed a little quieter than usual, but not to a great degree. Vamps went rogue sometimes; it happened, and the majority of the population had great faith in the ability of Hunters to take them out before things got really bad. One had eluded capture for five weeks by hiding out in the Brecon Beacons, but usually justice was swiftly, and terminally, dealt. My hand shook for a second. *Sil. What the hell happened to you?* There was that feeling again, as though my lower intestines had turned to glass, my heart stammered mid-beat and I had the most peculiar sensation around my midriff. Was this the connection Zan claimed I shared with Sil? Was *this* my demon inheritance? Blood that was a vampire narcotic – knocked out anything that bit me – and all the symptoms of typhoid? How rubbish. In the world of superpowers this made me something like Heroin Withdrawal Girl. My father ... my blood father, not Brian the ex-teacher now lying in York General Hospital with a dodgy heart, had been able to glamour and to create and use hexes for his own protection. I got an upset stomach and a Class A vascular system. Typical.

I made my way to Vamp Central through as many shops as possible, to avoid the possibility of reporters, noting, even in my distressed state, that Next had a shoe sale on. Zan was sitting in his office with a screenshot from the newsfeed on his computer. He was staring at the split screen, one half showing the grainy black-and-white image of a street littered with fallen humans; the other half was a portrait photograph of Sil. My heart squeezed. Face half in shadow, mouth unsmiling and hair unnaturally neat, it looked like the kind of pin-up picture that went up inside young girls' lockers or on bedroom walls. Only I had seen him sprawl into a chair, hook one leg up over the arm and lean his head back, bottle of Synth swinging loose between his fingers. Only I had seen him with his hair swept back and a grin on his face after we'd made the kind of love that made him feel human and me feel special

'How did this happen, Jessica?' Zan's voice was low. 'How could he allow himself to become so ... so *debased*?' He didn't take his eyes off the screen, although his fingers toyed with an iPad so up to date that it hadn't even hit the high street yet. It lay alongside the computer in a pigskin casing.

'I don't know. But we need to get real here, Zan.'

He turned around slowly. He looked, as ever, terrific. Carefully and co-ordinatingly dressed in clothes that all seemed to have their own tactile story to tell, which always made it seem as though he got dressed simply by touch: a white linen shirt and dark brushed cotton trousers with a silk tie cravat thing around his neck. With his dark hair and green eyes it made him look like a Victorian poet. Victorian he may be, but I would have taken bets against there being any poetry in Zan's heart. 'I fail to see how I can become any more "real" than is currently the case.'

My eyes flicked back to the screen. To that image of Sil. 'If this turns out to be … you know, a thing.' Zan looked me up and down and gave a tiny shudder, which I think he thought I couldn't see, or maybe he just didn't care. 'If the Hunters … if Sil gets … I mean, if it's not all some terrible mistake … He's going to be *dead*, Zan. What are you going to tell people then? There are reporters out there already, asking me how I feel … It's only a matter of time before they're offering a reward.'

Zan was looking at me steadily. His green eyes weren't at all human, they were cool and looked as though he was measuring everything for size when he spoke. Although, knowing Zan, they'd probably been like that when he was human. 'I am sorry. I know you care for him, and I'm sorry that I cast off your doubts about his whereabouts.' He dipped his head a little under the weight of the apology. 'If I had taken you more seriously, perhaps this could have been averted.'

'No, don't say that.' I moved jerkily, trying to shake off the implications by movement. 'Don't, Zan. I don't want to think that it was going to be any other way. If I start thinking that there's something we could have done then I …' I stopped before I choked. Zan's morbid fear of emotional displays would have driven him out of the building if I'd continued.

Zan fiddled with the iPad, stroking its casing. 'Hmm,' he said, without inflection. A sigh. 'Why is it that everything connected to you seems to become dangerous, Jessica?'

'I hope that's rhetorical.'

Another sigh. 'Not really, I was hoping that you may have some profound insight. I really should have known better. We must let things take their course.'

'In other words, he's dispensable. You're not going to try to save him?'

Zan's attention floated back to the screen. 'I very much

fear that he has put himself beyond our help, Jessica,' he said, and his voice was surprisingly gentle, for Zan. 'We must do what we can now to keep the Treaty intact until he is caught and justice is done.'

He was doing it again, treating me as though I was almost ... no, not an equal. Zan considered all forms of life to be mysteriously gregarious and unnecessarily emotional and therefore beneath him. But he was treating me as though I were *important*, somehow, which was only ever going to be true if there was a worldwide filing-related emergency or some kind of Otherworld uprising that could be beaten off with an electric pencil sharpener and a sheaf of expense claim forms.

'I'd better get out on those mean streets again, then,' I said, stiffly.

'Yes. It is essential to keep calm. This kind of thing happens; it is no reason for general panic or lower-class rebellion. And, Jessica?' he interrupted my attempts at a huffy exit. 'Remember, it is essential that you keep doing what you do. Do not allow uncertainty to creep in to the general populace. York must hold to the Treaty.'

'Yes, all right, I know. Cool head, even keel, blah blah.' And suddenly the streets filled with real, noisy people who didn't have to wear latex to handle loose change and who didn't regard receiving e-mails as a violation of their personal space was a much better place to be.

But I slammed the door on my way out.

I want my old life back. Even if it does mean wanting Sil but not being able to have him. I want to be human and boring again. I want to have nothing to bitch about but Liam's odd habits and a lack of HobNobs. I want my best friend to moan to on dull evenings when there's nothing on TV, and my sister to worry about Mum and Dad with. I want to be able to visit their little house on the moors, surrounded by sheep and brambles, and eat roast dinners and cheat my way out of the washing up. All those things that had seemed so normal and … well, normal before had suddenly assumed huge, wish-fulfilment size, as though they were all I needed to be happy and skipping around the place like a five-year-old with a new skill to show off.

Sunken deeply into thought, although nothing too forward-thinking, I didn't dare allow myself to consider what might happen next. I wandered along by the minster, where not a single Otherworlder was to be seen, through the tourist-jams of Petergate, where a human dressed as Dracula was advertising A Real Vampire Experience – which was, as far as I could tell, mostly standing around in overpriced nightclubs in overpriced Armani suits, trying to pick up girls young enough to be their great, great granddaughters – and my phone vibrated in my pocket as I got a text from Liam.

My hand went to it and then, as I remembered, stopped. *What if it's bad news? What if …* But my brain couldn't think any further, collapsing in upon itself with the possibilities, and duty cut in and took over.

There's a vamp out of area around the back of the minster. Female, name of Kitty Kelly, urgh, sounds like one of those manga characters, all eyes and tight sweaters.

I texted back. Okay, watcher-of-way-too-much-TV. On it now.

I dodged through the minster shop, flashing my library card in lieu of the proper identity cards we'd been promised but never got, out of the back door and into the minster yard, pausing only to wonder what they sold in a shop attached to, basically, a giant church. Then I saw her, half-crouched in the shade of one of the big trees that made the minster look, from this side, like a misplaced country residence. She was wearing a floral tea-dress and heels.

'You're out of area, Kitty. You need to head back, or I'll have to …'

She spun round and I recognised her vaguely, a recent incomer to York with a permit that kept her south of the river. Her taste in clothing had obviously been formed during the rationing when the Troubles reached their height in the forties, because she'd slathered her lips in the bright red lipstick that had been so popular back then. It made her mouth look tiny, but not in a good way, more in a 'one fang at a time' way.

However, I hardly had time to register this before she'd shot across the grass towards me, turning and moving with such speed that I was barely braced before she grabbed me.

Most vampires will try to get their victim on the ground before they bite. Humans are at a huge disadvantage when they're down and the vampires risk less damage to themselves from a prone human, so vamp attacks tend to follow a predictable pattern – and this one was no different. She locked an arm around my waist and tried to use her strength and forward motion to carry me down to the ground, but I was good at what I did, and I'd been attacked by quite a lot of vampires in my time. I put one foot forward, weight on the back foot, and then as she tried to sweep me down I folded in half. Then I straightened suddenly as she hesitated on the follow-through, used my bracing leg to kick underneath her and brought her crashing down to the cobbled surface, where she lay on her back and glared at me as I pinned her down with my body weight.

'What the hell was *that* all about?' I drew the tranq gun and held it above her.

'There's talk that there might be a fight coming. I mean, we're superhuman and yet we let you run around as though you were equals, it's not right,' she muttered. 'York should be run by people like us ... people who can take control ... You're Jessica, aren't you? Sil's girlfriend? Good grief, what was he doing with a human, when there are much more attractive people of his own type. I mean, look at you!'

'What, you mean, look at me, sitting on top of you and holding a gun to your head?'

'You're so … *scrubby.* Those shoes, really?' The highly painted lips curled in disgust, making her mouth look like advanced punctuation. 'He should have been with someone with style, someone with panache.' She wriggled to pull her dress down over her knickers. They were La Perla, the cow.

'Great. Sil's fan club is in town'—I fired the tranq into her neck—'and heading for home.' At least I hadn't ruined any clothing this time, I thought, dialling Enforcement. 'I've got a downed vamp here on the Minster Green.'

'Jess?'

It was Harry again. 'Are there actually any other Enforcement officers? Or is it all just you in different hats and rubber noses?'

'Minster Green? I can have a unit with you in ten.' There was a rustling pause, as though Harry was moving himself, or the phone, or both; then he spoke again, more quietly. 'What's this one's game then?'

I looked down at the sleeping vampire at my feet. 'Dunno. Think it might be the Vera Lynn Attack Force. Mad for Sil though, so obviously deranged.'

'Takes all sorts, doesn't it? Okay, catch you later.'

Lovely, kind Harry, attractive to the sort of girl who liked the idea of a big, strong man on whom to lean, and also, inexplicably, to Eleanor, who was more butch than the Incredible Hulk and whose only need for a big, strong man would be to have something firm to stand on when she was regrouting her bathroom.

'Thanks, Har—' But he'd gone, so I had no-one to talk to while I waited for the pick-up unit. I sat on the concrete path, one eye on the softly snoring Vera-alike, and hugged my knees. She was wearing cute shoes with a little strap across them, which would have made my feet look like a pair of hay-bales tied up with string, and her whole forces' sweetheart look was grating on me. Not only because the Troubles had been over for thirty years, so going around dressed like a Human Army supporter was nastily sarcastic in a way only a natty little floral dress could be, but also because she was neatly slim. I had a bosom that made me look like some kind of climbing hazard, so it didn't matter how skinny I might be I was cursed with the 'boob woman' look and an inability to run without a bra that reached from neck to waist.

I sniffed and hugged my knees tighter. What had she looked like as a human? The demon that infected the vampires gave them an enhanced beauty, although I suspected that neither Sil nor Zan had ever been hulking great ugs, so had she always been pretty? Or had she been a plain, overlooked girl who'd thought a demon would up her chances of meeting gorgeous men? Or had she fallen for some guy who'd used her as a free feed and not let her go in time, before his demon seeded into her bloodstream? Either way, she was right, even if she *had* talked about him in the past tense, the bitch. Sil should be with someone who could understand his way of life – the need for blood, excitement, the adrenaline rush that his demon got off on and that had made him …

I shook my head at how wrong this all was. Something must have happened to him in London. Sil was almost painfully law-abiding; for him to be running amok through a crowd of humans something … *please, God, something* … must have happened. And then the sensible part of my brain cut in. Vampires were vampires. With the demon came a whole new set of moral standards – well, more a whole abnegation of any morality at all, really – a new body, new abilities and strengths. Who someone had been as a human, *what* they had been, no longer existed, except in their repressed memories.

Sil was not who I thought he was. He professed to love me, to feel human with me, but ... in the end, he was vampire.

The circling blue light of the Enforcement van had almost never been so welcome. I clambered to my feet to greet the team, two officers I knew by sight, filled in the paperwork and let the irritation at this vampire's expensive underwear wash away any residual feelings of displacement as she was hoisted into the van and driven off.

Sil lay in the alleyway, covered with sheets of cardboard. Flat to the evil-smelling concrete, with his Ralph Lauren trousers in direct contact with something he really hoped was just rainwater and a pigeon giving him funny looks.

Oh gods. How did it come to this? Feeling relatively safe, from identification if not from dysentery, he let himself remember what he'd done. What the hunger and desperation had driven him to, the sheer power and high of the hunt and ... *Please tell me I didn't kill anyone. I don't* think *I did, or that I let my demon seed into a human ... Oh gods. What have I done?*

Desperation dropped his cheek against the rough ground for a second, and the pigeon eyed him again, perhaps hoping that he was going to die and provide it with a meal. *Out there, out in the world that once hailed me as the Vampire of York, there are going to be Hunters, Enforcement crew all looking for me. None of them willing to listen, to let me tell my side of things – that I was so hungry all I knew was that I had to feed to stay alive. Would they care? Would they even believe me?*

The gnawing at his belly wasn't hunger now. It was Jess, his connection with her making itself felt as a virtual pain. *So. She still cares. There is some hope for me out there in the world.* He called to mind her wide grin, her wild hair and the scent of her skin and he could feel himself smile, despite everything. *She* is *my world*. He remembered her dispassionate calm in the face of killing her demon father, and then the tears and the self-loathing that had come after. *Jess won't kill me*. He realised his inner voice sounded a little uncertain but the gnawing was a gentle ache now, an echo of that ever-present 'knowing' that ran somewhere between his brain and his groin, that whisper behind the eyes that told him she was out there, and that he was in her thoughts. *Jess. Will you stand not in condemnation but in pursuit of the mystery of what is happening to me?*

A pressure and a clicking sound told him that the pigeon had landed on the cardboard and was making exploratory pecks at it. *I need to speak to her.* Another brief exploration of pockets had so far, inexplicably, failed to turn up anything useful. *Someone has taken my phone, all my money, my cards. I need to see her. I need to see the look in her eyes, to know whether I disgust her now or whether she can see past this. I need her.*

Chapter Eleven

HQ was located in Town Hall, a Georgian building with more windows than sensible inhabitants and a blue front door that looked as though it had been ripped direct from the TARDIS. I went inside and waited at the reception desk while a young blonde woman with a proper clothing allowance and nice shoes rang through to the office and finally ushered me through the security door and up to the Hallowed Halls.

'Ah. Miss ... Grant.' I'd never met this man before, but then Liam and I were rarely granted audience with those who held the purse strings. Normally all communication was via telephone and e-mail, 'like cheap spies' as Liam always said. I suspected it was just to stop us shouting and demanding proper money instead of the loose-change salaries we currently got. That or they suspected that we smelled funny. 'We won't keep you a moment. Just a formality, you understand.'

I sat on the nasty wooden chair in front of the desk in this office with half-panelled walls, like a nineteenth-century stable, and the rest painted Institutional Green, and stared at him. Thinning grey hair was swept back – probably to make the thinning less obvious, but in reality making it look as though his forehead stretched round to the back of his neck – and was complemented by a grey suit and grey-rimmed glasses outlining grey eyes. If he'd stood still on an overcast day he'd have been invisible: the office walls were probably green just so that people could find him. 'Well, can it be a quick formality then, only I've got ... things to do.'

The office smelled of oranges, as though someone had eaten their lunch in there. It made my stomach rumble. 'Yes, of course.' This was said far too smoothly for it to be a good thing. 'We just wanted a quick word about your … position at Liaison.'

'That stuff in the newspaper was all just made up, you know,' I said quickly. 'And apart from that you can't have any complaints, our section has the lowest rates of any kind of Otherworld activity – even the ghouls steer clear of central York, our werewolves are all sourcing from the local butchers, we've got people on the inside of the clubs down by the river …'

'People on the inside. Yes.' The grey man, whose laminated badge proclaimed him to be David Hasterlane, Otherworld Liaison Supervisor, leaned back in his chair. 'And there is the matter for concern. You are currently … ah … *involved*, as I believe the press would have it, with the City Vamp? Sil? Tell me, Miss Grant, do *you* think your position may be compromised by your relationship with the vampires?'

Well, this had all come out of nowhere. I'd been with Sil for a couple of months now and nobody had raised any kind of concern up until this moment, so there had to be something going on, something underneath this sudden worry about my neutrality. I looked around the office but couldn't see anything unusual, apart from the ranked banks of neatly closed filing cabinets. In our office any closed cupboard was unusual, and probably hiding something *Doctor Who* related. 'I have no problem keeping my work and my relationships separate, Mr Hasterlane,' I said coldly, watching him carefully now. Apart from being relentlessly grey, he seemed a bit edgy. I know I sometimes make people nervous, but that's usually because they are waiting for me to either shoot them or shout at them; this man seemed to be randomly anxious.

'Then, can I take it that should the occasion arise you can be called upon to do your duty by the council? As a *human*? You would, ah … "bring him in" is, I think, the phrase used in these circumstances?'

I looked across the desk at him. There were papers, permits and movement orders all stacked up in volcanic heaps, a photograph of an unsmiling woman and a small child, a sheaf of business cards and … the computer screen, displaying thumbnail-sized stills of a video – Sil, somewhere, moving … 'Do you think I could have a glass of water?'

'I'm sorry?'

'It's all been a terrible shock,' I said, carefully holding my hand to my forehead and wobbling slightly as though I might faint. 'Sil being … terrible …' I half-closed my eyes and watched him through the gap. As I'd hoped, he leaped up and ran for the door, obviously of the *weak woman, water* school of thought, and as soon as he'd gone I flipped his screen towards me and noted down the web address of the film. I even had time to photograph the papers he'd got taped to the top drawer – covered in handwritten letters and numbers – and lunge my way back into the chair. I was sitting with my head between my knees when David Hasterlane came back in, carefully carrying half a plastic cup of warm water, which I was then obliged to sip at. 'May I go now?' I managed to ask after a few minutes of 'recovery'. 'Only, I'm not sure what it says in my contract about sitting around not working …'

Clearly worried that I might be about to ask for new rates of pay, Grey Man ushered me out of the office. 'You understand that this was not an official conversation?' he said, giving me a moment to wonder how unofficial it might be, given that it was held in our HQ, by the man whose badge said he was my supervisor. 'I just had to reassure myself of your loyalty to Otherworld Liaison, in the face of these very *challenging* events.'

Challenging? Seriously? He stood and watched me go down the mahogany staircase as quickly as was compatible with my recent 'faint'. I was very tempted to stop halfway down and wiggle my fingers goodbye, but I didn't think he'd see the funny side. I wasn't sure that he'd see the funny side of a stand-up comedian's entire set, actually, but then there probably weren't many giggles in trying to run Liaison, given our underpaid status and natural tendency towards unmanageability. Trying to direct us must be like trying to teach chickens to drive.

Chapter Twelve

'He had *what*?' Liam stopped mid-stride and a shower of biscuit crumbs fell off the side of the plate he was carrying.

'Not sure what it was. But stills from some other camera loop. I only had chance for a really quick look; was a bit worried they might have some sort of surveillance set up in there.'

'And you saw ...? Or is this twenty questions?'

I bit my lip and tried to twist the fear down, screw it up into a little ball somewhere I didn't have to feel it. 'Film from a private camera. Don't know where it came from but ...' I blinked hard. 'I managed to scribble down the web address. Oh, and if it's password protected'—I dragged my phone out from my pocket and flashed up the picture—'you might want to try some of these.'

'Wow, Jess.' Liam actually looked impressed, and it was hard to impress Liam without some quite specialist equipment. 'You're actually beginning to *listen* to some of the things I've been telling you.'

'Yeah, yeah, just not all that stuff about *Star Trek*, obviously. Quick, get on here before someone suspects that I might not be as stupidly girly as I look and changes all his passwords.'

Liam fiddled about with his computer for a moment, raising his eyebrows now and then. Eventually he swung the monitor around. 'Is this what you saw?'

The figure was stooped, folded up, like an umbrella that's been kept too long in a bucket in the hall. He held his arms in front of him, crossed over at the stomach, shoulders raised and head bent, like a mummified corpse walking. 'Something ... yes. But not this bit. Can you take it back to when he appears?'

'Can't see where he comes from. He just walks into shot from behind that tree like he springs up in the middle of the square.'

We watched the film as the vampire, hair straggled around the back of his head and shoulders, walked on, still hunched as though confined to an invisible box. There were a few more shambled steps, a gradual 'opening out' of his body and then he was running, so fast that the slightly shoddy camera film caught him in stop-frame motion, moving towards the crowded shopping area. 'And that's moving, even for Sil. Like he's heading for something irresistible.' I watched for another couple of seconds. 'So he was somewhere in that square. What's in Soho Square, apart from trees, a sort of shed thing, and grass?'

'Squirrels?'

'Liam, you had better not be suggesting that Sil was kidnapped by squirrels. Because there is a very special hell reserved for people who think like that, you know.'

Liam gave me a look. 'No. But he was walking as though he'd just come out of somewhere, and if it had been one of the houses then the camera would have picked him up before. Unless it was behind the camera.'

'But see how he kind of straightens himself up? Just here ...' I rewound the film.

'I suppose'—Liam began, very carefully—'if he'd just got the scent of blood from the main street ...'

I shivered and found that I was blinking hard. 'This is wrong. Just wrong, on so many levels. I mean, *Sil*, behaving like this? I know he's not Zan, but even so ... and if he wanted to bite, well, there's the clubs and the groupies and'—a sudden image of the Forces' Sweetheart and her designer pants—'his fan club. Running amok in Central London when he must know it's a death sentence?' I rubbed my hands over my face. 'Wrong.'

As though the force of habit was strong in him, Liam got up, collecting our mugs and heading out to the kitchen. Unwilling to be left alone with my thoughts, I followed him along the landing to the little kitchenette which sat beside the office and, I was willing to bet, the council didn't know about. They still forwarded any post to us labelled 'To Whom it May Concern', and if they thought we had a kitchen then they might start charging us rent for our own department.

Liam leaned against the wall, waiting for the kettle to boil. 'Okay, so what's the next step, Jess?' He was looking very hard into my face. 'I know you, don't forget, so please don't give me any of that "let's get out and blow the bastard away" crap that you're about to start. You love Sil. And him going rogue and tearing out throats isn't going to change that. Oh, Lord, this is what I've been worried about all this time ...'

'No you haven't.' I sniffed hard and tried to knock tears away from my eyelids with my arm as I pretended to stretch. 'And, if you remember, it was *you* who told us we should get together in the first place!'

'Jess.' He put a hand on my arm. The kitchenette was so tiny that he could do this while still leaning against the wall. 'This is real. This is the tough stuff now, the stuff we trained for. I know it's all been tranquing and admin up 'til now, I mean, apart from when you had to kill that demon, but that was just one of those things. This ...'

I took a deep breath. 'Hang on. I killed my *father*, not just any old demon, so it was not *one of those things* unless having demon relatives you knew nothing about is so common that Jeremy Kyle is about to do some kind of special on the subject. And what training? Why do you keep on about training? When? I don't think you've been out of my sight for more than a couple of days since you came on work experience; you've not had time to do anything more than a fire drill.'

'Stop it.' He tightened his hand on me. 'Jess. Please. Stop the gags. This is me, remember?' He crouched so that he could look into my face and his voice softened. 'You're the person who knows Sil best; you're his only hope of getting out of this. We need you to find him so that ... so we can end this. And it's your call, because I have no idea what to do now, go looking or wait it out or ... but it's not just us, not just York, not just Harry and Eleanor at Enforcement, it's the entire country, Jess. They're all going to be looking for him and, right now, we are the only ones who want him alive. Come on, show your badass side, here.'

'Liam, I'm an admin officer, I don't *have* a badass side. I don't even have a badass *ass*! I'm still afraid of the electric pencil sharpener, for God's sake.'

'Your father was a semi-immortal demon who had more magic than an entire Derren Brown show. You've got a badass in your genes, and now might be the time to pull it out and show it to us all.'

I stared at him.

'Okay, so maybe that came out wrong, and actually, now I come to think of it, a little bit pervy, but you know what I mean.'

Inside me, in the place that I rarely acknowledged because I wouldn't, *couldn't*, I felt a quick prick of fear. That part of me that held all the doubts about what I really was, underneath it all. About which side I would come down on, if it ever came to it, the part of me that held my demon inheritance, unexplored and unknown. 'It's not like a dog, Liam. I can't just suddenly decide to bring it out on its lead and use it to track him; I've lived with it all these years and never even known I *had* it, so why should a demon heredity be of any use now?'

I'd lowered my voice to a hiss, just in case anyone in the neighbouring offices might have a glass to the wall, and Liam lowered his to match. 'Because this is where you choose. Okay, yeah, I get why you ignore it, I get that you want to be human and pretend that you're nothing more than the daughter of a couple of teachers with a peculiar talent for spotting Otherworlders. But it's in you, somewhere, and if there's any *tiny little* part of you that can come out and do something about what's going on here – then now is the time to let it.'

'The car.'

'What? Are you just saying random words, or is there supposed to be a point?' The kettle boiled and Liam began pouring the water into mugs. The steam funnelled and twirled in his face like a thousand appetising ghosts.

'The car. Did he drive to London? Because you know what vamps are like for public transport.'

'I know what *Zan* is like, because he and I share a healthy appreciation for not sitting next to a nutter coughing "Abide With Me" while a small child attempts to push a crayon up my nose.'

'Sil is pretty much the same. Vampires are not really cut out for buses and trains; they don't have the patience. So he will have driven to London, probably in the Bugatti, and if he did ... where is it?'

Liam stared at me. 'Should I check with Vampire High Command? Ask Zan what he took?'

I went through into the main office and froze the computer on a frame of the back of Sil's head just as he moved through the gateway of the small square. Let my mind cast back into memories of his touch, the coolness of his skin against mine. The words he'd whisper when only I could hear. The way I could truly be myself and let go when his arms surrounded me and he held me so tightly against him. I pushed the thoughts away in favour of practicalities. 'No, let's keep it dark, shall we? Might be nothing and Zan ...'

'Zan wants him brought down just like everyone else.'

'Seems to. But then Zan has all the empathy of ... well, he pretty much defines lack of empathy just by existing. So, let's not bring him in on this, yes?'

Liam slithered down off the desk, rubbing his hands together. 'Okay. Sil usually drives the Bugatti, so I think we'll start with that one. Hmmm. Bugatti Veyron in London. Not exactly needle in a haystack, but coming close ... Do you know the registration?'

I tore my eyes away from the peculiarly hunched figure on the screen. 'Sorry.'

'God, Jess, you are rubbish. What colour is it then?'

'Um. It's shiny.'

Liam gave me a hard stare. 'Just stop it. That girly act doesn't cut any ice with me; I've seen you with PMT when we've run out of coffee and you make Godzilla look like a misunderstood gecko on a locust come-down.'

'No, seriously, it's a Pur Sang. You know, chrome?'

Liam did a complicated twisted-mouth expression, which managed to convey being impressed, annoyed and thinking deeply. 'Okay then. Registered to who?'

'Look, you wanted me to go badass. Checking vehicle registration is *not* badass. You're here for the non-badass side of things, I am going through this footage frame by frame for some kind of clue to what Sil's doing, which, given the level of eye strain I am enduring, is pretty badass.'

'That's a long-winded way of saying you don't know, isn't it?'

I advanced the film another frame. 'No, it's a long-winded way of saying find out yourself. Start by looking around the Soho Square area – he won't have left it far from where he was going. Vampires like casual walking about as much as they like public transport.'

Liam huffed, but started clacking away at his keyboard,

making occasional noises of disapproval, while I raked through the pixellated images of Sil walking through the green square and then running towards Oxford Street to begin his feeding frenzy. Frame by frame, watching his figure start out groping like a horror-movie zombie, gradually flexing and straightening until he accelerated out of the camera's range, then watching the whole scene in reverse, as though something would become apparent in the cartoonish walking-backwards images.

Then I called up Google Images. Checked as much of Soho Square as I could, seeing nothing more than a small park containing a shed, but not much else, surrounded by select shops, large trendy businesses and some houses. There was a vampire club on one corner, marked by the typical Goth-font of the logo painted above the door and the dark-tinted windows, but nothing else noteworthy, unless your tastes ran to blurrily-captured pictures of pigeons.

So why was he there? If he'd been in the club, why had no-one come forward to sell their story to the gathering press-hoards: 'My night of pleasure with off-the-rails City Vamp'? And it was eleven o'clock in the morning – the club would have shut at midnight, two a.m. latest … Where had he been since then? And what had he been doing? Because, with the way he was walking, he looked as though he'd been doing it in a box.

'Do you want the good news or the bad news?' Liam finally broke into my rapidly darkening thoughts. 'You may want to have the biscuits to hand.'

'Break it to me gently.'

'I've found the car. Well, I've found *a* car, registered to Vamp Central. SLS 63 AMG.'

'Is that the registration?'

'That's the *car*, you philistine. And the bad news is that it's been clamped and towed with a nice hefty parking fine;

that's how I found it. Do you want the "well, that's slightly surprising" news now?'

'Apart from the being clamped and towed? Which, to a vampire, is like admitting defeat? If you're going slowly enough to get a parking ticket you have failed in your basic mission to look cooler than the average fridge.'

'It was lifted from the Embankment, five days after Sil left here.'

'That's a fair way from Soho Square.'

'Yep. Which begs the question, why was he parked down by the river if he had business in Soho, or vice versa?' Liam raised his eyebrows at me.

'More coffee. Now.'

Liam hunched down into his 'oppressed mass' stance. 'Yessir!'

'I need to think.'

As Liam left the office with the mugs again, I put my elbows on my desk and massaged my temples with my fingers to stop the encroaching headache. *Think. Think, Jess. If he left you for a more exciting life, well he succeeded there, but why go to London, where his face would be recognisable from any one of* Cosmo's *'Eligible Bachelors' articles. Why not go abroad? And why take one of the cars registered to York; why not go and buy something new, something fresh, start again?*

I massaged harder as the headache threatened to kick in behind my eyeballs. *He took a Merc. A flash one, but not as instantly recognisable as the Bugatti, a bit more everyday. Was he trying to blend in? To pass as human in the crowd? Thinking he could blend in in a car that was bound to cost ten times an average salary would be a rookie vampire mistake though. And down at the Embankment? Why? Did he just fancy a quick look at the river before he went clubbing? Why not move the car?*

The headache twisted my eyes. This was ridiculous. Second-guessing a vampire was like trying to second-guess the wind: their motives were not human and they behave in ways we could never imagine. I cupped my eyes with my hands and groaned.

'Why don't you go home? Get some sleep.' Liam pushed a steaming mug my way.

'Because I can't sleep. And if I do, I dream of him, Liam. And then I wake up and he's not here and it was just a dream and …' I stopped myself before I blurted out any more of my fears that I was going to have to face the rest of my life without the only man who would ever truly understand how it felt to be me. The only man who truly *cared* how it felt to be me. And a life without him – would it even be a life? Or just days passing one after the other and knowing that the best thing to happen to me had happened and gone?

'So, go home and watch TV. Read a book. Chat to Zan, if you can remember enough classical Latin.' Liam started putting on his jacket. 'Only it's fast approaching six o'clock.'

'Yeah, you're right.' I got up too. 'We spend too much time in this place as it is. And besides, I'm going to pop into the hospital. Dad should be back from his tests by now, and I want to know how it all went. I want to take a quick wander round the streets as well, prove to Head Office that I'm on the right side.'

'Be careful, Jess,' Liam dug around in his pockets for his car keys. 'It must have occurred to you …'

'That maybe Mr Hasterlane left those images on his computer deliberately? To see what I'd do and where my loyalties lie? Yes, thank you, Liam, I have taken my paranoia-pills today, and I'm well aware of the lengths that York Council might feel it necessary to go to. But, for now, that film is all we have to go on, so, let's go on it.'

Chapter Thirteen

Sil hid until night. The cardboard had become soggy and the pigeon just a little too persistent by then, so he attached himself to a group of rough-sleepers milling around the back door of the restaurant at the end of the alleyway. Every so often someone would come and throw food out – a plate of overcooked pasta, some rolls that had gone stale – and they would fight in a desultory kind of way over the scraps. Sil pretended to fight too, the rising aggression pleasing his demon, but really keeping his head down, losing himself in plain sight, in the mass of unwashed bodies and stained clothes.

As soon as he could he borrowed a knife from a fellow sitting and chewing an out-of-date steak on a pile of bin bags and went into the shadows to hack at his hair, before returning to the unremarking mob with a ragged close-cut and a terrible wince. Later, after a bottle of something that tasted like an unresolved kidney complaint, he persuaded another one of them to change clothes with him, showing the designer label in his jacket as added incentive. And so by the time the restaurant closed and the group moved on, Sil looked almost completely different.

He's going to swap my Ralph Lauren suit for alcohol, he thought, watching his trousers moving off through the night, now held up by nylon string around a skinny middle. *But that's all to the good. Even though I am now wearing something that I couldn't swap for a gin and tonic and a can of flea spray.* He looked down at the too-small knitted jumper, which hugged his torso as far as the bottom of his ribcage, leaving a conspicuous gap above the waistband of a pair of denims so old that he was surprised the original cowboy wasn't still in there with him. On his feet were a pair of trainers a size too small, with one lace replaced by a frayed piece of elastic. His hair, which used to hang to the base of his neck, no longer even covered his ears, but that was all right because the Great Clothing Swap had included, as a bonus, a shapeless hat, of the kind worn by fielders during an overlong and overhot game of cricket. And, by the smell of it, had recently been worn for exactly that purpose.

A shiver of disgust ran up from his stomach. He pushed a hand into a pocket and, on encountering the edge of an obviously well-used tissue, withdrew it carefully. *Gods. Jessie, if you could see me now …* He shook his head, which gave him pause as he failed to feel the familiar swing of hair against his shoulder. *I am in fear for my life. I have done things this day that will have me shot on sight by anyone armed, no investigation, no recrimination, and my first thought is for my appearance and how my lover would react to it?* He sat on the recently vacated bin bags, head in his hands for a moment, the stirrings of panic in his chest sending his demon whirling again. *And now? What now?* For a moment the panic threatened to overwhelm him, powerlessness he had not encountered since the demon hatched inside him. *A century of supremacy. One hundred years of power, of strength and speed and unchanging looks, of sex and blood whenever and wherever I wanted, offered by those who were flattered and entranced. And now, here I sit.* His head dropped lower and he covered the newly bare back of his neck with his forearms, pulling his head in despair closer to his chest, tears threatening his closed lids.

And then he felt it. That tug at his solar plexus, the slow spinning of the silver thread that, in his imagination, connected him to Jessica, the thread that reeled and played, slackened and tautened as he moved through her thoughts. *Jessie. Thinking of me.* He touched his flesh, just beneath his ribcage, almost wonderingly, almost as though he could feel her through the contact. *Think of me. Because without you, without knowing that you believe I am still myself after the terrible deeds I committed … then I may as well turn myself over to Enforcement, or allow the Hunters to track me down and shoot me like something rabid.*

The connection vibrated and seemed to warm him along its length, but he feared that was simply his imagination.

Chapter Fourteen

My mother was knitting again, almost feverishly, while Dad lay in bed watching *Come Dine With Me* on mute. They weren't talking.

'Just passing by,' I said brightly. 'Everything all right?'

Two pairs of tired eyes turned my way. 'We saw the news, love,' my mother said quietly. 'What has he done?'

I felt my lip wobble as though I was five again. 'I don't know.'

My father patted the side of his bed and I sat down heavily enough to make one of the monitors signal an oncoming train. 'It might not be what it looks like, Jessie. There's something behind that kind of behaviour, I know.' He coughed softly and then carried on. 'In the Troubles we saw a lot of misinformation, misdirection. What you see is not always what happened, just remember that.'

I just shook my head. The words wanted to spill out, I could feel them clogged in my throat and my lungs, but my heart wouldn't let them past the lump in my throat.

'He loves you.' My mother came over and stroked the top of my head as though that inner five-year-old was visible from the outside. 'I've never seen anyone look at someone the way Sil looks at you.'

'I look at you like that,' my father interjected.

'Only when you want me to make you a cup of tea.'

I snuggled my head against the familiar scent of her shoulder and closed my eyes. Let myself imagine, briefly, that I was at home again, that this antiseptic-smelling room with the too-bright lights and the clicking machines was my bedroom in the farmhouse, that I'd suffered some stupid schoolgirl slight and that my parents, currently bickering lightly, would make everything all right for me again with a word, a glass of warm milk and a Jaffa cake. 'He's going to die, Mum,' I whispered. I felt her hesitation, her hand moved over my hair and I realised that she wasn't sure which 'he' I meant and was worried for both of them. It frightened me even more.

After a few minutes of sitting there being a little girl again, I straightened up and sniffed back tears which had yet to fall. 'Your sister and Rachel are thinking of going off on holiday in a couple of weeks,' my father said, as though this was the family dinner table. 'Why not see if you can go with them?'

'If you're better, Brian; they're only going if you're better.' My mother fussed his sheet straight. 'But that's a good idea. A holiday would be nice for you, dear. Where is it they're going; Spain somewhere isn't it?'

They're trying to make everything normal. Pretending that life will go on. Only you know it won't if anything happens to Sil – life might as well stop at that moment because nothing will ever happen again that matters.

'I'll think about it.' I took a deep breath. 'But leaving Liam in charge of the office wouldn't be a great move. He might get ideas above his station, and Liam's proper station in life is a bare platform with one train a week. In Wales. In the rain.'

Dad smiled at me. It was a complicated smile in which bravery in the face of pain was tinged with sympathy and something like fear. 'You go and do what you have to, love,' he said quietly. 'Just remember what I said.'

I hugged them both and left the hospital, not liking to ask for clarification on exactly which things I was supposed to remember. Probably not anything grammatical, I thought, wiping my hand over my eyes so that I could meet the outside world looking my usual self. Or about not staying out after midnight – that was years ago. My brain skittered around the things he'd said recently, about being careful and things not always being as they appeared, but those thoughts all came layered under the plastic sheeting of Sil, and what he'd done. They needed careful unpacking, consideration. Coffee would help, I thought, and turned to walk to the office.

As I passed under the ancient curved archway leading to High Petergate, I noticed a zombie walking ahead of me. Well, I say walking, it was more of a kind of localised shuffle: it looked as though he'd got his legs on backwards – not altogether unlikely given zombie tendencies to sew or stick on anything that had fallen off with more haste than mindfulness of biological design. I didn't pay him much attention; zombies usually worked the night shift, needing no sleep and not much in the way of wages, so finding one heading through the streets at this time in the evening was normal enough, and, since I hadn't had a call-out, he was unlikely to be out of area. However, *something*, call it the second-nature of someone who'd spent the last few years sharing an office with Liam and a series of unreliable electrical devices, made me look up. Jerked me out of my dark thoughts and worry and made me pay attention. When I did, I saw the man following him.

Not just following. Not innocently walking behind, looking for an opportunity to overtake, but actual *following*. I started to watch, one hand cautiously resting on the butt of the tranq gun – okay, shooting humans wasn't actually *allowed*, but it wasn't totally forbidden either since no-one had ever thought it would come up, and Liaison worked both ways.

The man ... the *human* man was vaguely familiar, in the way that sends up a mental flag saying 'not pleasant', and I ran through my brain's album of troublemakers. He was average height and stocky, with square shoulders and wide hips giving him the look of a walking shoe box.

My brain was suddenly flooded with memories. *A crowd, celebrating … fists raised in triumph*. Just like the gang of other like-minded souls preparing to harass Ryan, the zombie who'd been filling his veins with glue-mix. Those Britain for Humans nutjobs who really believed that Otherworlders should be despatched without mercy, 'Sent to the hell they came from,' as they put it in their sound-bite-friendly way. They thought that the vamps, zombies, weres and all the other species that had come through when the planet had suffered a brief magnetic flux, were a constant threat and should be annihilated, not tolerated or accommodated. This brought them into conflict with me on quite a regular basis – they probably had me on the 'to be dealt with as collateral damage' list, always supposing they could spell 'collateral' and, indeed, knew what it meant.

It was good to give my brain pure action to focus on. Watching these two, thinking about work, pushed the sick dread down from behind my eyes and I took my first deep breath in what felt like forever. Neither of them had noticed me. The zombie stopped walking suddenly and turned into the doorway of the pub; the Britain for Humans guy instantly pretended an interest in the window of the bookshop next door. I watched them over my shoulder, pretending my own interest in the window-displayed chalkboard menu. The zombie went inside, obviously for a night shift of cleaning and security work, while his stalker drew out a notebook and made a quick scribble before dragging himself away from the attractions of teen fiction and heading into the gathering evening crowds.

Right. So they were checking up on zombies' workplaces, were they? This was not good at all. I stared at the seafood section of the menu a bit longer. Zombies were fairly easy targets: slow-moving and clumsy and, best of all for anyone who wanted to take them out without suffering more than a nasty bruise, flammable because of all the glue. It looked as though Britain for Humans were planning some hits on the zombie population, but there was nothing I could do until something happened. I couldn't follow everyone all the time, not without being cloned, and I didn't think either the streets of York or Liam would survive if there were many more of me about. Anyway, we'd fight over shoes.

I pondered a moment more, still half-trying to improve my appearance with the aid of a reflection into which a seafood selection was embossed, when my phone rang. Unknown Number but, hey, it was chat to someone or hurry home to face Mister Sucky and a lecture on ... I dunno, how much better footwear was a century ago, or something. 'Hello.'

There was a pause so long I wondered if it was a crank call; I was just about to start shouting abuse when ... 'Jess?' The voice was so broken I didn't recognise it.

'Who is this?'

'It's ... I have stolen this telephone, mine is gone, Jess; all my money, my cards, they have taken everything from me ...'

'*Sil?*' My skin rose into goosebumps and pulled tight against my bones. 'Where ... what's happening?'

Another pause. 'I wish I could tell you something, Jessica. I wish I could make some sense, but I cannot. There is nothing I can say.'

God, oh God. 'I just want to know what happened, Sil. I want to know what happened to *you*. Can you ... where are you?'

The staccato wingbeats of a breaking signal. 'I am travelling.' His voice sounded tired, heavy with hopelessness. 'Travelling concealed, with a stolen phone and another's clothes, it is a twisted Purgatory that I am in, but at least I am moving.'

My stomach twanged, that weird window feeling opened up in my gut and I could feel his words, his fear, echoing inside me, feel the terror cooling his skin. 'Where are you going?' It was hard to get the words out.

'… coming.' The line broke, hissing and whining in my ear. '… meet me. Our place, after Malfaire, tonight.'

'But …' The line was dead. Killed by distance, by motion, by a desire not to talk any further, I couldn't tell. I had to stagger back a few steps and lean against a wall until the breath came back into my lungs and the pain that gripped at my heart lessened. I let myself fall forwards, hands resting on my knees, until the blood came back to my head and my brain started to work again.

My love scythed through me like Death making a house call, but I couldn't let it take me over, had to be practical, had to think things through, one step ahead, even though my heart was beating so fast that it whirred.

Sil. Not denying what had happened, but at least wanting to see me. Which is good, right? I mean, if he wanted it over he could just … just what, Jess? Everyone wants him eliminated for the good of the Treaty; he's hardly in a position to send a bunch of roses and a 'thanks for everything' card, is he?

A snatch of breath and I straightened up. The spool of whatever lay coiled in my belly wound itself a little tighter, and I smiled grimly. *Right. He wants to see me, does he? Well, he'd better be one fast-talking Suckface then, because if his excuses aren't more solid than Liam's rock-cakes, I'm going to kill him myself.*

I squared my shoulders and walked towards home, ignoring the treacherous little voice that whispered at the back of my mind, *Yeah, Jess, now think it like you mean it.*

Chapter Fifteen

When I got home, Zan was sitting on the sofa fiddling with his Blackberry. There was a half-drunk glass of Synth on the table and classical music filled the room through almost invisible speakers. Clearly a wild night *chez* Bitey.

He looked up as I came in. 'Ah, Jessica. There is some … human food in the kitchen, if you are hungry.'

I stared at him, grateful that my astonishment at his sudden civility allowed me to cover my distressed expression. 'Did I just come in the wrong house? Or are we starring in some kind of vamp remake of *The Odd Couple*?'

An inclination of the head and he turned back to the phone. 'I merely thought you might wish to eat,' he said. 'I didn't realise we were going to be partaking in *Mastermind*.'

'Sorry. Yes. It's been a bit of a weird day.'

'Another one?'

'I think it's my default setting. Look, I'm a bit tired and I've got a killer headache; I think I'll just go to bed, Zan.'

A totally unreadable look from those green-marble eyes; then a slow nod. 'Of course. I sometimes find myself forgetting your human bloodline. You need sleep. Of course,' he repeated.

Should I tell him? 'I had a strange phone call on my way home,' I said carefully, watching his face, although I didn't know why – Zan could have given snakes lessons. 'I think it might have been Sil trying to make contact.'

He looked back down to the phone in his hand. 'He has attacked humans, Jessica. For the sake of the Treaty there is only one course of action open. He must know that, and for the sake of your position I trust you understand what must be done.'

I sighed. 'Empathy, Zan. It's a real thing you know.'

He didn't look up. 'Alas, like a flat of your own and a car, it is evidently one of those things you cannot afford.'

'I meant *you*,' I said and he looked up again.

'And how long would this city remain if I were empathic, do you think? All those pleas for clemency, all those "It was just the one ..." How many times could we allow the Treaty to be broken before it became commonplace – or do you feel it should be different because it is *you*?' There was a surprising tightness around his mouth as he spoke, a betrayal of some emotion, and, as far as I knew, Zan had had all his emotions removed a long time ago. And probably pickled. He stood up, surprisingly imposing. 'If it starts with your lover, Jessica, where does it end? We excuse your family, then your friends, then someone you once met at a party?' He was angry now, his fangs covering his lower lip, his breath hissing in and out. I found my hand travelling to the tranq gun in my pocket and I really hoped I wasn't going to have to use it: knocking out my housemate would be horribly embarrassing, plus I'd be on washing-up duty forever.

'I know, Zan. Really, I do.' That still image from the camera footage was stuck in my mind like a fishbone in a throat; Sil, with blood in his hair and on his cheek, lips curled back over reddened fangs.

'I hope you do, Jessica.' The fangs betrayed his remaining anger, but he sat down and picked up the phone again. 'I hope you do.'

There was nothing further I could say, so I left him to his reprogramming and went upstairs to lie on the bed and to speak to the one person who would understand.

Liam was clearly doing something with the hand not holding the phone but, since I knew Liam quite well, I didn't want to ask what it was. 'Did he just ring in?'

'Yes. But he sounded really *weird*, Liam. Kind of ... strung out, if a vampire can *be* strung out without having had second helpings of my arteries. He wants to meet me tonight, at "our place".'

'So he's heading north, then? Unless "your place" is Hyde Park.'

'I'm not a hundred per cent sure where "our place" is, actually.'

Liam made an incredulous noise. 'Seriously? Jessica, unless you have all the romance of an A to Z, surely you must know where it is? Like you know what your song is and all the significant dates in your relationship from first drink to, well ... I've got a spreadsheet for me and Sarah.' He added, smugly.

'And that's romantic?'

'It is if you're me.'

'You have no idea how glad I am that I'm not.' My fingers prickled with the desire to know Sil's skin again, the touch-memory of his hair, the sensation of his demon firing up with the desire that crackled when we were together, and the smooth understanding that ran like a current between us. I gave myself a mental kicking. He'd gone. Left. And now he was in trouble ... *But he'd called me. There's not much trouble that a vampire can get into that a human can get him out of, so there's something else, a reason he wants me.*

'You okay, Jess?' Liam's voice held all the concern that Zan's hadn't. 'Have a coffee. Doesn't sound like you're going to be sleeping much anyway, so another caffeine-overload isn't going to hurt.'

'He left me. And now he's in trouble ... presumably thinks I can help, because that was not a phone call to remind me to put the rubbish out.' I chewed a nail. 'But why? I mean, two weeks without a word, no e-mails, nothing, and then suddenly he goes mental and I'm supposed to jump when he says so? Why the hell should I?'

Something squeaked at Liam's end of the phone. 'Well, for

one thing, you might be the only person he can turn to; you might have some specialist knowledge that could help him—'

'Only if he's in the kind of trouble that requires sourcing a phenomenal number of paper clips.'

'Which he might be, we don't know. And, also, because you are crazy mad in love with the guy, and him just buggering off isn't going to change that any time soon.'

I rested my forehead in my hands. 'I just want to see him, Liam.' My voice sounded broken, even to me. 'I just want to know ...'

'And you should.' The squeaking carried on – it sounded as though he was squeezing a hamster. 'I know it looks bad but ... well, no, there isn't really a "but". Oh no, I've just thought of one ... you are a kick-ass woman, and you are *not* going to sit around pining for some bloke without knowing what happened. You are going to get in there, give him a hefty kick in the bollocks and ask for an explanation, because it's what you're owed, all right? And if he still wants your help, once he can talk again, *then* you can decide what to do. Sound reasonable?'

'I don't know about *reasonable*. But it sounds like a plan.' I managed a weak grin down the phone. He knew, and I knew, that my trying to find Sil had never been in question, whatever the reason, however dubious my motivation. How could I not? 'By the way, what are you doing?'

'Pumping. Look, he's a vampire – we can't second-guess his motives. Hell, we can't even first-guess them. You're right, you just need to know what's going on and we can take it from there.' There was a pause and Liam panted down the phone a couple of times. 'Sorry. Sarah's mother is coming to stay and I'm blowing up the spare bed.'

'Which I am very relieved to hear, because you are making some very weird noises.'

'Story of my life. So, what are you going to do?'

Chapter Sixteen

I hadn't been entirely sure until now what I intended to do. Sit and wait for Sil's inevitable capture, telling myself that it was what he deserved? Ring the papers and tell them he was heading for York? Or head out for the only place that I could think of that might qualify as 'ours, after Malfaire'. After the demon had tried to kill us, the place we'd hidden, the place where ...

I shook my head and walked on. It was late, somewhere around midnight, the air was cool and smelled of stale beer and the river. The only people on the streets were those out enjoying themselves, or those for whom enjoyment wasn't much of an option. A ghoul, spinning along in a dark circle of air, ignored me, which was fine: I didn't want to have to think about work tonight.

It was even cooler by the river, and there was a vampire about: I could feel it, somewhere. But that was nothing unusual, most of our local vampires were so image-conscious that they only came out after dark, so they got the maximum boost to their 'mysterious and gorgeous' auras – even *I* looked mysterious after dark, although my gorgeousness depended on very low lighting levels and a high intake of alcohol. I walked down to where the river sloshed up a high cobbled slope designed for launching boats and parking ice-cream vans, and then further down, almost to where the murky waters met the concrete. The river was low for the time of year and I could clearly see the storm drain where Sil and I had ...well ... we'd ... My body gave a little disloyal shiver of pleasure as I remembered. *I'd been so, so cold, and there he was, heated by the effects of my narcotic blood, offering to warm me, to touch me, to give me what I'd burnt myself up with wanting. And I'd fallen. Lowered all the barriers and let myself drop, hoping he'd catch me. And he had. Or, at least, he'd* said *he had …*

This had to be the place. But no time had been mentioned, had it? Still. No harm looking. No harm retracing my steps to the place where I'd found that a vampire could feel loss and guilt. Such pain that they chose to keep their emotions locked away, out of reach even of themselves, rather than suffer centuries of feelings, centuries of blame.

I bent down and looked into the drain. There was a tidemark up the walls where the spring floodmelt had briefly caused the river to rise, and a huddled bundle almost out of sight further up.

Vampire.

'Hello?' I stayed at the mouth of the tunnel.

'This must be a truly amazing disguise.'

'*Sil?*' I took two steps inside before I remembered. He'd left me. Gone, without a word. I stopped, fingers just brushing the grip of the gun.

'You came.' His voice sounded hoarse, broken over words that should never have been said. 'That's good. I wasn't sure …'

I strained my eyes through the darkness at the slumped shape. 'You look …'

'I'm wearing jeans, Jess. *Jeans.* Can you imagine how distressing that is? They aren't even *designer.*'

'Sil, what happened to you?'

And then the tiniest noise, just a loud swallow followed by a muted indrawn breath. 'Jess.' And his voice was strained wide around tears. '*Jess.*'

I forgot the hunch, forgot the gun. Forgot everything other than that my lover was hurting, and moved forward along the sandy floor of the tunnel. A pair of arms like steel grasped me and pulled; a ribcage heaved against my cheek and retching sobs were muffled into my hair. '*Jess.*'

And I forgot that he'd left me. I forgot all those people he'd bitten. Forgot Zan's words about there only being one end to this – I forgot everything but the need to hold him close and feel the cool smoothness of his skin, the rough pebbles of stubble against my forehead as he put his lips to my face. I moved my head and brought my mouth to his, feeling an affirmation of our love in the depth of his kiss. And it was only after we'd breathed in one another and held that breath like two people in a smoke-filled room trying to hold on to the last gasp of oxygen that I moved away until I could look at him properly.

Even allowing for the nasty neon illumination from the riverside lights he looked terrible. 'What the hell did you do to your hair? It's not some trendy London cut, is it?' I touched the shorn, lopsided locks that littered the sides of his head and down his neck. 'Believe me, fringes are *not* going to make a comeback, whatever you were told.'

He kept a hold on my hand, a slightly desperate grip, as though he was afraid I might run. 'It's disguise. And it has worked, so far. I managed to hide in the back of a lorry heading up to Aberdeen; jumped out when he stopped at a service station. Then I stole a phone and called you and got in a horsebox heading for York Races. I walked here from the racecourse when it got dark.' He paused. 'It's a long way, isn't it?'

'It is if you're dressed like Val Doonican after a hot wash.' My fingers traced the line of his skin where the shrunken tank top didn't meet his waistband. The touch of him, knowing from the writhing of his demon that he was excited, despite himself … It was all I could do to stay sensible. 'Sil …'

A short, ragged breath. 'Look, Jess. Things are really bad for me.'

'Oh, you don't say. Well, I would never have known that, what with me living at the bottom of a bucket and everything.'

I pulled my hands away, now was the time to forget what he was to me and get some serious answers. I hadn't *quite* ruled out the kick in the bollocks either. 'What's going on?'

Another deep breath; then he folded his head forward into his hands. Uneven hair tumbled, hiding his expression. 'I really have no idea. Seriously. None. I remember us, being here, being ... in bed. The next thing I remember is being ... somewhere ...' A headshake. 'Coming out starving, all I could think was ... blood. And then ...' He stilled, even his demon was quiet. 'Those poor people. I was crazed, starved, so hungry and they were ... warm.'

There was a tiny sinking inside me. I'd hoped, *somehow* against all the odds, that the film of his attack had been, what? A mistake? Faked? To hear him admit what he'd done made my heart flop in my chest. 'So you fed from them. Couldn't you have got some Synth from somewhere?'

His head fell lower. 'I had no money. No cards, no phone, nothing, and I was *starving*. I think my demon just took over to save both of us, feed first and face the consequences later. I am mortally sorry for what I did and I would never have had it this way.' He looked at me and his eyes flashed grey to white in the strobing lamplight. '*Never*,' he repeated.

I took a deep breath. Professional. I was a professional. And there were two ways that this could go: I could shoot him now, call Enforcement, have the whole thing over by morning. Shrug off the memories, start again – try to fall in love with a human this time round. Or, and my fingers fell away from the gun with the inevitability of it, I could try to sort this out.

'The car was towed from the Embankment,' I said. 'Any idea why it was there?'

A silent headshake.

'Or why you'd gone to London? You didn't tell Zan or me, you just ... went.'

He slowly dragged his head up through his hands. 'Gods, Jess. All I remember is ... a girl, I think. And ... books? Just stupid little fragments, like pictures, images that mean nothing. If I was human I would have said they were dreams but ...' But vampires don't sleep. His voice tailed off and he stared at the wall of the man-made cave, eyes flickering. 'The last time I had an experience like that was'—he looked at me from eyes narrow with confusion—'when I fed from you.'

My blood. The only drug that had any effect on a vampire. 'What girl?' I said, focusing on probably the least mysterious element of the whole thing. 'Why were you with her? Did you leave me for her, Sil, was that it?'

'I don't *know*!' The shout filled the drain with sound, echoes of the glamour, the only magic a vampire had. The magic to make humans powerless, to entice, to do the vampire's bidding. The magic that had never worked on me. 'I don't know. Do you understand how that feels for me? With the exception of the time I drank from you, my actions have been under my control from the moment my demon hatched inside me, and now there is a blank space in my head, actions I cannot recall, intentions that will not be brought to mind.' A hand snaked out, touched mine. 'And all I can think of is you.' Fingers linked, and our joined hands were lifted to his lips. 'I need your help. I need to know that whatever I have done, you will help me.'

Choose a side, Jess. Either help your lover, or turn him in. For or against. Human or Other. Now is the time to decide.

I felt the pressure of his fingers; saw the desperation in his eyes. Those eyes and the touch of him. Things I had longed for since the day I met him. 'Okay,' I said, in a voice that sounded stronger than I felt. 'This is what we're going to do. Find out what the hell happened to you in London, why you felt you had to go there and what you were doing.'

'Yes.' A half-laugh. 'Yes.'

'Although I warn you, if it turns out you left me for some floozy with a short skirt and her boobs on display, I am going to turn you in to Enforcement there and then.'

'I …' Sil increased the grasp on my hand. 'I feel … it is you, Jess. *You*. Underneath, somehow, that it was all … for you?'

'Hoy, bitey-boy, don't you go loading all your guilt onto me. I'm fairly sure I never even mentioned so much as a dirty weekend in Battersea, so I am not taking the blame for any nasty little secrets you've gone and got yourself, all right?' But I increased the grip on his hand regardless. 'It can be sorted, Sil.' I reached up and moved his hair so that I could see his face properly. 'It can.'

He raised our joined hands to his lips once more and then touched my face. 'Please, Jess.' And now his voice was a clotted whisper. 'Please.'

'Right.' *Organise, it will stop you thinking* … 'We need to get you out of here and somewhere you won't be found.' My mind was buzzing. He couldn't go home: Zan would turn him in in a heartbeat. Liam had his mother-in-law coming to stay, and the office was far too public a place. Rachel had a spare room but I didn't feel that turning up late at night with a smelly vampire in tow would be a great move. 'Okay. You'll need to wait here while I get some transport.'

He nodded slowly. 'And some Synth? It has been some while since I … fed last.' He drooped his head in shame. 'Oh gods,' he whispered as though the horror was coming home to him again. 'I fed …'

'Yes, all right, shut up about that now. I'll be back in half an hour, sit tight.' And reluctantly I unwound our conjoined fingers, gave him a brief flash of a smile I didn't feel, and headed out into the night streets.

Chapter Seventeen

Sil lay under the blanket in the boot of the car and allowed a tiny glimmer of hope to illuminate his heart. *She can do this. She can make it all right.* He felt his demon give a little jerk as it sensed the adrenaline coming from her and wished for a moment that it would lie still, let him pretend that Jess was cool-headedly sorting things, putting things right, rather than betraying her anxiety.

'Where are we going?' he called across the dog-haired acres and wriggled uncomfortably – a supreme predator should not be shut in the back of a Volvo. 'Because it isn't very nice back here.'

'Shut up and lie still,' came the answer, to the accompaniment of grinding gears. 'This is the world's worst car to drive, and having you nagging from the back doesn't make it any easier.'

He lay back again, until the overwhelming smell of moist canine got the better of him. 'Can't I sit in the front, with you?'

Graunch. 'No, you can't. If I drive through any security cameras the Hunters will be all over me like ... like a bunch of tight-shirted muscular men with guns. Okay, I'm sure there's a downside to that ... oh, yes, you'd be dead.'

Sil closed his eyes and remembered the sheer relief he'd felt earlier, burying his face in her hair and holding her close. That weak, human frame that seemed so frail compared to his demon-enhanced hawser-strength and yet held such power, such unbounded certainty that her path was the right one.

He laid his head against the bumping floor of the car and closed his eyes. Let himself feel almost safe for a second, let the screw of tension that was sending his demon pirouetting around his chest uncurl just a fraction. *I trust her. More than I trust myself, in fact. What was I doing in London? Why do I have a fraction of a memory of a girl, smiling, flirting with me? I would not be disloyal to Jessica, I would NOT, and yet … the memory comes with a feeling of hiding, concealment … gods, Jessica, if I have done anything to hurt what we have, never mind the Hunters, I will shoot myself where I stand.*

And then another memory, this one ringing with clarity. *A child. Stopping me in my tracks, attacking the monster who had bitten his mother …* A wave of nausea climbed his throat, fuelled by the hasty bottle of chilly Synth he'd chugged down in the tunnel. *Monster. I have become again that which I tried so hard to leave behind, a blood-crazed animal who disgraced my attempts at humanity – so who am I really? A few bottles of Synth away from being a beast or a man struggling for compatibility with a demon that drives me to lengths I should never consider?*

The car bumped once more and he heard Jess swear, then speak to him over her shoulder. 'Sorry. Got to pull over.' He was thrown to the side, banging himself against the spare tyre as the car lurched and stopped on an angle. 'There's trouble. You stay there.'

He heard her open the driver's door and shout something; then voices, male, raised in aggrieved complaint. He sat up and peered like a cautious spaniel through the rear windscreen to see Jess, her hand on the shoulder of a doubled-over zombie, facing down two of the bronzed, muscled brutes who pretended to patrol the streets 'to keep order'. Sil vaguely recognised their faces from the office, where pictures of those 'likely to cause nuisance' were Blu-tacked to the wall in one of Zan's rare lo-tech forays into the world of detection.

'He's a dead glue-guy, yeah?' one of them was saying. 'Out after curfew? We don't allow that kinda thing round here.'

Jess bent to the zombie and spoke quietly; then stood up again. 'He's on his way to work, you morons,' she said, and Sil's demon grew positively frisky inside him on her rising anger and the overload of testosterone the two thugs were giving off. 'You know perfectly well that the zombies run the night-shifts because they don't need sleep.'

The other shorn-headed youth did a double-footed shift. 'Oh yeah? Still on our patch, still after dark, so I say we bring down a world of pain on Uhu-boy here.' Sil watched the fists bunch, and the lighters held within them flare, saw Jess straighten her stance, head up and chin set.

'No, I'll tell you what happens. You apologise to Richard here and then go on your way.' Her voice was remarkably gentle, she sounded almost deliberately feminine and unoffensive, he thought, trying to defuse the situation through calm. 'All that's going to happen otherwise is trouble. Richard has his permits and all his paperwork in order; you are in the wrong here.'

The zombie managed to get upright. Sil gave him a cursory glance, didn't recognise him, but then zombies had the kind of faces that tended to change quite quickly, a nose off here, the lopsided look of injected silicon sealant there. He knew that zombie-ism had come through the dimensions with the Otherworlders on infected food, and that it had almost died out since the source had been identified, but since the zombies could, theoretically, and given large enough supplies of Araldite and other fixatives, live forever, there were plenty about. He couldn't, even as City Vamp, be expected to know them all. But Jess did.

As he gave the zombie's face another quick scan in case it was someone he *ought* to know, one of the brawny-brothers swung a punch. There was a sound like an accident in a meatpacking factory and the zombie went down. Jess shouted, 'Hey!', and then the two men were on her and he lost sight of her in the melee of fists and feet and general mayhem.

'Shit. Jessie …' he slithered around. The boot didn't open from the inside, so all he could do was press his face to the window and watch, occasionally rubbing the smeared glass to improve his view, his demon cantering through his chest with impatience, like a racehorse in a too-small paddock.

Jess was down on the floor, one of her attackers next to her, bent double and groaning over his gonads. She had the other attacker in the kind of headlock he wasn't going to get out of with both ears intact. In one movement Jess pulled out the tranq gun, fired a single bolt into the neck of the man she'd got in the complicated wrestling hold, who went limp with what sounded like a grunt of relief, and then was up on her feet, facing down his compatriot, who was still writhing on the ground. 'Get your friend home,' she said, and her words were quiet again but distinctly unfeminine this time. 'And get the fuck out of town.'

The writhing one gyrated a bit more. ''S fuckin' *illegal*, that is.' His reply was a little strangulated. 'Tranquing humans. 'S not allowed.'

Jess came in really close now. Sil caught the scent of her hair through the crack in the car window, a combination of jasmine and coconut, and his demon danced at the arousal it sent through him. '*Only if somebody sees*,' she whispered, and smiled a smile so nasty that even Sil felt his hackles prickle. 'Okay, off you trot, boys.'

'Bitch,' Mr Groinally-Challenged spat, from his position on his knees.

'Remember my name. You'll be screaming it later, followed by the words, "Help me, please."' She pocketed the gun. 'Now, *go*.' Amid much rebellious muttering the man picked up his fallen companion and began dragging him along the pavement towards the centre of town. Jess watched them go, and then frowned at the zombie, who was watching rather sheepishly. 'And, Richard, what have I told you? In *pairs*, you go out after dark in *pairs* at the moment.'

'My mate went on earlier; was his turn to open up.'

'Then you go early with him, understand?'

His nod was combined with a splash of almost-anger. 'It's not right! I was minding my own business – why should it be *us* creeping about!'

She sighed and patted his arm. It made a hollow noise. 'Yeah, I know, Richard. Life's not fair, yada yada, just deal with it, okay?'

'But ...'

'Go on, you don't want to be late.' She bent to pick up the dropped cigarette lighters and the zombie shuffled off into the night with a rather wobbly shrug and much muttering. Then she turned and wrenched open the car's rear door, and rounded on Sil as he straightened himself out into the moonlight. 'I thought I told you to keep your head down!'

'I was concerned. You were fighting.'

Jess blew her unruly hair from her eyes, eyes which blazed at him with an anger and a fire that sent his demon rocketing again. 'I'm *always* fighting! It goes with the job, like paper cuts and Liam's horrible jokes!'

I wanted to protect you. I want to keep you safe from hooligans like that. Oh, gods, Jessica, I want your life to be happy and filled with cake and beautiful things. I want you never to have to fight or risk so much as a broken nail. I want you in my bed as you are in my heart, my lovely, feisty, infuriating woman. He thought the words but knew better than to say them. Instead he cleared his throat and gave her a small nod. 'Yes. I am sorry; I did not intend to demean you by watching.'

The anger drained from her face and she pursed her

mouth in an expression he thought meant she was trying not to laugh. 'Bloody vampires,' she said. 'All about the dominance.' And then she stepped in close; the press of her body was delicious as she hugged him. 'Thank you,' she said quietly. 'At least they didn't see you. But then, it's dark and you look'—a quick grimace—'horrible. Come on, back under your blanket.'

'Now that is an offer I cannot refuse.'

'Alone, bitey-boy.'

He tightened his grip around her waist and felt the tremors running up her spine, the delicious rucking of her skin beneath his touch. Her body was betraying her, whatever her mouth may say. 'I have missed you, Jessica.'

'Well, yes, I've missed you—' He cut off the sentence, moving his mouth against hers, feeling her try to speak against the pressure but giving up and giving in to him. She opened her mouth wider to his and stretched her body the length of his own, it felt like hot wire pressed to his nerves. He caught her more tightly and moved them both back until she was resting against the side of the car, and he could lean in without the risk of knocking her over backwards; grasping her hair to move her head back so he could flick his tongue along the slope of her neck, down to her shoulder. *Does she trust me? Truly?*

For one, sweet second she relaxed, her legs buckling against him, her body sagging in his arms and then she was up, rigid, arms no longer wrapped around his neck but pushing against his shoulders until he stepped away. She was panting, her cheeks pink with blood and the little vein in the side of her throat pulsing like a cheap motel's Welcome sign.

'Hey, steady. This is almost an act of gross indecency.' A glance down. 'Enormous indecency, anyway.'

He nearly laughed, but his eyes were caught by the blue tracery that led through her skin. Caught and held, trapped.

'Sil!' She pushed his shoulders again and he became fully aware once more. Tore his eyes back up to meet hers, and found them soft amber, filled with an understanding he had no right to. 'I am not afraid,' she said. She turned her head slightly to the side, so the flank of her neck fell bare, tilted almost level with his lips. 'Whatever happened back in London, it wasn't you, Sil.'

'But—'

'No. It might have been your body, your demon, but it wasn't *you*.' She knew what she was doing, tempting him there with her blood, that sweet narcotic that would not only feed him but allow him to rest, to blank things out for a while, to forget. He knew it. For a second the temptation rose with his demon ... *sleep, memory, peace* ... but he forced it away and took a small step back.

Her fingers traced his cheekbones, ran lower, over his lips. 'Did you ever really doubt me, Sil?' And her voice became a whisper against his breath. 'Seriously? Did you worry that I'd be afraid of you now?' Soft lips upon his. '*Never* doubt me.' Fierce now. '*Never*.' And then she was away, sliding back into the driver's seat. 'Come on. I want to get you hidden away somewhere safe; then we can start to work out whatever is really going on here.'

Sil shook his head slowly to give the feel of her fingers time to drop from his skin. *I will, quite simply, never understand women, particularly this one.* He climbed back into the car, over the rear seats and repositioned himself under the dog-smelling blanket with a sigh.

Chapter Eighteen

It hurt to leave him. Physically. I ached as I drove away, leaving him dishevelled and disorientated, watching me go from the doorway of my family's farmhouse on the moors. I kept his dark form in my mirror as long as I could, until the final bend in the farm track took him from me, and I had to pull the car over on the cattle grid that met the main road and let some of the tears fall from the burning agony in my chest. I didn't dare stay in case Zan missed me. Not that Zan and I were exactly sharing a toast rack and morning paper over breakfast, but I wouldn't have put it past him to have some kind of secret 'clocking in' arrangement fitted to the front door.

Sil was safe, for a while at least. The house was empty, since my mother was staying in the hospital with Dad, and she had been pathetically grateful that I'd offered to go and check on the place to save her the trouble.

I slept properly for the first night in what felt like ages, and, in consequence, was late for work. But judging by the fact that there was no crowd of journalists waiting on the step, this was probably a good thing.

'Ah, Jess,' Liam said, with a brightness so artificial it should have been checked for E-numbers. 'Good morning.'

'What have I done now?' I hung up my jacket and flicked Liam a quick look, while my heart broke like waves inside my ribcage. *Liam wouldn't have told anyone about my phone call, would he? No. Really, no.* His expression was more exasperated than guilty and my heart gradually slowed, until I felt I could turn around and sit on the edge of my desk. 'Forgotten to submit your expenses claim again? Although I really should mention after five years of working together,

Liam, that claiming for "wear and tear on trousers" isn't making you any friends at Head Office, you know.'

Without answering, Liam placed a folded newspaper on the desk.

'Oh, not again!'

'Afraid so, Jessie. On the plus side, you made the front page today.'

I flopped the paper flat across my keyboard. They'd used a picture someone had taken of me leaving the office yesterday. My hair was caught in a panicking breeze and looked as though it was being pulled slowly upwards, and I had the wide-eyed stare of a hit-and-run bum-pinching victim. I scanned the so-called 'article'. It reported the bare facts of Sil's attack on the humans in London and then speculated on my allegiances, 'Oh bugger.'

Liam ducked his head lower. 'I rang Head Office, in my role as your Excuser. They're feeling a bit ... sensitive at the moment, with you being associated with a vamp that's gone loopy down south.'

Despite actually having had real sleep, I felt tired. 'I dunno, Liam. It's all looking a bit hopeless. I know York Council don't exactly have us on their Calendar of Useful Departments, but, at the moment I'm getting the feeling that I'm completely out of my depth. I mean, usually I have all the handle on things of a Jack Russell, but right now ...' I stopped and just shook my head. 'Right now, even a Jack Russell has the edge on me.'

'No!' He looked up quickly. 'Why do you keep doing yourself down? You're gorgeous, you're funny, you are absolutely *amazing* at your job ... oh, hang on, there's barely room for the two of us in here, we don't want to have to start knocking down walls just to accommodate your head.'

'Shut up, Liam. And, thanks.'

'What for?'

'The compliments.'

Liam raised an eyebrow. 'Me? I said nothing. You're a hideous old battleaxe who runs this office like a brothel – only without the interesting equipment – and who can barely string a sentence together. But haven't HQ already had words with you about split loyalties?'

'Maybe I should just take a leave of absence. Go and hide under my duvet or something. Tell Zan I've got a notifiable disease to stop him busting in every three minutes for one of his "chats", and just ... oh, I don't know, catch up with my woefully behind reading of *Heat* magazine.'

He gave me A Look. 'Jessie, you attract trouble like this carpet attracts unexplained stains – and those two things, now I come to think of it, are probably not unrelated. So maybe you're best off where your trouble is at least work-related, did you ever think of that?'

I stared at him. 'You're very bossy all of a sudden. Did you get a pay-rise to cover making decisions and being definite?'

'My inner geek has moved over a bit to let my inner office manager have a turn. It's like being possessed by a firm of accountants, for the record.'

I lowered my forehead until it was touching my desk. 'I don't know what to do,' I said to my feet and then closed my eyes.

Liam jumped up. 'You've always done your duty, you've always bagged and tagged and never let the bastards get away with so much as a *toe* over a boundary without the paperwork signed in triplicate! Ever! And I should know, because I have to do all the admin for that, and, let me tell you, it would far easier on you and me if you just kept schtum, because some of those buggers are so daft that they're out of area because they actually *forgot* they needed a permit. So you go out and send them home, either walking or in the Enforcement van, when it would be far easier to just have a quick word, and that wouldn't result in five forms and an online checklist every single time. I really *hate* those checklists.'

I glared at him. 'They are your job, Liam. You aren't paid to like them.'

'I'm not paid to do anything with them. I'm paid just about enough to unlock the door in the mornings, with a possible option on pressing one random button per day. Everything else is out of the goodness of my heart, which is being strained into cardiomyopathy at the moment.'

I sighed. 'Don't. One heart attack per year, I'm on a quota.'

He slumped back down into his chair. 'Yeah. Sorry, Jess. It just makes me angry. You put in all that effort and subject yourself to all that danger, and the council behave as though you're about to sell us out for two Kit Kats and a high-street voucher, and the press treat you as though your life is there for them to poke around in whenever they want.' A raised eyebrow. 'And you really *do not* want that, do you? The press poking around in your life, turning up ... well, who knows what?'

My mouth had gone dry at the thought. *They could be watching me, cameras at the ready ...*

'I shall do my best to live a suitably boring life then. Listen. What Sil has done deserves investigation. Going off the deep end like that, biting his way through a street full of shoppers in broad daylight? Not very Sil, you have to admit, not the MO you'd expect of a vamp who's normally so smooth that he looks like a Fair Isle sweater model. And why Oxford Street, of all places?'

He shook his head. 'You are way too close to ground zero on all this, Jessie. Way too close.' He bit his lip and scrunched his face up. 'But, yes, you do have a point. It's a little bit odd that Mister Bitey took himself off to London before going mental. Long way to go for a bit of sucky-action – why not stay here and let loose in one of the Blood Clubs?'

I opened my mouth to tell him that Sil couldn't even remember going to London, let alone why he was there, but realised that might not be a great course of action. 'Just go and put the kettle on,' I said. 'Just because you're getting all opinionated doesn't let you off making coffee. And you can bring out those emergency HobNobs too, I can feel a concerted think coming on.'

'First time for everything, then,' he muttered, not quite under his breath, and collected the mugs.

Chapter Nineteen

Sil roamed the farmhouse like a corporeal ghost. He caught Jess's scent and found her old bedroom, half-tidied into an office space but still retaining the bed, the poster-covered wall dotted with train tickets from forgotten journeys and a cupboard that held a collection of old school books and photographs that kept him busy for several hours.

You were so young. He traced the outline of her face, plumper with youth and cheekier with innocence, his heart uncomfortably heavy with the knowledge that he and his kind were one of the reasons she'd lost that. *So sweet back then, in that ridiculous school uniform, tie under one ear and your buttons done up wrongly, hanging on your school friend's arm and mugging at the camera as though life was just one big joke.* He flipped the pictures over, seeing images from her life in scattered order, one minute she was a bony-kneed seven-year-old on a small, fat pony, all earnest eyes and screwed-down pigtails; the next she was late teens, flaunting a body she didn't seem to know what to do with. Then back to being a ten-year-old, blowing out candles on a cake; then a toddler squinting up at the camera. Sil felt that weight on his heart again. *All these ages. And while you were growing up, growing … I was this. A twenty-nine-year-old vampire. The person I was then is the person I am now.* He put the pictures back into the cupboard. *I barely remember what it was to be like you, young, life stretching like the world's most exciting unread book, all I had to do was to turn the pages and …*

He turned. Walked out of the little room and back downstairs to pace around the kitchen, watched by an impassive series of cats, who sat along the worktops like a scrambled set of Russian dolls. 'This is ludicrous,' he said aloud, the sound of his voice making cat ears twitch. 'Why am I even here?' Once more around the table, the contrast between the homely domesticity of rag-rugs and pine furniture and the twisting mass of his demon as it pirouetted in his chest tugged at his heart. 'There must be something ... some way I can achieve something useful, to my cause, to hers.' He stroked a matriarchal tabby, which dipped its head as if in agreement. 'Some way to find what I hoped to acquire in London?' The cat narrowed its eyes beneath his hand and gave a punctuating purr as he performed one last circuit of the room and headed out into the flagged hallway, trying to walk sense into his thoughts.

I left the car on the Embankment. His vision swam for a moment, a fluid memory rising and falling like a dream of mercury recalled through mist. An emotion, almost like the tug at his soul he got when Jess was thinking of him, a niggle, almost like pain, and an image of a girl sitting at a desk, flirting with him, came floating into his head. *Is this memory? God knows, a hundred years of life means more memories than I can call to mind ... Who is she, this girl? And, more importantly,* what *is she to me? Friend, acquaintance ...* An awful possibility crept in and he forced it down. *No. I would never take another woman now I have declared for Jessica. Never.* But the fear still flared under the flickering edges of memory, that dread that something may have turned him, some unknown affliction may have played him until he betrayed both himself and his love.

A shiver, and his demon revelled. *No. I must hold true. I must find a way of doing something about this goddamned mess.* With the heels of his ghastly trainers squealing on the stone, he turned sharply into the low-ceilinged sitting room. A wood-burning stove stood cold sentinel and, on a table, a computer whirred its impotent fan into the dust.

Sil's heart began to rise. All was not lost if he could access the internet. Despite what Zan might think, he was no slouch in this new computerised age; he watched, he learned. Zan might have the edge when it came to technology, but Sil held the blade.

He hunched himself down in front of the keyboard, ignored the audience of cats that had followed him in from the kitchen, and began to search.

Chapter Twenty

I made up my mind to go and patrol, just in case the zombie-hating thugs had decided to groove the streets with their knuckles a bit more, but as soon as I got out of the door I walked smack into Zan.

My mind was still whirling from my conversation with Liam, and there were two ways my sudden encounter could have gone. In one universe I burst into tears and threw myself at virtually the only creature in the world who would wonder what the hell the fuss was all about, since Zan and feelings hadn't had a passing acquaintance since 1875. Thankfully I chose the universe of anger. 'What the hell are *you* doing here? Don't tell me you've taken a job as a Secret Shopper and you're popping into Next to check out their policy on trouser returns.'

Zan looked down at me. He was wearing a leather coat, which flapped gently in the breeze and made him look like the figurehead of a tea-clipper in full sail. 'I came to find you,' he said.

'You could have just come into the office. Or telephoned? Or e-mailed? Good God, can't I even do my job now without you trailing along in hot pursuit? Just get yourself a security blanket, Zan; it will be cheaper in the long run.'

Cold, green eyes, like the depths of the sea, held mine. 'Get into the car, Jessica.'

I'd never really been afraid of Zan before. He was too … pernickety. Liam and I quietly made fun of his hatred for physical contact and his obsession with all things technological; being scared of him would have been like being frightened of the guy who invented Facebook. But here Zan was no laughing matter; he was tall and rigid and *angry.* And ever so slightly scary.

'Look, I've got Liam in there getting all "I am Manager, hear me roar",' I said, trying to conceal the fact that he was making me nervous. 'So if you're going to get all mean and moody on me, be warned that I'm *this* close to trashing someone's entire DVD collection of *The Office*. I think it's giving him ideas.'

'Your petty quarrels are of no interest to me.' Zan waved a hand towards the car park.

'Oh, bugger. So you didn't come to rescue me from health and safety lectures and having to laminate procedural directives to stick on the back of the door then?' I fell into step beside the vampire, whose fangs I could see showing just a little behind lips pulled into a tight line. His demon was quiet though, which was strange; he should be getting a whole banquet of stuff from me: my blood felt like battery acid and disappointment. So, he looked and sounded angry, but his demon wasn't reacting to it, or to me? Strange. 'So, you came to fetch me, why?'

'Be. Quiet.'

Woah. Zan knew that vampire glamour didn't work on me, so he hadn't even tried to pull it. He'd just used pure, old-fashioned, alpha-male command, which – coming from a guy who made scarecrows look a bit plump and who seemed to have had all his butchness removed and replaced with slippers – was a bit of a surprise. I shut up and buckled myself into the Veyron, which he had driven into the pedestrian area, almost as though he owned the city. Which, I suppose, he did.

He swung the car out between swiftly dodging pedestrians and we slunk along the main road into town like a metal ferret on steroids.

After half a mile of stop–start traffic, I weakened and turned to look at him.

'Zan?'

He looked normal, well, as normal as a man who's been a demon-infected killer for over a hundred years can be: pale, intense-eyed and floppy-haired. But he also had a kind of tension about him that made him look leaner and tighter, as though all the sinews in his body had drawn together. 'Where are we going?'

'I see no reason to tell you.'

'Apart from the fact that, if you don't, this is kidnap and, you know, all illegal and stuff.'

Zan made a short laughing sound. I didn't think I'd ever heard him laugh before, and, since Liam and I had concluded his sense of humour came in somewhere around *The Hills Have Eyes*, it was disturbing. 'Jessica. You know as well as I do that, as a half-demon, you are subject to the laws and controls of the Otherworld. You are under my jurisdiction; therefore, to whom would you make these allegations?'

'I'll think of someone,' I said darkly. I still wasn't terrified, just afraid enough to be annoyed and defensive. Zan had never seriously harmed anyone. *That I knew about*, muttered my treacherous subconscious, but this behaviour was definitely not normal. For a start, if separated from his various computerised devices, Zan always carried on as though part of his brain was missing; actively removing himself from the office and its various flashing lights and beeping noises came close to voluntary lobotomy.

'I am simply distancing you from influences.' He twisted the little car down a side-street and over a small bridge, pulling over in a lay-by from which I could see the river.

'I don't have any influences. Except Liam, and I influence him, so that's more of a negative influence. An affluence. Outfluence. Effluence.'

'Be. Quiet.' He did it again, that cold command. I hated to admit it, but it made Zan just that tiny bit sexier. But that wasn't hard – he usually had all the sex appeal of a sarcophagus. 'Jessica.' He turned in his seat and his green eyes were narrow. 'We have been compromised.'

'Well, if you will go driving off with me and parking up … oh. You don't mean the old-fashioned way, do you?'

A single shake of his head. Zan had long hair for a man; like Sil, he tended to favour the styles he'd known when he'd been human. But while Sil's was untidy and always looked as though someone had run their fingers through it, Zan's was usually neat and off his face. Today it was showing signs of unruliness. 'The Otherworld computer system has been hacked.'

My first thought was Liam, and it must have shown on my face, because Zan gave another of those mirthless laughs. 'Did you think I was unaware that your office regularly creeps around our software?' His eyes were hard. 'I understand computers, Jessica. They are not like people, changing, given to flights of fancy and unreasonableness, they are singularly reliable and trustworthy; thus I find them perfectly easy to comprehend. Computers do not indulge themselves …' He tailed off for a moment with an expression of pained disgust. 'They are my domain,' he said. 'And I regard someone breaking into my files with the same emotion that I believe you would feel on learning that someone had raided your rooms and read your private documents.'

'I never knew vampires could feel violated,' I said. 'But then, I shouldn't suppose you get many burglars pissing in your kettles, do you?'

Zan tapped his fingers against the steering wheel. 'I was last burgled in 1934,' he said, almost dreamily. 'His fear made him utterly delicious.'

'Great. *Crimewatch* meets Jamie Oliver. So. The system has been hacked. If it's not Liam, and it most certainly isn't me because I've only just found out how to use the Search function … why are you telling me? Presumably you don't just want sympathy and a cuddle.'

Zan looked at me, and there was something in those deep green eyes that sent needles of cold into my veins. 'Whoever has done it has taken care to cover their tracks, using different ISPs to make it hard to trace back to source. I believe it is Sil,' he said.

'It … he … I mean … he's *alive*?' And now I knew why Zan was keeping his demon quiet. He needed it to read me, to react to any emotion I might give off; somehow he'd managed to suppress it so that he could use it as a kind of lie detector. I fought with everything I had to prevent my heartbeat speeding up, or my breathing from betraying me. 'But surely … there would have been news of him from somewhere?'

Zan's demon was moving, circling, feeding off my anxiety and confusion. 'You seem upset, Jessica,' Zan said and his demon swooped and dived. 'Do you have news of Sil you are keeping from me?'

Grit your teeth and hold your nerve. 'No! I'm just … well, it's a shock, that's all. I mean, he ran off, attacked people and now he's …' I shook my head. Hopefully my guilt and horror at the fact that Zan knew Sil was alive could be mistaken for fear and general upset. 'If it is him, of course. I mean, anyone with the ability could hack your system, couldn't they?'

There was a moment of steady regard and then Zan dropped his eyes. 'But they would need the ability and the inclination. Why should anyone wish to hack into Otherworld systems, unless they required information particular to us?'

'Why would Sil? What could he want to find out that he couldn't get from, I dunno, reading the papers or something? I mean, he must know that the entire world is out to get him; what are you running that he might need to know about? Anything that might help?'

Zan reached out and grabbed my face. It was so fast

that I didn't even have time to turn away, and found myself being held steady as he leaned in, so close that I could see his demon flickering behind his eyes, and the gold flecks in the green, like chips of moonlight floating in poison. 'I shall ask this question of you once only, Jessica. Do you know where he is?'

Careful ... so careful. You know this vampire, Jessica. You know him. I let my mind move from last night, leaving Sil in his terrible clothes looking vulnerable and shaken, sitting in my parents' kitchen, head in hands. 'Right now? I have no idea where he is,' I said, letting my body show the absolute truth of that statement. *He could be anywhere. In the garden, in the yard, up with the sheep.* Zan's demon took my certainty and dropped, feeling almost disappointed. *There, you clever sod,* I thought, but kept my expression hovering around the 'confused and hurt' mark. 'Why would you think I'd know?'

He let go of my face, letting his hands fall to his lap and dipping his head forward so that his hair swung against his totally smooth jawline. 'I know that you think I am cruel,' he said, in a quiet and, for Zan, almost emotional voice. 'To pass judgement on your lover; to call for his end. But bear this in mind, Jessica: he has been my friend for many years. We hunted together in the heady days before the Treaty and worked together in the days since; he had declared for me as I have declared for him, many times. He was the only thing walking this earth that I trusted. Now, knowing how I care for him, knowing what he has been to me, and that, even with this, I would see him die for his crimes – do you not understand?' He closed his eyes, as though he was trying to blank out his words, to disassociate himself from what he had to say. 'Do you understand how it hurts me?'

There was a huge, physical pain in my throat. I could feel the words rising, the urge to tell him where Sil was, to ease the awful sorrow that I could see etching itself into that ageless face; as my brain forecast a future response to my words, I bit them down and forced them away. His demon reacted, I felt it glide gleefully on my turmoil, giving me away to the vampire, who opened his eyes and turned to face me, mouth open and accusation clearly lined up on his lips. I did the only thing that I could think of, and I impressed myself with my own daring, I reached out a hand and touched his cheek. 'I never thought, Zan. I'm really sorry, I wish I could help.'

He responded as I'd thought he would, jerking away from the physical contact with an expression that indicated I'd not so much stepped across as hang-glided over some massive boundary. But at least it seemed to make him put my demon-feeding burst of feeling down to sympathy, rather than guilt. 'Your compassion is not necessary,' he said, stiffly, from the far edge of his seat. Thankfully he didn't pull out his handkerchief and wipe the offending cheek, but I had the feeling it was a close call. 'I told you merely so that you would understand the severity of the situation.' He straightened. 'Where may I take you?'

'Well, you could drive around a bit, maybe slow down past all those snotty girls I was at school with who didn't think I'd ever get anywhere in life,' I said, reckoning that slipping back into my usual persona was my best defence. 'You can beep the horn as well, if you like.' Zan gave me a pained look. 'Or, failing that, just drop me back where you picked me up, please. There's stuff kicking off: a bunch of guys with too much time and too many tattoos on their hands causing trouble and I want to take a walk around.'

Zan started up the supercar and I leaned back into its luxurious upholstery to think. *So Zan thinks Sil is guilty too. I really have no idea what to do now.*

Chapter Twenty-One

Sil stood at the window watching the darkening sky. He sipped occasionally from the bottle of Synth that swung between his fingers and tried to pretend that this was just a holiday, just a break from the everyday world. After all, many people would pay to stay in a place like this: a cosy, tastefully furnished house standing with views over the point where the fields blurred into heather and bracken. It was achingly picturesque and he'd not seen a soul all day, apart from a Barghest out hunting in the form of a giant black dog. It had been trotting up to some sheep, which had predictably reacted by becoming hysterical. Sil had waved a hand at it, whereupon it had transformed into the shape of a headless man and, rather sulkily, vanished in flames.

Is this loneliness? I don't believe it. Haunter of the dark places, the terror that comes from within, child of the night ... and I am seriously prepared to put early evening television on just for company. He took another swig of the blood and let his head fall forward, trying to make sense of his thoughts. *Otherworld office doesn't know anything about what happened to me, and they don't seem to be trying too hard to investigate. Gods. I cannot conceive how Zan can believe that I have run amok, but all information on the system shows that he is willing to hand me over to the human authorities, to the Hunters.* Sil tried not to remember the e-mails, Zan's promises of co-operation, his assurances that Sil would be found and brought to justice as a rogue vampire. Despite his snug surroundings, his isolation from the world, Sil gave a tiny shiver of fear. *I found nothing, nothing to help me. That means I am relying on Jessica.* He thought of her strength, her unwavering devotion to whichever path she set herself on. Remembered her desperation in the face of the knowledge that she was going to have to kill her father, and the single-minded way she had done it. And then he remembered her tears, her helpless misery, when the deed was done. *Is she strong enough? The situation looks hopeless: if I can't find a way out, how can she?*

Perhaps I should go. Yes. Leave this place to its memories of her as a little girl, innocent of the world that made her. I should run north, head for the border, maybe lie low somewhere in the mountains where I can't easily be tracked, try to keep my head down and … And what? He dipped his head again. *Die in a filthy bothy somewhere, wrapped in a dead sheep?*

He felt the connection with Jessica give a sharp tug. She was thinking of him, concentrating on him, not as a passing thought but as a serious consideration. He gave a half smile, which vanished from his face when the tug came again, hard enough to cause a thrust of pain this time. *Jess? What …?* And again. This time the connection felt like fire, like red-hot metal that spiralled and sparked somewhere in his gut, a line of flame that ran between him and her, a bond that felt as though it had been forged in hell.

He doubled over and the bottle of Synth fell from his fingers, spilling the remaining blood over his shoes as he crouched, arms wrapped around the pain's centre. A few words wheezed from his throat as the agony built and his demon reacted by sending out a shot of adrenaline that would have killed a horse, or at least enabled it to win several races concurrently, and his fangs lengthened in response.

Sil dropped to his knees amid the blood, feeling his demon building to take control, to remove the threat, and had just about surrendered himself to the loss of consciousness when he heard the door slam back against the wall of the room.

'What the *fuck* did you think you were doing?' Jessica

stood there, framed in the doorway, hands drawn into fists and her face pink with anger. 'Zan knew you'd hacked the system and he bloody nearly got me to admit I knew you were here!'

The connection exploded. In his stomach, in his head, pinpricks of silver embedded in his skin and behind his eyes, but the pain died away and he found that he could move. 'I … needed … to find out …' he gasped, still cupping his abdomen, afraid that if he stood up too quickly, his entrails may slide out. 'I cannot … just *sit* here …'

She kicked the door shut. 'Well, tough, bitey-boy.' She almost snarled. 'You came to me for help, so you should … what the hell are you doing down there anyway?'

'Indigestion.'

'Seriously? There's some Rennies in the kitchen cupboard … Hey, hang on, I'm really angry with you here, this is no time for medical advice! I almost had to make a pass at Zan to get him to stop thinking about you and, okay, so we were sitting in the Veyron at the time, and there's a lot of things I'll do to keep sitting in a Veyron but, let me tell you, shagging your boss is *not* one of them!'

Now Sil wasn't sure if the buzzing in his head was the after-effects of the fiery connection, or his brain's attempts to make sense of what Jess was saying. 'You … and *Zan*? You … and *ZAN*? No, I'm sorry, I'm not even sure that's physically possible.'

'I only said *almost*. He is so not my type, with the green eyes and the hair and pulling the alpha-male stunt and that body … Okay, not doing myself any favours here. Let's just leave it at *almost*, shall we? And then I can go back to being terrified that you are going to give yourself away and they are going to come for you.'

She whirled away from him now, going to stand by the window, watching the night. He suspected that she didn't want him to see her cry. 'I was careful,' he said, quietly. 'I used at least three ISPs to disguise my trail. He could probably track back to here, but only after a lot of hard work, and I didn't do any damage in his system, I just looked up a few old files, checked out what he was working on to see if he was ...'

She turned again and he could see the tears bubbling in her eyes. 'He's not trying to save you, Sil. He wants you dead.' Her voice rose at the end of the sentence, almost in surprise, and her shoulders gave a small shake. 'Even Zan.'

He nodded. 'I already know.'

For a moment she stood there, the dark sky behind and her dark hair tumbling over her face. Then she just said, 'Shit, Sil,' and closed the space between them, wrapping her arms around his neck and resting her forehead against his chest, pushing herself into him as though she wanted to possess him, to force his demon to relinquish charge and take him herself. 'You stupid bastard,' she muttered. 'You stupid, stupid *bastard*.' And all thoughts of running, of leaving this woman behind, disappeared, burned off by the heat of her body, the scent of her skin and the pain in her voice.

He pulled her in tighter, feeling the silk of her hair beneath his chin like the beginnings of a noose. 'I am sorry. I didn't think that ... I underestimated Zan. I just have to think now ... to break it all down until I can find a way out of this.'

Her arms clung. 'Maybe there isn't a way out. Did you think of that? Maybe there's nothing more to it than – you went off the rails.'

'Which you don't seriously believe.' His demon was spinning around inside his chest like a sample in a centrifuge, feeding off her doubt, her fear, her desire. It made his mouth water.

'And what makes you think I don't?' She stood back a little in order to look into his face. He felt the pull of those amber eyes almost as though she held a glamour of her own, a power into which he was falling.

'Because if you did, you wouldn't be here now. You would have killed me yourself, Jessica, when I first came to you. You would have been swift and you would have been merciful, but you would have killed me.'

She looked deep into his eyes, moving her hands to the back of his head. 'You keep remembering that,' she breathed, raising herself so that their mouths were level. 'You just keep remembering that.' He leaned in and their lips made contact, hers softly parted, his slightly puckered by the fangs that occupied his mouth.

Chapter Twenty-Two

I was still angry with him, and that anger made me kiss harder than I should have. His fangs nicked against my lower lip and I heard his soft moan as the taste of my blood ran against his tongue. Clearly not enough to incapacitate him, just enough to inflame, because he suddenly pulled me in tighter, so tight that my ribs could hardly move enough to get air in, and I found myself gripped against his horrible sweater so hard that the Aran pattern was embossing itself against my neck. I moved back as far as his grasp would allow. 'Back up, bitey.'

'Or what?' His eyes were black, flashing to occasional glimpses of grey, dominating that pale face, making his cheekbones stand out like running boards. 'Hmm, Jess? Bottom line?'

'Bottom line is I kick your ass all the way to Otherworld Central.' He was rigid against me, physically excited and mentally too, if the look on his face was anything to go by. 'I don't think this is a good idea right now. We're both too ...'

'Too ...? I think we're always *too,* Jess. Yeah, we're too wound up, too edgy, too fucking *scared*, but that's rather the point of being us, isn't it? Always on the verge of something.' He let me go suddenly and I almost toppled backwards. 'Remember before? Before we got involved, when we used to tiptoe around each other, both wanting and neither of us really knowing what it was we wanted?'

'Oh yes, I remember,' I said darkly. The watching, the wanting, all the time knowing that I couldn't have him, that he could never love me ...

'Well, now I *do* know.' He stepped in again, cool and beautiful. 'I know that it's you. And I want you, here and now, in case it's the last chance I ever get. If they take me, tomorrow, the next day, at least I can go knowing that we had this – that it was all real, you and me.'

'So you want us to have sex here, in my parents' living room, in case the Hunters come and get you? That is the most ridiculous reason I have ever heard.'

'We need a reason now?' One thumb trailed over my lips. 'I don't think we have *ever* needed a reason.' And he kissed me, gently this time, making my heart skid inside my chest and my breath stop in my throat. 'Love. It's the reason we've always had.'

'I don't want to lose you. I can't bear it, Sil.' My voice was still backed up, pulled down with the weight of unshed tears. 'But I can't see how we're going to get out of this.'

He drew me down onto the sofa, fingers cupped under my jawbone, holding my head steady as he kissed me again, harder now. 'No. Neither can I.' His eyes were burning now, clear and cold silver heated by an expression that called to me. '*Jess …*'

And suddenly I didn't care that everything seemed hopeless, I just wanted him to keep doing what he was doing. Sil's mouth raked over me, his fangs bumping against my skin and sliding, carefully, never even so much as nipping, his fingers gliding along after them until I was coiled tightly as a spring beneath him. My hands reached up and pulled his horrible jumper over his head, revealing that glorious taut body, pale skin almost gleaming in the moonlight.

'You're shining,' I murmured.

'If you say one single word about sparkles, I will bite you right … now.' His voice fell into a moan as I unfastened his equally horrible jeans and his cool flesh settled against mine, like nightfall.

'Jonathan.' I used his name, his *old* name, blew it into his hair as he raised himself above me. 'Remember who you are. Not a vampire, not here, not now. Here you are Jonathan.'

‘I wish …’ But whatever he wished for was lost in the rising heat as our mouths came together and I felt his hands slide down me, his body pushing us both down into the couch. Then everything became a pulse of bodies and heat and pressure, a labyrinth of limbs as we wove around each other, I became rootless and weightless and finally murmured his name again as the climax took me over; then clung to him as he fixed his eyes on mine, driving into me with a desperation that he could only show here, now, like this. ‘You, Jess. Just you.’

And then his demon was cartwheeling and spiralling, and he came on a moaned outbreath, gathering me to him and holding me so tightly that I could feel his bones pressing into my hips, burying his face against my hair. The smell of his skin seared into me, dark and deep, the mysterious smell of ancient papers with an undercurrent of thyme and rue. We sank back on the sofa and he was stroking my hair as I lay my head on his chest and tried to catch my breath.

‘So, what do we do now?’

His ribs heaved as he laughed. ‘It’s a little too late for me to offer to buy you dinner, I think. Perhaps some wine?’

I raised my head and gave him a hard look. ‘About’—I waved a hand—‘all this. You can’t hide here forever. Mum and Dad are going to come back eventually, and Zan is going to get suspicious if I keep dodging up to the farm all the time. Actually, scratch that, he already *is* suspicious.’

The laughter stopped. So did the hair stroking. Sil lay still beneath me. ‘I don’t know,’ he said. ‘And I am afraid.’

We lay for a while longer, wound around each other, without speaking. The simple rise and fall of his breath was enough for me, for now. Just to know he was here, that in this second we were safe.

‘Did you find out anything at all from the Otherworld system?’ I asked at last. ‘Or was it a complete waste of time?

Apart from me getting to hear Zan pull the Big Man voice, of course.'

Another moment of silence. 'I was trying to find out what I might have been doing on the Embankment. Whether I parked the car there purely for convenience, or whether I had business at that end of London.' He was speaking into the dark; I could hear the slight tremor in his voice. Sil wasn't just afraid, he was terrified.

'And did you?' I decided to give him the dignity of pretending I hadn't noticed.

'I scanned all the businesses within a mile radius of the point at which I was parked. Government offices, mostly, two riverside clubs'—a catch in his voice—'and a boat-hire place.' I stayed quiet. That quiver in his tone told me more than I wanted to know about his self-doubt regarding the clubs. 'I have no reason to visit any of those places,' he went on. 'None.' A sudden jerk of movement as his demon reacted to his uncertainty. Or mine. 'But I did establish one, small fact.'

'Go on.'

'Zan had been looking too.'

I struggled to sit up without leaving his embrace. 'So, Zan hasn't quite given up on you, then?'

'I didn't say that. All I know is that he had also been trying to track my movements. We cannot know whether that was to help establish my innocence or my guilt.'

A thin trickle of moonlight slid through the uncurtained window and illuminated our bodies, as though the couch was a stage set. He lay, full of the grace and ease that his demon lent him, as fine-boned and tautly muscled as a thoroughbred, but his eyes, black in this false light, were shadowed with anxiety. 'Use our system,' I said. 'I'm sure if you can hack into the Otherworld system, you can hack into ours. Then you can carry on looking without worrying about Zan tracking you.'

This probably counted as treasonable behaviour as far as York Council was concerned; there was probably some law on the statute books that said I could have my firkins crushed and my swoggle removed in public for doing this, but right now I would have done, and said, anything to help remove that tightness from his face.

'But Liam will know, Jessica. I cannot move through your system as easily as my own; there are passwords and ...'

'I'll give you the passwords.' And say goodbye to my one groat a year donkey allowance. 'And I'll deal with Liam.'

'*Jess* ...' He turned and breathed my name into my hair, pulling me in close again, as though he needed every molecule of my scent. 'I cannot let you expose yourself like that.'

'And I can't let you get shot down without at least knowing why.' Reluctantly I drew myself away, off the couch, and rummaged around in my jeans pocket, until I found the only piece of paper I had and, on the back of an old bus ticket, I wrote out the passwords to access the various parts of our system. 'Liam thinks I don't know these. He thinks I never pay attention when he's logging in, but I have to, otherwise I'd never be able to hack his Amazon account. That boy has some seriously strange reading habits, and I have an entire set of Terry Pratchett paperbacks he hasn't found out that he's bought yet. Thank you, one click purchasing.' I scribbled the last code and held up the ticket. 'Here.'

Sil raised a hand to take it; then closed his fingers, empty. 'Do you know what you are doing? In effect, handing over the tools of your destruction to the enemy. I could blow your system open to all comers, infiltrate your Tracker program, alter all your files. I could—'

'Yes, you could. But there are two reasons that you won't.'

'Which are?'

'You are Jonathan Wilberforce. Oh, yes, you might call yourself Sil these days, you might have a demon that lives off thrills and you might drink blood and all that, but ... at heart you are Jonathan. Husband of Christina, father to Joseph and Constance.' At the sound of his children's names, Sil became very, very still. 'You are a good man.'

Lips brushed my cheek. '*Thank you.*' Barely a breath. 'What is the other reason?'

'Oh, because you know that if you did *anything* to compromise my systems or to put the Treaty at risk, I would hunt you down.'

'Oh yes. That.' After a moment, his fist closed around the paper. 'I will not forget.'

'Better not, bitey-boy.' I began to slide my jeans back up my legs and fumbled my head and arms back into my shirt. 'And now, I have to go.'

'Can we not have this night, at least?' He ran one hand up my arm. 'We may never—'

'Yes, I know. But if I stay out all night and it's not to rattle my chains at the office, then Zan is going to know that something is up, and since I haven't had a night off since we went decimal, it won't take him a millisecond to work out what's going on. So ...' I turned, half-dressed, to face him. 'I have to go.'

A long, slow nod, and then Sil was slipping back into his nasty jeans, wincing at the cheap chain-store label as he eased it over his hips.

'Why don't you change into something else? I'm sure there'll be some clothes around here that would fit you better.' I finished climbing back into my generously discarded stuff, trying to ignore the fact that all this clipping and zipping held the coldness of a last meeting.

'No.' Sil turned to face me. Bare-chested he looked more 'vampire', composed and powerful. But then, that truly awful tank-top would have made Dracula look like a train-spotter. 'These remind me of what is at stake. They remind me how much I have already lost, and how much more I stand to lose if I cannot solve this problem.' Suddenly his arms were around me with a desperate strength. 'I promise you, Jessica, I will find out what happened. And then, if necessary, I will hand myself over to the Hunters, for due process of law.'

'They'll ...'

'Yes. But it will be what I deserve. If ... if I cannot be trusted. If I have ... lapses, if I refuse to be bound by the Treaty, then ...' He stopped speaking and kissed my shoulder. 'Then I am better off dead.'

The weight of the hopelessness came crashing down again, but I wouldn't let it settle, refused to give it roosting room. 'Then we'd better find out what happened fast, because, seriously? Those jeans? With that jumper? You are going to be looking for a new girlfriend – probably one who regards Walmart as a top-flight fashion emporium.'

He gave me a solemn look. 'That will be no more than I deserve.'

There were no more words. Nothing to say that we couldn't hear from the silence and feel in the desperate hug and the kiss that made both our cheeks wet. I held him to me, felt his taut frame trembling against me; felt his demon brush lightly against my hands as if in another farewell kiss. All I wanted, *all* I wanted, was to lie down with him, close my eyes and forget. Sleep in his arms and wake to the familiar dark scent of his skin and the knowledge that this was forever – however long our forever might be.

And, as I drove away, it felt as though I left my soul behind.

Chapter Twenty-Three

Mum and Dad were pleased to see me. Mum waved her knitting, which now looked set to beat her *Doctor Who* scarf records, and Dad smiled vaguely from behind his mask. I read Dad a few of the more salacious headlines from the copy of *The Times* that I'd picked up on my way in and then, when he seemed to drop into a doze, I took Mum to one side and stilled her knitting with one hand.

'Any idea when they're going to let Dad go home?'

A sharp, blue-eyed look. 'He's doing well, so hopefully the end of the week.' The wool coiled onto her lap. 'Jess?'

I shook my head. It wasn't safe, *it wasn't safe* ...

But she was my mother. She'd known me for the entire thirty-one years of my life, she'd known me since my pregnant teenage mother had turned up at the shelter, afraid of the demon who'd fathered her child, she'd pretended that I was her own baby for my safety. She knew me. 'Is he there?' she whispered, barely more than a breath.

I gave one, short nod.

'Oh, *Jessie.*' It wasn't exasperation, it was fear with a little bit of hope mixed in. 'We saw the news. Can you do anything?'

'I don't know, Mum. But I'm trying.'

The door opened and my sister came in. 'Oh, hello, Jess.'

We gave each other slightly awkward air-kisses. It wasn't so much the fourteen-year age gap that made us stiff with one another, more the nasty things she'd said about me when I'd had to pretend to kill my best friend in front of her. It was to save the world, but obviously Abigail didn't regard that as a suitable excuse. She gave our mum a much more exuberant greeting and went to check on Dad.

'He's sleeping,' I said, unnecessarily, but to distract Abbie from wondering why I looked a bit shell-shocked.

'Mmmm.' She made some notes while Mum picked up her knitting again. 'We're just a bit concerned about that seizure ...'

'Oh.' Mum's hands stopped. 'It was a bit odd. I didn't think people had fits when they had a heart attack.'

Abbie, looking like an efficient sausage in her slightly-too-tight uniform, I thought disloyally, fiddled with the monitor. 'They don't, usually. And he's no history of fitting or seizures either. What exactly happened, Mum?'

Half of me listened to my mother detailing how she had taken the post through to Dad, gone into the kitchen and heard a crash, gone running and found my father on the floor in the living room clutching his chest. How, as soon as she'd come into the room he'd started thrashing his limbs about. The other half of me could only see Sil, stretched out on the couch in the same room, eyes flickering from silver to metal grey. I bit my tongue.

'Look, I'll come back later,' I said. It was beginning to sound like an episode of *Casualty* in here, and while I could be *fairly* sure that a handsome doctor wasn't going to come in and be involved in our family affairs, I really didn't want to take any chances. 'When Dad's awake.'

After elbowing my way through the rather jaded hacks still camping out on the office step, groaning at my customary 'No comment,' I went to take out my anxieties on Liam.

Who had no nose.

I did a double-take that nearly knocked me out of the door before I realised that it wasn't Liam, it was Richard sitting in Liam's chair. And he seemed to be lacking in the finger department too. 'Hello, Richard.'

'I was just about to text. Richard wants to talk to you.' Liam popped up from behind my desk and drew to me to one side. 'He seems upset,' he murmured. 'From what I can tell, anyway. There are things missing, you know. Bits. Parts.'

'And I am most expressly not going to ask any questions about that,' I muttered back, and then perched on the edge of Liam's desk and took a closer look at the zombie. As well as lacking nose and fingers, he'd got a gaping gash down the side of his neck, and the overalls he wore for his warehouse job were ripped down one seam. His head was slumped forwards and his cartoon-chick hair was completely awry. 'Trouble?'

'Those two blokes that you had a word with last night. They came back.' Richard held up his right hand to show that his two middle fingers were missing, and the tip of his thumb had gone too. 'It was … I couldn't fight them, Jess, they had fire and knives and—' He stopped talking suddenly.

I jumped up and laid a hand on Richard's arm. It felt like a roll of carpet, but was shaking slightly. 'Liam, pop across the road for a tube of superglue, will you?'

'I think there's some ordinary in the kitchen.'

'We can push the boat out for Richard, I think. Besides, he can't drive a forklift with his fingers missing, so it's an allowable expense, unlike your bloody trousers.' When Liam, muttering, had run off down the stairs, I turned to the zombie. 'What's happened?'

He looked directly at me, his lower eyelids stretching upwards, which was the nearest a zombie could get to crying. 'They threatened to harm my wife.'

Shit. I moved closer to him. He smelled of the PVA wash that all the zombies used, with a faint, desperate overlay of Lynx covering the surprisingly sweet scent of corpse. But he *wasn't* a corpse – just because he couldn't feel anything didn't mean he wasn't a person. He was just dead, that was all. 'What happened? Richard?'

'They … they waited until morning, until I got back from the warehouse and they jumped me. Had a knife to Suze's throat while I … I tried, I honestly tried to fight but …' He held up the mangled hand. 'Said it was "to teach me a lesson", so I'd know my place, something like that.' His spiky hair flopped, as though it too had lost heart. 'When they left we … I … I took her to a friend's, and came here. They said they'd be back, you see.' He stopped talking, as if his throat had run out of words, and raised his head so that his deep eyes met mine. 'They said they'd be back.' His voice lowered to a miserable whisper. 'I didn't know where to go. These … blokes are human, it's me being – well, what I am – that's got them so angry. If I start reporting things and making it all official and getting the vamps involved …' His eyes flickered as confusion reigned behind them. 'I'm afraid of where it will end. I just want it sorted … I didn't know where to go,' he repeated, elongating the last word as his emotion strangled the sentence.

I took another breath. 'Okay, you did the right thing. We can sort this out without getting Otherworld Central involved. Course we can.' I patted the log-like arm again. 'I just need to think. Your wife, is she somewhere she feels safe? With people who will look after her?'

'Her friend is taking her to the Centre.' The place where zombies went to get professional patching-up and any other death-care needs.

'Well, that's good, she'll be protected there. But they won't intervene; they won't do anything practical, you know that?'

'That's why I came to you, Jess. I want Suze safe.'

I felt slightly sick now. I'd dismissed those men as just chancers, random attackers picking on a zombie out alone and unprotected, but, combined with the man I'd seen following the zombie through town, and the group watching Ryan, it looked as though they were part of some concerted hate group against the zombies. Had I complicated things by intervening?

'We need to get you fixed.'

'It's all right, I've got some mastic at home. It's the fingers that are the real problem, can't do those single-handed and without them I won't be able to load the forklift and I can't afford …' The reality of the situation seemed to crash around him. 'I can't afford to lose my job.' He reached into a pocket and pulled the recalcitrant digits out, laying them down on the table, where they rolled like tipped wax crayons.

'I'm sorry, Richard,' I patted his arm again. 'If I hadn't got involved the other night …'

'No. That's not it.' The zombie gave me a small, and slightly scary, grin. Zombies are largely harmless, motivated pretty much by the need to keep everything – literally – together, but even so there's something unnerving about the undead baring their teeth at you. 'It's been worse lately anyway. They're going around, picking on any of us they think they can damage – if it hadn't been me it would have been someone else. I just wish …'—his head dropped forwards again—'this life. *My* life, such as it is … all of us, we're just trying to make the best of it. To be useful, to earn ourselves a place … It's so *easy* for you humans, you think …' His eyes flickered again as his long-defunct tear ducts tried to respond to his emotion. 'I only wish they could walk a mile in my shoes. See what I see. Know what my life is like.'

I pulled a face. On my computer the Tracker program was running and everything looked normal; not for the first time I cursed its stupid bias, I could have done with tracking a few humans right now. I wondered if Sil was already in the system, flicking through the files, using our software to search.

I need him. At first I thought I was only feeling like this because I wanted him here, helping, his knowledge of the anti-zombie fraternity, his insight. And then it struck me. *I want him here just to have him here. Even if he knew nothing, even if he could offer no more help than holding*

Richard's arm steady so we could stick his fingers back on straight. I'd want him because he's Sil. The realisation that I'd become so completely unobjective made me wobble for a moment. When had this happened? I'd been so sure that if Sil turned out to be unreliable, unpredictably given to moments of blood-savagery, I would turn him in for the final justice to be dealt ... and now it was slowly dawning on me, the feeling rising like the return of a bad kebab at three in the morning – I couldn't.

Up until now I'd half thought that our relationship was something that burned so brightly that it would die in a flame of its own making, splutter and peter out into hello's on street corners and the occasional 'do you remember'. But now ... Now Sil was somewhere in my heart, as he was in my head. We just needed to work out how to move to the next level, the trusting and accepting level. Oh, and the not being shot by Hunters for breaking the Treaty bit, as well.

Oh bugger.

My temporary vulnerability vanished when Liam arrived back, carrying two new tubes of glue. *Someone* had to be in charge here, and I'd rather it wasn't a man who thought *Doctor Who* should be declared a religion. 'Right, that's the last time I can show my face in that newsagents: they either think I'm an inveterate glue-sniffer or I build *really big* plastic models.' He tipped the superglue onto the table. 'And I don't know which is worse.'

'This coming from a man with a TARDIS in his living room. Which, I have to mention, you built yourself.'

'We're going to use it as Charlotte's play-pen when she's older.' Liam busied himself with neatly snipping the lids off the glue rolls and throwing the plastic discards into the bin.

'You're unnatural, you know that?' I watched him pick up Richard's first finger and examine the gristly surface for stickability.

'But unnatural in a good, and overall efficient, way.' He married up the two ends and pushed the joint together.

'I was an extra in *Doctor Who* once,' Richard said. He seemed to be feeling better now that something was being done. 'Me and my mates. We had to get blown up. Got a bit boring after the third take, and, you know, they promised us they'd put everything back the way they found it, but I've still got a kneecap somewhere in Cardiff.'

Liam and I exchanged a look and a grin. 'Right. That seems to be attached.' He stood back to examine his hand-made hands.

'Head back to work, but be careful,' I said to the zombie. 'Make sure you always go around together: these bully boys won't tackle you in groups.'

Richard sighed. It made a kind of church organ sound. 'It's not right, Jess,' he said, standing up. 'They're making us into second-class citizens. But who is it that they call for if some nuclear power station needs clearing out, or someone wants some old explosives got rid of? You humans, you need us for the dangerous stuff but you don't want us to have any rights or anything. Oh, present company excepted, obviously.'

'I know.' I showed him to the office door. 'Something has to be done. I'll have a think, okay?'

The zombie shuffled out and down the stairs in a backwash of PVA. He was right, that was the problem. Zombies did the unpleasant, deadly jobs that no human would, or could, do – being already dead was a huge advantage in lots of professions. But they weren't paid or treated like humans, just expected to get on with it and be grateful that the humans had found them a niche. It made me grind my teeth with the unfairness of it all.

Liam had gone back to his desk, but when I came back in he got up, without a word, and headed to the kitchen. I heard the kettle and furtive rustling as he fetched the biscuits he fondly imagined to be cunningly concealed behind the emergency bucket.

I pulled up the Tracker program and sat watching it for a few moments. Sil, like Zan, was allowed to move without permits, so didn't register, but that didn't stop me from zooming out on Google Maps and staring at the farmhouse. The picture had been taken about three years ago, Dad's old Land Rover was parked on the driveway and the big tree still grew alongside the top barn. *God, I wish I could go back to that time. Everything was simple then.*

'Talk to me, Jess.' Liam nudged a mug towards my hand, making me jump. I'd been so deeply sunk that I'd not heard him come back, and I hurried to minimise the incriminating picture.

'About what?' I drank a mouthful of scalding coffee to give my face time to assume an innocent expression.

Liam raised one eyebrow and knocked his hair away from his face with the back of a wrist. 'He's in our system. And there's only one way that could happen ... Well, no, there's two ways, but one of those involves Daniel Craig, two albatrosses and an enormous quantity of rubber bands, so I'm betting on you being involved.'

I stared at him. 'How did you know?'

He rolled his eyes dramatically. 'Jessica Grant, I've been here five, nearly six years now – and I want some kind of celebration when I reach the anniversary, not an In Deepest Sympathy card like last year.'

'*I* thought it was funny.'

'Hmm. Anyway. When I came you were trying to get by with a defunct Casio calculator and a word-processing machine that York council must have found on a skip somewhere. I *built* this system! I know this computer like I know my own daughter, better probably, given the length of time I spend in this office, and you expect me not to notice that someone is remotely trawling through our files and then hiding his trace by using a load of ISPs from all over the country?'

'You and Zan, do you two get together and compare the size of your motherboards or something?'

'Technology, Jess. Just because you think it's all done with magic and kittens doesn't mean the rest of us don't get it.' He came and sat down in front of me, perching on the edge of my desk with his legs crossed. 'So come on. Tell Uncle Liam what laws you've broken this time.'

I leaned right back in my chair, threw my head back and let out a huge breath. 'How long have you got?'

'That depends. Is crying involved?'

I thought of Sil's face, those huge grey eyes full of anguish and hopelessness. 'I can't promise it's not.'

'In that case I've got all day.' Liam leaned forward, catching the arm of my chair and swivelling it so that he could see my face. His voice was lower, serious, and his eyes were full of concern. 'If you've let him into our system, you are going to need me to cover his tracks, otherwise Head Office are going to be in here in— Well, knowing them, about ten years' time. But they are going to want answers, whenever they get round to finding out that they need them. Tell me; then you've at least got one person to watch your back.'

I told him. About Sil contacting me, about my hiding him, about ... oh, about all of it. It was such a relief to unload, to let out the misery of my dad's illness, Sil, Zan, all of it. I splurged it all in possibly the world's longest unbroken sentence, with gulps of coffee to help me over some of the more unpalatable statements, and an occasional tissue-usage. 'It just feels as if it's all coming at me at once, Liam. All directions, just shit flying towards me, and here's me armed with nothing but the latest council print-out and some very unflattering newspaper articles.' I finally forced myself to meet his eye. I'd been so afraid that I'd see censure there for my actions, I was steeled to start justifying myself again, but the only expression in those chestnut eyes was thoughtful consideration. 'What?'

'Thinking.'

And, incredibly, I felt the air start to move in my lungs again. As though I'd started holding my breath on the day the news about Sil had broken and only just let it out. Knowing that Liam was firmly on my side, that he might actually be able to help me through this mess, made the day seem just a tiny bit brighter. 'Well okay, but don't let it become a habit.'

'I'm not paid enough to have habits. Even biting my nails got too expensive,' Liam said, without losing that concentrated expression. Then, still staring into space and frowning slightly, he leaned further forward and touched my arm. 'We can sort this, Jess,' he said, and his eyes finally came back from staring at some computerised version of the future. 'We can. I'm not sure how much we can sort, but I can at least make sure Head Office don't know that your boyfriend is playing fast and loose with our darkest secrets.' He pushed away from the desk and sat in his own chair, cracking his knuckles over the keyboard. 'Some of us have far too much to hide to let Head Office have the run of the system.'

'Liam, you are a star,' I said quietly.

'And please remember that next time the pay comes up for review.' He started typing, staccato bursts as though answering on-screen prompts. 'I'm also putting a false track through into the Otherworld system, it won't hold Zan forever but it might just make him think he's been hacked by some random crawler for long enough to give us a break.'

'You think so? He's pretty clever. Plus, he really doesn't have a life.'

'You are underestimating my complete lack of hobbies,

social activities and interests outside the home.' Liam thought a moment; then started typing again. 'I grew up with computers; Zan had to pick them up from scratch. Let's just hope that those critical years that I spent clicking on the image of a teddy-bear's stomach to get giggle noises paid off.'

'Yes, let's.'

'And I know that every fibre of your nearly-human body is screaming at you to get out onto the streets and hunt down those lowlifes that attacked Richard, but, for the love of everything Whovian, please be sensible.'

'Wow, and they cloned my mother while I wasn't looking! I should tell you now that I'm not tidying my bedroom, however cross you get.'

Liam glanced around the chaos on my side of the office: strewn papers, sandwich packets and biscuit wrappers mingled with forms and printouts. 'I sort of guessed that,' he said in a pained tone.

'I need to be out there, Liam. I need to be showing them that we're not taking this lying down, and we're not afraid of bullies. If I'm out on the street, even if it's just walking around, it will send the right message. And, besides, I've kind of promised Rachel that I'd pop in and I've been putting it off for weeks.'

Liam gave me a straight look. His untidy bush of hair crept back over his eyebrows again and he shoved it away. '*Just* walking around, Jess,' he said, sternly. 'No shooting anyone. Even if you see those blokes, even if they're burning down the minster and casting aspersions on your entire family, you just call the human police, right?'

'Wise words, Yoda.' I stood up. 'You're right, of course you are. How did you get to know so much about these things?'

'From breaking the law on an almost daily basis,' Liam said, vaguely, stirring his mouse to life. 'Now, go. And please be careful.'

'Have you always been this paranoid?' I pulled my

jacket on and shrugged my arms down into the sleeves. The familiarity of the action and the knowledge that I was able to do *something*, even if that was just walk around trying to look unconcerned, reassured me.

'Hanging around with you has given me a healthy understanding of the phrase "trust no-one". Since your demon dad turned up, I've sharpened up my reactions a bit, that's what nearly getting killed will do for you.'

'Okay. Right, I'm off to go and drink artificial tea with soya milk in and eat pretend biscuits. Honestly, it's like playing cafes with a three-year-old.' I turned around to leave the office, but stopped in the doorway. 'Thanks, Liam.'

'As I've said before, I always have one eye to the Christmas bonus.' A sudden smile gave him a schoolboyish look. 'Besides, my God, this is better than filing.'

I ran down the stairs to the road outside with a lighter step and a heart that, while it wasn't singing, was at least beginning to hum.

Sil stared in amazement at the screen. A message box was flashing in one corner, its closed envelope managing to look like both an implication of hope and also of deep dread. *Has Zan traced me? If I open it, am I setting myself up for Hunters piling through that door, doing their slick-suited efficiency thing; then taking me out to the yard and shooting me?* His demon was moving so fast that it seemed to flicker inside him, preparing to save itself by separating from his body, although that would mean his death, bullets or no bullets. He laid a hand against his chest, trying to remember how it had felt before, being human, nothing operating inside his body save his own will and heartbeat. *Shit. Too long ago for me to remember. Vampire is what I am now, however I try to persuade myself and her that I remain human enough. I fed on humans. How long can I hide, how long can I avoid the punishment?* Without giving himself any more time to think about the consequences, he clicked the flashing box and the message opened.

'I'm opening all the files to you, plus the recently loaded software that Jess didn't have the protocols for. Just, you know, stay out of my e-mails, mate, okay?'

The instant rush of relief slackened his muscles in a slump of relief. *Liam. She's brought Liam in.* Technology was no longer the enemy; now he might be able to make some use of it instead of tiptoeing through the random files he'd had access to, scared of leaving a marker that would lead straight back to him. And Liam, his friend, his partner in crime in dubious adventures they both hoped Jess wouldn't find out about, who was now settled with a girlfriend and a baby and still as willing to put himself on the line as ever ... Sil grinned, and for the first time in a long while it was a proper, human grin, not something that showed fangs.

'She's got you on board? Blackmail again?' he typed into the flashing line below Liam's message and waited, realising as he did so how much he'd missed interaction with others. *Jess, naked, eyes dark with concern and her body consuming mine with the kind of fire that comes from loss of hope. Tears on my skin, the connection between us running like water, like a silver chain of faith ... The only thing that stops me falling on my sword, walking out into the world and surrendering myself.*

'Nothing on me, mate. And, hey, stop chatting and get searching. Want you back in the world so she can start nagging you and leave me alone. L'

Sil settled back in the chair and stretched out his legs. *I'm not alone. Jess and Liam are out there for me.* 'On it now,' he typed back, and split the screen, as half of his life set out to delve into the further reaches of the Liaison office computer system, while the other half watched the news channel.

Chapter Twenty-Four

The streets of York were full of tourists photographing buildings and each other, tripping over the cobbles in the Shambles and buying extortionately expensive key rings. Every green space was packed with people picnicking and toddlers chasing squirrels, a policeman was frowning at a double-parked van and everything was wonderfully, *humanly* normal. I could feel a ghoul somewhere, out of sight, trying to stay undercover until nightfall, but it didn't seem to be up to anything furtive, so I ignored it and felt its shudder of relief when I walked past its hiding place.

The sun was high, had burned the shadows back to stumps in the undercrofts of churches and the basements of the shops, and the humans, lulled as ever by the mistaken sense of security that full daylight gave them, were going about their businesses. I stood on the minster steps and looked around me. Yep, people being people, and a couple of vampires thankfully *not* being vampires but strolling along with only the usual number of heads turning and tongues lolling as they passed by. Situation normal.

And yet. Out there, somewhere, a sub-set of humanity was rising like the green scum that grew on the river every summer, floating on the surface suffocating life and causing a nasty stain along the banks. The Britain for Humans party. Equal-opportunity haters – vampires, ghouls, were-creatures, they'd bring equal violence to bear on any member of any race that was not human or no longer human.

I walked down to the riverside, opened the door to the building I had known so well, and climbed the stairs that still smelled of cabbage-dinners and unwise amounts of alcohol. Even the smell stirred memories of normality. When the worst

I had to deal with was a frisky out-of-area vampire trying to get to the designer sales without a permit, or a Shadow hanging around the Job Centre, feeding off the desperation and unhappiness that pervaded all government offices. And now ... I shook my head and hesitantly knocked on the door.

It was answered by a buxom blonde; the bux was natural and the blonde wasn't.

'Hello, Rach.'

We'd shared this flat until I'd moved in with the vamps, although not many meals since Rachel's vegan, non-biscuit diet and mine were almost fatally incompatible, but she probably hadn't noticed I'd moved out yet, since she spent her downtime obsessing over her cat, who was less of a pet and more of a psychosis in fur.

'Oh, Jessie, you came! I'm so glad, it's been *yonks!*' She grabbed me by the arm and wheeled me through the door and into the flat. There was a nasty mark on the carpet from the demon attack a few weeks back, and the place still smelled of a cat who uses a litter tray only when all other surfaces have let him down. 'You said you'd come over *ages* ago.' She wandered into the kitchen and made rummaging noises. 'Is it really posh, where you are now? I mean, the vampires, they've got loads of money, haven't they?' Her words held an edge of envy, but underneath them ran a tiny wobble of insecurity.

'No,' I said, and then, more quietly, 'it's horrible, Rach. Sil has ...' My eyes stung with the tears I wouldn't, *couldn't* allow. If I folded now and let the knowledge of everything that was going wrong fall upon me, I'd never get up again. The only way I could keep going was to keep going – there would be time enough for tears later.

And suddenly my five-foot-two, vegan, cat-obsessive friend snapped back into her old role of wary comforter. 'Oh, Jessie! I'm so sorry. I saw the news, it must all be dreadful for you.' A waist-level hug knocked the breath out of me for a second. 'I'm going to put the kettle on. There's only soya milk but it's better for you anyway; your blood pressure is probably off the charts, and your stress levels must be scary.'

The tears pressed at the back of my eyes again and I followed her into the kitchen, where Jasper, the most malevolent ball of incipient moult outside a convention of really bad-tempered werewolves, was rumbling gently to himself as she poured him a saucer of pretend milk. 'Rach, I came to say ...' My voice faltered, dammed up behind all the stuff that lay between us, 'I'm so, so sorry for what I did.'

A moment's hesitation in the stream of milk. Maybe she hadn't heard; my voice sounded, even to me, hoarse and unnatural. Less like an apology and more like a phone call from the Other Side. But then, I didn't often apologise for anything, did I? Saying 'sorry' wasn't part of my skill set ... Maybe I hadn't sounded convincing; maybe my tone had still held too much self-righteousness.

'Jessie.' For one nerveless moment I thought she was going to reject my words, tell me what a nasty, selfish, heartless excuse for a person I was, and my skin stung with the heat of my blood as I prepared to acknowledge the truth of the situation. But then she abandoned the milk carton on the worktop and flew to hug me, her boobs distressingly embracing my ribcage until I felt as though I were being sucked into a sofa. 'It's okay. Abbie and your mum explained it; you had to pretend to kill me to save the world. It's pretty cool actually – I saved the world by being dead! Like Jesus or something!'

'Um, yes, okay, I suppose, if you want to see it like that ...' I took a mouthful of the tea. It wasn't that bad. 'So. What have you been up to?'

We fell easily back into our old parallel-chat-streams; I talked about work, about vampires and Liam and patrolling the streets, without making it sound glamorous, or easy or particularly fun, and Rach talked about people I'd never met doing things I'd never do in clothes I couldn't afford. The high point of her life at the moment, it seemed, was becoming a union rep at work.

'So you haven't tried to re-let my room yet?'

'Well, I did want to, once I knew you were ... when I knew you'd got somewhere else,' Rachel said with, for her, a remarkable amount of tact. 'But no-one seemed very keen – do you know, it's surprising how many people are allergic to cats?'

I managed not to look at Jasper, who'd followed us back into the living room and was scratching behind the sofa in a way that usually preceded a nasty smell. 'Really?'

'So, are you going to pick up some of your stuff, while you're here?'

I opened my mouth to say that I didn't need it any more, but then stopped the words with another swig of tea. Yes, all right, I had some new clothes; Zan had started to make sniffing noises when I came in wearing my old gear and I'd had the feeling he was only a few minutes away from laying down newspaper before I was allowed to sit. But my old stuff was *me*. The proper, human me that I'd been before. 'Yes, might as well.'

Back at Vamp Central I unpacked the box we'd borrowed from Rach's job in the chemist. It indicated to any interested onlookers that I'd either decided to buy enough Tampax to last the rest of my fertile life or that I might need some kind of gynaecological intervention, but it had been the only box large enough to contain my photo albums, diaries, a selection of my less-damaged footwear and my surprisingly large collection of books about vampires.

Zan wandered into the living room just as I reached the 'boot and shoe' layer, and almost visibly recoiled. 'Jessica?

What in the world has possessed you to bring that … bric-a-brac into this house? Would a garden bonfire not be sufficient?'

'Just because you lot regard memories as something to be ashamed of, it doesn't mean we all have to carry on like something out of *Memento*.' I didn't add that only memories were keeping me from packing up and moving back in with Rach – that, and the knowledge that leaving this house would be like an admission that Sil and I were over. That he would never come back. 'These things remind me of the days before I came to live here. All the things I had then that I don't have now.'

'Body lice?' Zan sat in front of me on the leather sofa without even a reassuringly amusing farty sound.

'Freedom. The ability to come and go as I wanted without the local press trying to grill me for news about Sil. This.' I brandished the scrapbook of clippings, stray wisps of dusty newsprint trailing and waving loose from its pages like a tattered flag of humanity. 'What?'

Zan was staring at me, his eyes as cool, green and unemotional as fathoms-deep water. 'Do you wish me to assist you?'

'I …' Good grief. Zan was offering to *help*? When that help consisted of his emotional equivalent of a rat-infested sewer? 'No, it's all right.' Then, because he still hadn't moved, and was still staring, 'Thank you.' And then, because the staring was *still* going on, 'What?'

Zan shook his head and let his gaze fall to the perfectly aligned seams of his trousers. 'Ideas. Possibilities. Posits. Nothing to concern you, Jessica. Yet.'

'Oh,' I carried on sorting, without feeling reassured. It was like having a peckish tiger watching you cut your toenails. The scrapbook creaked open and I started to turn the pages slowly, pausing occasionally to read snippets, or smile to myself at half-forgotten images. There, laid out in black-and-white, was the history of my time in Liaison, the newspaper coverage of my successful cases, my intermittent failures; pictures of my attendance at various council functions, always alone, always with a wary expression and a borrowed dress, and some peripheral events that I'd thought worthy of note.

There were also some pictures of Sil. I'd hoarded these like snippets of gold, clipping and pasting them into my book whilst persuading myself that I was doing it to keep an eye on his comings and goings, his various alliances and his sporadic dating of, apparently, every eligible female in the Otherworld fraternity. I tried to flick through these more quickly, although my eye kept getting snagged by images of those silver-grey eyes staring out beyond the camera to reach into my soul. Something inside me pulled again, that curiously umbilical feeling, and I put a hand to my heart as though to steady it.

Zan leaned forward. 'Are you ill, Jessica?'

'No, I ...'

Those frosted-glass eyes flickered to the page I'd been looking at. Took in those newsprint sheets pasted so carefully, to ensure they didn't wrinkle or tear, and scanned over my handwritten annotations of date, setting and other, more personal, notes. 'The connection is open between you, then. He must be experiencing something pertinent to you.' Zan seated himself back firmly on the sofa, but I knew him too well to assume he'd dismissed what he'd seen as the jottings of an extraordinarily dedicated Liaison officer. He knew me, after all.

'It's ... it feels more like a lively case of heartburn to me.' I gave my chest one quick final rub and flipped pages more quickly.

And then, suddenly, there was a cold hand on my wrist

and Zan was jerking me upwards until I stood facing him, the scrapbook falling at my feet like a tatty remnant of another life. 'This is no joking matter.' Zan's voice was very deep, very even, and he was standing way too close to me for it to be an accident. 'Jessica, your connection to this vampire, it is not to be taken lightly. Do you imagine that every female who'—his voice tiptoed over the word—'*loves* a vampire has the same reaction? Those deluded women who paste our pictures on their walls, who create a fantasy in which we feature, night after night; who read those fictions that even you collect so avidly – do you believe that they too feel something when the object of their desire allows them to stray across his mind?'

He smelled of something acerbic, something lemony that cut through the alluring 'vampire' odour of darkness, as though the night had been turned into an exclusive perfume and marketed only to *really* good-looking people. His hand was still chill on my skin and his eyes, when I met his gaze, were drawn down green, no longer a light, almost human shade. 'I realise that you can tear my throat out any time you like, Zan,' I said, steadily, 'but we humans have a little thing called "personal space" and you are invading mine like an alien task-force, so firstly, please back up a little.'

The hand dropped from my wrist and fell to his side, like a defeat. Then he took a prissy, markedly small, step back and gave me a curt nod.

'Thank you. And secondly, whatever Sil and I have going on, whatever runs between us, is none of your business. Just because you run Otherworld York, it doesn't allow you to indulge your repressed mother-in-law tendencies, all right?'

'It is not the fact of your connection which is noteworthy; it is what that connection implies.' Zan looked as though he was about to touch me again, and whatever movement I unconsciously made must have looked slightly threatening, because he pulled his hand back and interleaved his fingers at groin level, possibly protectively. 'It, and your incredible ability to sense Otherworlders, are not a human thing, and therefore must be a legacy of your bloodline. We must ask ourselves why your father, a ghyst demon, would have ever needed such an ability.'

'Must we.'

An elegant eyebrow arched. 'Well, those of us with any interest in the future of this world might. Those whose main topics of interest seem to include cheap hosiery and a rather'—a pointed look at my scrapbook—'*adolescent* approach to desire, may not care, of course.'

I gave him a look. 'You really do spend way too much time thinking about my life, don't you, Zan? Can't you just take up stamp collecting?'

'And then there is the matter of your blood being so ... ah ... *affecting* to us.' There was a slight edge to these words that made me think this was the real reason he was bothering to have a conversation with me. 'Jessica, has anyone ever mentioned the Twelve to you?'

I stared at him. 'The twelve what? Like, the *Twelve O'Clock News*? Or the twelve disciples? Twelve days of Christmas?'

Zan sat on the farty sofa again. There was a slope to his shoulders that might, to a susceptible onlooker, have looked like worry. 'We vampires have ... tales ... just rumours, whispers, that the human government discovered twelve humans who were immune to vampires. Nothing we could do would touch them, not glamour, or demon seed or anything, they were ... impervious.' Zan's voice slowed. 'They were our bogeymen, during the Troubles. An elite force that we could not affect.'

He stopped and looked at me expectantly. I looked back. 'Am I supposed to be going "Ooh, yes," to this?' I said.

'Because, so far, all you've done is give me visions of vamps telling one another scary bedtime stories.'

He stood up again. 'No, Jessica. I merely wondered if this had been mentioned to you. I can see that it has not. Since you do not wish my help, and you are beginning down a path that will only lead to further argument, I will bid you goodnight.'

'I'm not beginning any—' But he'd done the vampire thing and faded his way out of the room, leaving nothing behind but that bone-cold sensation still around my wrist and the smell of citrus fruit. 'Weirdo. Don't let the Twelve come and get you!' I called and went back to turning the pages of my journal. And then stopped. I stared, unprepared for the rising of the emotion that came with the headline: 'Werewolf Threat Prevented' above the standard-issue head-and-shoulders shot of Cameron James MacDonald, his rumpled hair above wide brown eyes and a cheeky grin. My heart pulled itself close to my ribs for protection as I skim-read the article I already knew word for word. Cameron, my gay best friend and, for his protection, my pretend boyfriend, had been alleged to be forming an alliance of were-creatures in order to overthrow the Treaty – and had been shot down by Enforcement. More than a year had passed and I still felt that horrible, powerless dread. I couldn't wade in and tell everyone that Cam was gathering together all the gay shifters so they could form their own, self-protecting pack without setting the homophobic were-world into a general panic, so I'd had to keep it all to myself. Let Cam go down as a loose cannon, a rabble-rousing troublemaker, when he'd been the gentlest, sweetest man, and a well-behaved and surprisingly house-trained wolf.

Under the picture of Cam was a photograph of the aftermath of the Enforcement attack. A crowd of Britain for Humans supporters were triumphant at what they saw as another element removed from the planet, waving pre-Treaty flags and cheering. Mouths open as they yelled their delight at the death of someone who wouldn't have harmed a human if his life depended upon it, and their names pencilled underneath; I'd found out who they were and made sure I would remember, for their joy at Cam's destruction, for their sheer hatred of the Otherworld. My stomach ached for a moment with the wish that time could be turned back, that I could have seen what was happening then and prevented it somehow. That I could have told Cameron not to go that day. I gritted my teeth. Heard, in the back of my memory, that laughing Scots voice telling me not to be so scared of everything, things would work out, he knew what he was doing ...

I'd failed Cam. Another sharp tug in the region of my ribs, and I closed my eyes. *Sil alive and safe, that's all I want, and I truly can't see a way out of this ... but I will not fail you too.*

Sil stared at the CCTV footage. Felt the black hole where he should be able to recall, the shivering mirage that was his memory of London as he watched himself, suited and business-like, parking the big Mercedes on the Embankment, getting out and locking the door. Glancing each way down the road for oncoming traffic and then walking confidently across and in through the doorway opposite.

And I remember nothing. This film is as strange to me as those photographs of Jess in the cupboard upstairs. Was I truly there? With an effort he could feel running down the connection between himself and his demon, he tried to remember. But there was nothing. Just a seamless transition between being here, being with Jess, curled around her body, watching her sleep – and the blood. The sudden, heaving hunger and a new freedom which had beckoned him into the crowd ...

He shook his head. *I will not remember that now.* With practised ease he pushed the memories down, deep down, beneath even those of his wife and children. *More pain to forget, more emotion that I dare not allow.* And a sudden memory that he *had* to allow, Jess turning to him with her golden eyes flashing an anger he rarely saw, her reckless hair trailing a marker behind her as she spun round, her lips already framing the words 'don't you *dare*' and, despite it all, he smiled. *It's all right, Jessie. I've learned that particular lesson; I learned it hard and I learned it from you – let yourself feel. For without feeling, there can be no love, and the love we have is the only thing that keeps me going right now.*

He rewound the film, taken with the protocols that Liam had sent down to him, one of the many hours of footage he'd forced himself to sit through, scanning for anything which might give him some clue as to what he'd been doing in London ...

Chapter Twenty-Five

The dream had doughnuts in. And one of them was beeping.

I opened my eyes to see my phone, screen flashing, right up against my forehead and took a few moments to remember that (a) I was in bed, in my room in Vamp Central, a bed like something that Louis XIV might have come up with in a fevered nightmare, (b) my mobile was ringing and (c) it was somewhere to the left of the middle of the night.

'What?' I irritably tapped at the screen until the phone stopped ringing, and reasoned that I must be talking to the person who'd woken me from a rather nice, if fattening, dream. 'Am I the only person around here who ever needs to sleep?' And then, with a sudden fear dawning, I said, 'Mum? What's happened, is something wrong?' Clutching at the duvet as though the stuffing could shield me from awfulness.

'Jess.' A single outbreath, containing more emotion than should be possible for one syllable.

'*Sil*,' I hissed in a whisper; I was very aware that Zan didn't sleep, and regarded the night hours as a suitable time to pace the landings. The Addams family could have used him as a mascot. 'You—'

'I have been reviewing security camera tapes from London.' His voice was back to normal now, each word equally weighted. I clutched at my phone so hard that the plastic made a little cracking sound, trying to force myself closer to him through electronics. 'And I think I may have found something.'

There was a jolt in the middle of my chest, my heart catching in its rhythm. 'Found something in a good way, or bad?'

'I am unsure.'

We breathed at one another for a moment. 'I feel I should point out that being enigmatic is lovely, very cool and everything, but it's not going to stop a Hunter putting a bullet through your head, whereas I just might be able to, if you *give me something to work with*.' I swung my legs over the edge of the bed. 'So, start talking, bitey-boy, or I shall give them your address right now, and I'll probably offer to hold their coats while they aim.'

'Why are you so irritable, Jessica?' Sil's voice held a guarded amusement, as though he was relieved simply to be able to talk.

'Because it's the middle of the sodding night, your boss could come storming through this door at any minute, and I was having a really nice dream, which you interrupted for no real reason other than that you seem to be a bit bored.' I began hunting around the floor for clothes. 'So you either give me something solid to go on here, or I'm hanging up and putting my head under the pillow for another five hours.'

'I have found out where I went. Before I ... before the attacks.'

I dropped the phone and then had to paddle around in the darkness that filled this cavernous room, patting the floor in search of it. There was no lamp and the light switch was over by the door, five acres and a swamp away. I think it was deliberate on Zan's part, giving me a large, dark room, where the furniture all looked as though it had been stolen from a Goth version of Versailles. I eventually kicked against it, and snatched it gratefully to my ear again. 'You've ... how?'

'Used Liam's protocols to hook into the council. Thought I'd try to find the moment when I left the car, see which direction I walked, whether I was alone or ...' He stopped and coughed. I carefully didn't say anything. 'Trying to obtain a clue, some idea as to my state of mind, my motives.' Now his voice held a shiver, his demon was making its presence felt;

either nerves or excitement or dread were driving Sil now. 'I went into the Records Office, Jess.'

Well that explained why I hadn't seen him on any of the loops I'd looked at, I'd not considered that he might have gone into any of the government offices alongside the Embankment; I'd thought he'd only parked the car there because there was a space. I'd been looking for him in the wrong place.

'And what did you do there?'

A swallow. 'I … I don't know. I'm …' He stopped talking; even the sound of his breathing at the other end of the line became faint, as though he'd covered the handset. 'I think I may be afraid.'

It wasn't unheard of for vampires to drop in at the Records Office, the place where human births, deaths and marriages were filed and had been stored since before the Troubles. A lot of vampires liked to keep in touch with family, although I thought there was something decidedly odd about turning up to visit your great-grandchildren when you were younger than them and infinitely sexier. 'Okay. So. At least we have something.'

'Why would I go there, Jess? My family … my line is gone. I had no siblings; my children …' Another small swallow.

'I know,' I said gently. His children had died in a flu outbreak and he, as vampire, hadn't even been allowed to attend the funeral. 'But this is good: finally we have a lead. Would the Record Office have anything on why you might have been there? Any signing-in documents or anything like that?'

'I checked – there is an online booking system, but it appears that I turned up without prior arrangement and searched without assistance. I need help on this one, Jessie.'

'Sssssshhhh!'

'I beg your pardon?'

'I heard ...'—I dropped my voice to even more of a whisper—'outside my door. I think Zan is shuffling around on the landing.'

'So why do I have to be quiet? He can't hear me.'

I listened again, but there were no further sounds. Either Zan had moved on, reassured, or he was standing with his ear pressed to my door. 'We need Liam,' I barely breathed down the line. 'I daren't come to you; I think Zan might be suspicious.'

'Zan is always suspicious. It is how he has remained alive for so long.'

'That and the fact that he's mostly hidden behind huge pieces of electronic equipment. To do Zan any damage you'd need a tungsten-carbide round and a map. Stay put, Sil, and keep trying to track yourself down.'

There was a sigh from his end of the phone. 'And where, exactly, would I go? Bearing in mind that I am wanted by more people than Mick Jagger right now?'

'*Mick Jagger?* Seriously? That's the best you can come up with?'

'Forgive me for not keeping up to date with desirable males, but I am largely heterosexual and also just a little in hiding. If you wish me to be more current, then I suggest you give me twenty minutes alone with your magazine collection.'

I hung up. Sil and I were still new to this 'relationship' thing, and arguing had been our default position for so long that we were better at it than coy acquiescence; we could be bickering over the latest sexy hunks for the rest of the night. I rang Liam.

'I need you to phone me in three minutes. Loudly, please.'

'Wow.' Bleary fumbling sounds underneath his words indicated that he was trying to get out of bed. 'We're not having the "shouted argument that leads to phone sex to embarrass anyone listening into hanging up" thing are we? Because I might need a bit of a warm up for that one, it's three a.m. and I didn't get Charlotte off to sleep until midnight.'

'Good thought, but no. I need to be a bit more direct on this one,' I said. 'This is important. Sil has found something out, and we need to get right onto it, I'm not sure how much time we've got before someone finds him up there. I can't just jump up and go because ... old fang-face suspects that I know something, and he'd probably follow me, so ... I need you.'

I heard a sleepy comment as Liam's girlfriend, Sarah, muttered something. 'What did she say?'

'Nothing.' Liam's voice was tight. 'She's just a bit ... upset at the hours I'm putting in. I'm getting dressed now. Presuming you're going to want me, yes? I mean, no chance I get to lie in and wake up when it's all over bar the shouting, screaming and the obligatory slap-up dinner? I only went into this job because it was this or car mechanics, and I wouldn't know a head gasket from a ... well, that's pretty much the only bit of a car I can name.'

'If you call me to the office, I'll meet you there. Even Zan can't be suspicious about me going to work since it's pretty much the only place I ever go. Put a note in the diary, would you, when we get there, under tomorrow. "Get a Life." '

'Right, okay.' There was the scuffing, underwater sound of the receiver being covered and a private conversation being held. Then Liam was back, sounding a little artificial. 'So, what are we going into the office to do? Seriously, Jess, if I'd known that being a sidekick was going to get me out of bed at this time in the morning I'd have auditioned for villain, you know. At least villains get a straight eight hours.'

'We need to look over the footage he found. It might all be a red herring – he might have gone on somewhere else – but I need to know the exact timestamp on the thing. And you're a five per-center too, so we'll be able to spot any Otherworlders in case he wasn't alone.' *Or in case he was with a woman but doesn't want to tell me that bit.*

There was a small pause. I didn't want to break it because I thought it was occasioned by Liam putting his clothes on, and I really did *not* want any elucidation on that subject, but eventually he was back on the line, slightly breathless.

'Okay, I'm ready. Calling you back in five, four, three ...'

I hung up just in time for my phone to start ringing again. I answered it, and almost shouted down the line. 'You REALLY expect me to come into the office at this time of night?'

'Do I have to talk, or can I do the usual thing of keeping quiet and hoping that you shout yourself into submission?' Liam said cautiously.

'Well, yes, I suppose so,' I answered, one ear on the subtle lack of noise coming from the other side of my bedroom door; Zan was there, I knew it. Listening.

'You know I've always liked dominant women,' Liam went on, conversationally. 'But it's nice to have a chance to chat and know that you really can't answer back.'

'Oh, really?'

'Yes. I mean, this thing with Sil, you know I'm on your side, Jess, whatever happens, if everything goes completely mammaries-skywards, I'll still be here, but you need to be careful if anyone from York Council finds out. Could be your job on the line, and while I'm more than happy working for you, I'm not sure I'd want to work for *another* shouty person with control issues.'

'You ...' I started, and then remembered the point of the conversation. 'Right. Office in ten minutes.' And then, eavesdropper or no eavesdropper, 'I do *not* have control issues!'

Liam just snorted and hung up. I waited for a moment,

gave a heavy sigh, and began making loud noises as though I were just dragging myself out of bed and searching for clothes, rather than standing up already half-dressed.

When I opened the bedroom door, Zan was nowhere to be seen, but as I reached the front door he loomed up out of the subterranean darkness of the hallway, like the Gatekeeper of hell waiting for an Amazon delivery. 'Jessica? It is late.'

'Technically, it's early, but since I'm not getting overtime anyway it doesn't really matter. Liam just rang, we have to get into the office – there's some kind of problem with the Tracker program. It hasn't switched over to Head Office and they can't see what's happening on the streets.'

This had happened a few times, perhaps something to do with Liam building our computer system out of shoeboxes and gaffer-tape and powering it with something that made clockwork look like cutting-edge technology.

Zan nodded. 'It is time your system was upgraded. Perhaps we should enquire into merging our two offices: running the city from one location would be far more efficient and we could use the same resource-base.'

I pulled my jacket down from where it hung behind the front door. 'Nice idea, Zan, but I'm not sure I could stand sharing with a man who thinks chaos is putting some of your pencils the wrong way up in the box.' I gave him a grin which, from his expression, encompassed my belief that bedlam and anarchy were the two essential operating systems for any council department, and left the House of Grim.

Chapter Twenty-Six

I stared down at the York streets from the office window. Dawn was beginning to glaze the rooftops and I was feeling the lack of a good night's sleep. Behind me, at his machine, Liam tapped his way through yet another stream of film from yet another camera, as we tried to find out what time Sil had left the Records Office. If we knew how long he'd been there we might have some clue as to what he'd been doing.

'Nope. Still no sign and I'm at half an hour after they closed.'

'Could he have come out another way?'

I turned to see a shrug.

'Maybe, but everyone else has used the front door, even the staff. And I've checked all the other cameras around, doesn't look like he snuck out of a fire escape either. And besides'—he stood up now—'wouldn't that line us up a whole new set of questions?'

I leaned the back of my head against the office wall. The plasterboard rocked slightly under my weight and I briefly wondered whether we should take up Zan on his office share suggestion. All the Otherworld offices were properly built, and didn't shake like an earthquake zone every time an overweight person walked past outside. 'Such as, why would he want to sneak out without being seen?'

'You got it.' Liam flipped his wrist and squinted at his watch. 'Are we considering Kit Kats to be a suitable breakfast food? Because I've got the feeling this is going to be another of our legendary "long days", and I'm not sure that confectionery is going to get us through. At least not without the sugar rush from hell and another layer of podge around thighs that can't take much more without having to go up a dress size.'

'Are you calling me fat?'

'No, I'm trying to get your attention. Jess, we need to think here. We have to know why Sil went to the Records Office, because this whole memory loss thing – is it because he *can't* remember, or because he doesn't *want* to remember? And, if it's the latter, then ...'

'Shut up, I'm still focusing on you calling into question the size of my thighs, and wondering how I can punish you without the screaming attracting the neighbours.' I perched on the edge of my desk and stared, without really seeing, at the assorted papers, Post-it notes and files that lay in a sort of wafer-layer effect over its surface. Much as I hated to admit it, Liam was right. I knew, first-hand, how good vampires were at repressing bad memories and emotions – good enough that most people believed they didn't *have* emotions at all. Keeping it all down, out of conscious thought, was the only way they could function without being driven mad by the thought of all the evil they'd seen and done, all the pain they'd caused and been part of. *Could Sil have managed to push the memories of his time in London so far down that even he believed they were beyond retrieval?*

'Jess ...' Liam said, but shook his head when I looked at him expectantly.

'No, what? You know I hate unfinished sentences almost as much as I hate an unfinished HobNob, don't go catching my attention and then tailing off.'

He picked up the mugs but didn't head to the kitchen, instead he leaned against the wall opposite where I perched, and looked at me seriously. Liam's face, with its wide mouth and gentle eyes, wasn't made for 'serious'; trying to be solemn always made him look as though he was searching for a punchline. 'I'm worried about you.'

All of a sudden I felt horribly, terribly tired. As though I could lie down on the carpet, or what passed for a carpet, and fall into an endless sleep. I think I even slumped slightly, because suddenly Liam was there, arm around my shoulder and nearly-empty mugs sliding cold coffee down my back. 'Jess?'

He sounded almost panicked. It told me all I needed to know about the face I had to show to the world. If I – daughter of the almost-immortal demon Malfaire, vampire-spotter extraordinaire, and able to 'down' Otherworlders faster than I could eat a HobNob – if I began to give in to the feelings of hopelessness and powerlessness that were threatening to overwhelm me … where would that leave everyone else?

'Get off, I'm just feeling the effects of being woken up by Mister Angst and his scarily elusive memory, that's all. I mean, it's still not even time we should be here and I haven't had a *single* cup of coffee yet, so what do you expect? I thought you had to sign something that said you'd always do your duty, and your duty is making coffee, so come on.'

'You're thinking of the Boy Scout promise, not a work contract,' but Liam let his arm fall away casually, as though it had been workaday contact, not reassurance. 'But you're right. Coffee and some thinking and we can put everything right.'

'But we've had more practice at the coffee thing, so let's start there and work up.' I flopped down onto my chair, which spun its customary half-circle underneath me, like a fractious pony, put my elbows on the desk and rested my head in my hands. 'I'm okay, as long as I can keep thinking about one thing at a time, I can cope. So, we have Sil going in to the Records Office two weeks before he … well, before he turns up on camera again. There's no sign of him coming out, and the next time he's seen *anywhere* is up in Soho Square, which is not that far away but …'

Liam headed for the kitchen, mugs rattling. 'He goes into

the Records Office, doesn't come out as far as we can see, and then turns up going all Dracula on the population's asses.'

'Thanks, Mister Continuity Announcer.' I stared at the freeze-frame image of Sil walking towards the office doors, just before he vanished from the camera's view. 'There's no chance that he didn't go in? Walked off somewhere else?'

'Could have done, I suppose.' There was a sound like a small bell ringing as Liam levered the lid off a tin. 'If he crouched down and ran with his knees bent along under the concrete canopy in front of the offices and I think someone doing a Groucho Marx impersonation for half a mile along the Embankment might have been remarked on. There's nothing, Jess. No reports of unusual activity down there, no Enforcement calls or Liaison work, nothing. I double-checked with all the London branches: it was like a dead zone the whole time. I think the Merc being illegally parked was the most exciting thing that happened during the entire fortnight, I'd take bets that there wasn't even any litter dropped.'

The fragrant steam of overdue coffee preceded Liam's re-entry by a considerable margin, and my sleep-deprived ears detected the dull rattle of chocolate-coated biscuits accompanying him. Life was looking up. 'We need to know what he was doing down there.'

'He doesn't remember, Liam. Nothing.'

Liam put the mugs down, and the distance he placed mine from my hand, plus his carefully neutral expression, told me that he was about to say something I wasn't going to like and he didn't want me armed with a cup of recently boiled water when he said it. 'Are we sure about that? *Seriously?*'

'Look.' I tried to keep my voice steady. *It's not his fault, he's only voicing what you've already thought.* 'If he weren't telling the truth'—the doubt tasted sour on the back of my tongue and lay like an unacknowledged weight on my heart—'then why didn't he just set himself up a cover story? Or even just lie? Why pretend not to know?'

He chewed his lip, paying very close attention to the biscuit delivery system. 'What did he say about it all? I mean, you know vamps, especially the old ones, they're pretty much remembering systems in fancy suits; the only things they can't remember are the things they don't *want* to remember. Not being able to remember something that only happened a few days ago … well, that just doesn't happen to a vamp. To you, yes, because your brain is some kind of chaotic system, but not them.'

'He said …' I raked through my chaotic system in an attempt to remember. 'He said it felt scrambled. Like … well, like the time he fed from me.'

'Your blood being vampire heroin?'

A momentary flashback to last night, to Zan's words, but I brushed that thought away; there was no time for worrying about vampires' scary stories. 'I was attempting to skirt around that, but, yes. I presumed he meant he felt as though he'd been drugged. But, apart from the tranqs – which basically just put them to sleep without any after-effects – there aren't any drugs that work on vampires on account of their demon filtering everything out before it gets to their brains.'

'Except your blood.'

'Yeah. Zan's been fussing on about that too. Muttering something about "the Twelve" in the same tone you usually use for muttering about overtime.'

'While he's looking at you and dribbling, presumably.'

'Liam, Zan thinks a drug habit is something worn by headachy nuns. He really does sit down and think quite hard about me only being half human, you know. He keeps bringing it up, as if it's something I'm supposed to do something about, like … I dunno, getting a licence to go out in public. It's almost scary, if Zan was ever really scary as opposed to really really irritating.'

'I think we need to talk to Sil.' Liam looked surprisingly serious. Well, as serious as possible for a man drinking coffee out of a 'Bazinga!' mug with a Twix biscuit clamped between his fingers as though he were a genteel confectionary addict. 'We need to sit down and work this out, logically and face-to-face. Get him to go back over what he *does* remember in the hope it loosens something up.'

'It's nearly time for me to visit Dad, and besides, I daren't go up to the farm again. Zan's already stalking around keeping an eye on me, and I don't think the presence of four-foot-deep mud and two collies is going to put him off. He might take a while to work his way through the sheep, but, believe me, he'll be there.'

'Yes, but he's not watching me, and neither are the press vultures. Look, you drop in to the hospital and I'll sort something out.'

'You've got a plan?'

'Okay, drop the squeaky emphasis on the first and last words there, and remember that I've seen every James Bond film ever made. I'm actually *very* sneaky, and ... well, that's pretty much it, but we need to do this, Jess, and, as your wingman, it is incumbent upon me to do *something* before we all fall into a black hole comprised of angst and bullets, all right?'

I stared at him. 'Sometimes, Liam, you're so butch it scares me.'

'Yeah well, it terrifies me too, but before I'm forced to hand in my subscription to *Metrosexuality Now*, get your sorry ass out there and let's get things moving!' He drained his coffee in one swig and slammed the empty cup down onto the desk. 'Move it!'

'Yes, all right, I'm—'

'Ow, ow, hot hot hot! God, that burns! Jess, if I show any signs of coming over all Jean-Claude Van Damme again, just shoot me, please. I'm really not cut out for it. Or at least take the temperature of any beverages I may be holding.'

'Well, that's reassuring.'

And, leaving him clutching at his throat and making little coughing noises, I headed off to the hospital.

Chapter Twenty-Seven

Dad was 'resting'. It crossed my mind to wonder how much actual rest was needed by someone who was hardly ever allowed to get out of bed, but it did give me a chance to have a cup of coffee with Mum, who took much pleasure in telling me that Abbie was, apparently, seeing quite a lot of the doctor from Urology, a small Scotsman – we called him the Wee Man, in a linguistic triple-whammy.

'And how are you, Jessie, love?' She opened a sugar packet and squeezed the contents into the hospital-issue saucer. My heart sped up. My mother hadn't taken sugar since 1990.

'I ... busy. You know. Working, trying not to think.'

'Is he safe?' She lowered her voice and the words were breathed at the table top.

'For now, I hope ...' Nothing else would come out of my mouth. I took a deep sip of too-hot coffee to try to force the tears back down. Her fingers were busy with the sugar. Heaping it into tiny piles, moving grains with the tip of a nail from one side to the other. 'Mum?'

A sudden flash of blue eyes as she looked at me and said, 'Do you ever think about her? About Rune?'

My real mother. Who had abandoned me – oh, to the care of my lovely adoptive parents, but still. Abandoned. Out of fear, I'd been told, fear that my demon father would find me; fear that I might be ... not quite human. 'I try not to.'

'Would you have wanted to meet her? If she'd still been alive?'

'No.' The coffee was bitter, stinging the sides of my tongue and moving past the widening of tears in my throat.

'*Jess*.' Just my name, whispered with such gentle concern

that it broke me and suddenly I was sobbing, coffee spilling from my mouth and cup while I tried to catch a breath, bringing my hands up to cover my face. To hide everything I was trying so desperately to keep away from – the huge emptiness that the fear of desertion had exposed inside me.

'Why ... do people keep leaving me?'

A tissue was produced from the maternal handbag. 'She didn't want to leave you, Jess. She had to. She never talked about where she came from but, from what we could gather, her life hadn't been very good even before she met Malfaire. She had nowhere to go and no job.' A gentle dab at where my nose was running. 'And I don't think, for one minute, that Sil would have left you voluntarily. Not for any length of time. You and him are made for each other, my love. There is more to what he is supposed to have done than his simply going mad. Are you going to try to find out what that is?' The tissue raised. 'Now, blow.'

Obediently, I blew. The sheer childishness of the action made me feel better, almost as though I *were* a child again, and my parents could make everything better. 'I just feel ... a bit like nobody really wants me. *She* didn't want me; Sil says he does, but he went ...'

'Jessica.' Her voice was stern. 'I did *not* bring you up to feel sorry for yourself. Your father and I gave you a stable background and a nice home; the best Rune could have done for you was to keep moving you from hostel to hostel and even then you probably wouldn't have been safe, knowing that ... that *demon* who fathered you. Yes, she would have liked to have known you but that was just not to be. And something has happened to Sil, to the man you profess to love; something so bad that he is being hunted. Now, are you going to sit here and indulge yourself in thoughts of what could have been, or are you going to do something about something you can do something about?'

I opened my mouth and closed it again as little bits of damp tissue rained into it. 'What?'

'Oh, you know what I mean!'

'Thankfully, knowing Liam has given me a thorough grounding in boll— I mean, in nonsense,' I stopped myself before I got pulled up for swearing and a hefty frowning-at. 'Yes. You're right. I'm sorry, Mum.'

Now I got a smile and the tissue wiped quickly over my cheeks. 'You're allowed to be fragile, Jessie; you're allowed to have doubts. It's the way you overcome everything that counts. Remember, you may not have had the greatest start in life, but from thereon all anybody has ever done is to try to protect you. Don't let us down now, will you?'

My resolve did whatever it is that resolve does, and forced me to stand up with a slightly wobbly smile. A deep breath drew in more tissue fragments. 'Thanks, Mum.' My phone vibrated against my thigh, and I was so tempted to ignore it, to let this bubble keep me a while longer in my pretend world of humanity and horrible beverages, where I was my mother's younger daughter. *Just let me stay here ... let this be real life and everything outside be someone else's problem ... just this once ...* And then I thought of Sil. Of his dark, anguished eyes, his desperate touch on my skin, of his unvampire-like fear.

'Sorry, Mum, better get this.' I reached into my pocket and pulled out the phone, feeling its planetary weight against my palm. 'Liam and I have something on at work.'

She launched into a monologue about how I worked too hard as I dragged up the text.

I've laid a false trail for you. Zan thinks you're staying at the hospital today. Can you get out round the back and come up to the farm?

I rolled my eyes.

Do hospitals have a 'round the back'?

Try the Proctology Department.

I shoved the phone back in my pocket. Bum jokes are so not my thing.

'Duty calls?' My mother said on a sigh, as though I'd spent my whole life running out of the house to the bleep of a pager, rather than dragging myself to the office twenty minutes late via the newsagents and any shops with a sale on.

'Sort of. Can I borrow the car again? And, yes, I'll pop over to the neighbours and check that the dogs are behaving themselves and the sheep are ... I dunno, doing whatever it is sheep do.'

'Die, mostly.' The keys were handed over on another sigh. 'It's practically their hobby.' And then her fingers clasped around my wrist in a warmer, more human echo of Zan's grasp last night. 'Jessie, I meant to tell you. The vampire ... he's been here.'

My heart slid along the inside of my ribcage in its attempt to get out. 'Sil? He was here?'

A wave of a hand, barely raised above table height as though she was too tired for the motion. 'No, the other one. The one with the eyes like ...' She frowned. 'Actually, I couldn't say what they were like, but green. Very green. And he had a computer thingie with him, like a book, he could write in it and everything.'

My heart rolled itself back where it belonged. 'Oh, that's Zan. What did he want?'

Another frown. 'He ... he was asking questions about you. Odd questions. Things about what you were like at school, as a child, something like that. I just thought I should tell you, I'm not sure if it's important, or anything to do with what you're doing but ...' She shook her head, almost as if a troubling memory was stuck somewhere at the back of her mind and could be dislodged by movement. 'I didn't tell him very much, was that right of me? I mean, he's very ...'—even though she was nearly eighty my mother's eyes flared with a sudden passion—'very *tasty* isn't he? But even so—'

'And that is an "even so" of such huge proportions that I'm surprised it can fit inside this room.' I stood up and patted her shoulder. 'It's okay, Mum. Zan's weird at the best of times. Now with Sil ... I think he thinks I'm up to something.'

'Well you are.'

'Only a bit. Nothing more than usual. Look, give my love to Dad, got to go now or Liam panics; panic makes him spend money, and I've had to get so creative with the petty cash receipts that they're almost a Booker contender now. See you later.' Dropping a quick kiss in the direction of her dry cheek, I headed off down the corridor towards, hopefully, a back door, or at the very least some laundry trolleys in which I could make a comedy exit.

In the end I found that my usual approach of being inept worked just fine. Some lovely kitchen workers believed my story of getting lost coming out of Gynaecology and, with disturbingly sympathetic remarks about my 'lady bits', ushered me out between the cookers and fridges and down a little lane that led straight to the car park. There was no sign of Zan, no hint of any journalists, so, keeping low to avoid any cameras, I drove out under the barriers and headed for the moors.

Chapter Twenty-Eight

Sil sat on the bale of hay in the big barn and waited, his demon almost mirroring his necessary patience by lying quietly at his centre. In the doorway, Liam was leaning against a piece of machinery, updating his Twitter feed with, Sil could see, innocuous banter. Keeping up a pretence of being in the office, half his tablet device still tuned to the Tracker program. Convincing all that he was where he should be, not lurking in a chicken-infested straw-stack that, if Sil's eyes did not betray him, was set to leak mightily if the predicted rainfall should arrive.

'Why do you consider this to be a more secure location than the house?' he asked eventually, wondering if the relentless itching that was causing his legs to twitch came from the hay or the trousers. 'Are we not ridiculously exposed up here?' He peered again past Liam, out through the open double-doors and across the paddock which separated them from the house.

'If you're going to be exposing yourself, then better out here than in the house,' Liam fiddled with the tablet, turning it sideways and giving what Sil considered to be a slightly sinister, thoughtful nod. ''Sides, up here we've got a better field of vision. Can see anyone coming, y'know the kind of thing.'

'Oh.'

'She'll be here.' Liam didn't even look across. Sil wondered what it was about himself that was betraying anxiety and tried to lean back in a 'careless' attitude.

'I don't doubt it.'

'You know Jess: she won't walk away from a problem, not until she's kicked it to death, anyway.' A quick glance. 'You lucky bastard.'

'Liam—'

'Yep, I know.' Liam slipped the tablet back into its protective sleeve. 'You and Jess, the air practically boils when you're together – oh, bloody hell, that sounds like something out of one of Sarah's books, disregard above comment, please. I just mean ... it's you and her. Always has been, whatever you might say, whatever you might have done, she'll be there for you, mate. If it turns out that you've ... don't expect her to walk away, will you. She won't go easily, our girl.'

'I know.' Sil slithered off the hay bale and sank his hands deep within the pockets of the jeans, the fact that the pockets were deep made him shudder inside his skin, no designer worth his salt would *ever* produce jeans with usefully workable pockets. 'But I may have to make her, do you understand? If ... if there truly is no solution to this problem, I cannot expect any mercy from any quarter, and I will not have Jess brought down with me. She ... I ...' Sil felt the words, their shape and meaning, but could not allow them their freedom and stammered into silence, pushing his hands up to his head and using the distraction of feeling the ragged ends of hair where once he would have run his fingers through skeins of silk.

'Yup, well, they're going to terminate your shampoo advertising contract, that's for certain.' Liam inclined his head and Sil was grateful for the lack of emotional follow-up. Vampire he may be, but he was also a man, and if Liam had decided to follow his feminine side to a discussion about feelings and how much Jess truly meant to the pair of them, then he was rather afraid that he might have had to bite him just to shut him up.

The sudden jerk in his abdomen felt like temptation and he was flooded with a sudden, sweaty sickness. *Is this it? Is this what I felt – is this what drove me into that crowd? Is this blood-lust?* Then he recognised it, welcomed it. 'She's here.'

'What?' Sil didn't know whether Liam realised that he was straightening his shirt collar and shaking his hair into shape. 'Where? Can't see anything ...'

'Nevertheless. She is here.'

'You really can feel her? Shit, man, that's a useful ability, could do with that round the office, stop her from—'

'I am waiting for the end of that sentence, Liam.' Jess spoke from the far side of the barn and Sil felt his face relax into a smile. She wore the tension of the situation lightly, only betraying it in slightly raised shoulders and a small, new crease of worry between her eyes. She had her hands on her hips and a 'waiting for a male confession' expression – he was glad he wasn't the cause.

'I was just going to say that it would stop you creeping up on me, but the picture was worth a thousand words, I thought.'

Her eyes met his and his demon rose to greet her, flashing into life behind his welcoming smile. Sil could feel the way it twisted and rolled under the weight of her gaze, like a dog greeting a returning owner, and his mouth carved itself into a grimace, despite his best efforts to keep the smile active and engaged. *By the gods, loving this woman is turning me into a shadow of myself ... but I never liked that shadowed self. She is making me a better man.*

'Right, bitey-boy. Liam and I have approximately twenty minutes of our most valuable time to spare you, and if your fang-faced leader gets onto us it will be a lot less than that. So let's talk.'

'I was hardly about to suggest a tea party.'

'Ooh, sarcasm! Look, Liam, this is what being vampire turns you into, forget the whole demon thing, it gives you an excess of irony masquerading as cool.'

Liam flashed him a glance. Overtly it said, 'You see? I *told* you this was how she'd be,' but beneath, in the dark space that humans could not cover, Sil could read his fear for Jess. The terror that there was nothing to be said here that would make a difference. 'I double-checked what Liam saw on the film. There is no evidence of my leaving the Records Office. I went in and I did not come out.'

'Until—'

'Yes, all right, Liam, I think we all know what happened next, you don't need to do the DVD commentary.' Jess's tone was as sharp as the words, and Liam subsided into silence, his raised eyebrows serving as his only rebuke. 'I've had ... no, it's not as much as an idea, it's ... well, I was at the hospital earlier and ...'

'No anal probes.' Liam bowled the reply and Sil felt a little more tension leave him. If these two could banter, then nothing bad could happen. 'At least, not unless you warm them first.'

'Liam! No, it's ...' Jess turned to him. 'Do you remember when we had that boy that killed Daim Willis? He'd been glamoured, and Zan got you to re-glamour him to try to overcome the first glamour?' Her gaze flicked quickly back to Liam. 'Keep up, Liam.'

'Can I take notes?'

'Shut up. Well, I thought ... you said, when you tried to remember ...' She tailed off.

She was nervous, shifting her weight like a horse about to shy and his demon tangoed on the feelings. *Why is she ... Oh, no. She wouldn't suggest ... would she? Madness. Utter—*

'Madness. No.' Sil turned away so he didn't have to see her expression. Afraid and yet pushing the fear away, overcoming it for the sake of ... what? For him? Did she not remember? 'I cannot guarantee your safety, Jess.' And now his voice was almost a whisper, the words containing all that he felt about her, bulging with the emotion like an overpacked suitcase. 'I dare not. After London ... I fed to surfeit. I did not stop.'

'All right you two.' Liam knocked against the wooden door, the sudden rap of his knuckles making them both jump. 'Let's back up about a decade here, and someone explain to me what *exactly* is going on; I accept both diagrams and line-schematics if words fail you.'

'Jess wants me to bite her,' Sil said, hoping that the simplicity of the statement would prevent any comeback; then he rolled his eyes at his own stupidity. *I know these two. They could argue over the colour of socks.*

'I just thought ... Sil said that when he tries to remember what happened to him, it feels like he's been drugged. The only thing that we know will drug a vampire is my blood, and if glamour counteracts glamour, then maybe ...'

'Drugs will counteract drugs? That's bloody ridiculous! It's like saying if you get savaged to death by a lion, getting savaged again by a tiger will bring you back to life!'

'That is a stupid analogy, Liam, and you know it.'

Sil felt himself bound to interject. 'Can we all keep our voices down? I am supposed to be in hiding out here, and I fear that your current volume will make us audible to anyone with sophisticated listening devices or, in fact, an ear trumpet.'

'You are *not* going to let him bite you!'

'Or even just quite good hearing.'

'Look.' Jess sat down on the bale of hay that he'd recently vacated, hitching herself up so that her legs swung. 'We've got absolutely nothing to go on here, and Zan is probably only one shave and a Spartan breakfast from working out where Sil is.' She turned to him again. 'Seriously, what the hell is it with him? Does he really never sleep? It's like living with a spring-loaded Dracula; he's only missing the sinister accent and the cloak and we could enter him in competitions.'

'Zan would look great in a cape.' What frightened Sil more than anything was the slow way that Liam spoke, as though he'd seriously considered her suggestion. 'He's got that whole tall, dark, mysterious thing ... you could be on to a winner with that one. Oh, if he wasn't so *Rainman* in social situations, obviously. Oh, and no, I'm still not going to let him bite you.'

'Then what else have we got? Eh, chaps? Because from where I'm standing, letting Sil take a little bit of my blood to see if it counteracts whatever was done to him is looking an awful lot better than just blundering around in the film archives like we're trying to win fifty quid from *Vampires do the Funniest Things*!'

Liam dropped his head forwards. Sil could see that his fingers were twitching, hitting keys on an imaginary keyboard, which didn't have any answers either. 'I don't know,' he said, quietly. 'It's dangerous, Jess. He might not ...' His glance slid over Sil, chilly as a winter breeze. 'What if he can't control it?'

'I am no happier than you about this.' Sil had to weigh in. 'But she is right. We haven't got anything else.' And as he accepted the truth of what must happen his demon dived, hovering low down in his stomach region like a swimmer waiting to break surface. *Waiting for me to feed on the ultimate. On the absolute joy and elation that her blood brings* ... Sil raked through the memories that brought his demon such anticipation, finding that he remembered little of that feeding, only the memories of the aftermath, of the sex and the remembrance of his long-gone family. An uncertainty such as he hadn't felt for decades crept its way into his veins.

'What's the worst that can happen?' Jess's voice broke through the raging memories. 'Seriously?'

'He can go mental again, tear out your throat and ... and I want you to bear this in mind above all things in your considerations – he can come after me. And I'm a third-generation coward on my father's side.'

'That won't happen.' Jess was beside him, her skin as smooth as a mirror untroubled by reflections, her eyes like syrup. 'Will it?'

And he knew. Knew that if they stopped and debated that they would keep on debating, arguing this way and that, pros and cons, for and against; up and down and round the houses. This was Jess, giving him the power. He took it, and was grateful.

Chapter Twenty-Nine

Even though I'd seen the demon rising and braced myself, the actual blow came as a shock. Sil's demon knocked both of us to our knees and then bent over me, no trace of my lover in those eyes now, nothing but the desire for blood and a cold acknowledgement that I was food. I heard Liam shout, 'Jessie!' and then the faint sounds of his moving towards us. But by then my body had hit the shock-barrier and I could do no more than move a hand in a vague 'go away' motion.

The demon moved faster even than a vampire: there was a sudden heat at my neck and then he was against me, anchored by those fangs deep in my skin. There was an abrupt pain that made me jerk back, and then his body wrapped hard around me, as though Sil was trying to claim my skin. Rigidity forced itself down my veins and kept my head angled away from his, and, gradually, a gathering dizziness broke through from the back of my brain. 'Sil ...'—I tried to speak without moving—'that's enough.' No reaction, apart from a gathering up of the body above me, and an increase in the speed with which the dizziness was marshalling. His skin was heating now, I could feel the warmth beginning in his lips and radiating out until it reached the hands that held me still, or perhaps it was the chill that was starting to invade my extremities that made him seem warm, made his scent intensify until it almost echoed inside my head and made my body feel as though I were dropping towards some cold centre, my limbs spiralling outwards as I broke into fragments, falling ... falling ...

A commotion, and my eyes flickered upwards to see the demon's head being dragged backwards, my own following because of the fangs still embedded in my skin, until we moved like a pair of conjoined twins. There was a loud smack, followed by such a sudden retraction of fangs that I fell away and ended up draped across the hay bale with Sil crumpled down on the floor. Liam was walking away, one fist gripped firmly under an armpit, and a hunch of agony dipping his shoulders.

'Did you …' My voice was barely more than a sigh. 'Did you punch him?'

'No, I gave him a goodnight kiss!' Liam spun around, still cradling his hand. 'Of course I bloody punched him! He was going to … well, I thought you'd passed out, and someone had to stop him.'

I inched my way up the bale, dragging myself by the string until I could sit and watch the grey veil before my eyes start to tatter and the world become more real. 'That's actually quite brave.'

'You'd think so, wouldn't you? Turns out it's a set of broken knuckles. Vampires are really *hard*.'

I looked down at where Sil lay on the barn floor, his mouth hidden behind a smear of blood and his whole body relaxed into an almost-human posture of sleep. 'You … er … you might not want to be standing around here when he comes round: he might be a bit … cross.'

Liam sat, pointedly, next to me on the bale. 'Nope. I've asserted my masculinity now; I'm going to see this right through to the end, whatever shape that comes in.' He withdrew his hand from his armpit and shook it gingerly. 'Although if he goes all fangy again, he's your problem. This is the hand I use to wa—'

'Don't you dare.'

'I was going to say water the plants, oh great jumper-to-filthy-conclusions.' He looked down at Sil. 'They look pretty good when they're out cold, don't they? Plus, it's nice when he's not constantly being all dour and rational at us. Perhaps we could market your blood to anyone with a particularly sarcastic vampire problem.' He laid a hand on my arm. 'How are you feeling?'

'A bit dizzy still, but not too bad. You stopped him before he seeded and before he took too much blood.' To Liam's evident surprise, I laid my hand over his. 'Thank you.'

'Oookaaay, either you want something, or you've lost so much blood that you don't know what you're saying, because I don't get gratitude as a general rule. In fact, I'm thinking that you had your gratitude genes removed when you took the job – hell, with York Council it's probably an employment requirement.' But his hand stayed under mine and we sat, Liam squeezing his damaged fist between his knees and me breathing deeply and trying to force the mist of hovering faintness back where it belonged, until Sil gave an involuntary jerk and his eyes flickered open.

He stared upwards for a moment, his eyes a blur of black and grey, like wet newsprint; then he let out a long, open vowel sound, almost a groan.

'Are you all right?' Removing my hand from Liam's and fighting my wobbly knees, I moved to crouch down beside him. My blood had crystallised around his lips, his skin was warm to the touch but tinged almost blue and his eyes moved quickly from side to side until following their motion made me feel sick. 'Sil?'

A short, inward gasp, stopped on a held breath and his eyes closed again.

'It's just like you when you've had one HobNob too many,' Liam observed from a precautionary position over by the door. 'Try rattling a gin bottle. Always brings you round.'

I ignored him and bent lower, trying not to yield to the urge to run my fingers over his cheekbones, to trace his beautiful mouth. 'Sil, are you all right?'

The speed with which his arm came up and grabbed the

back of my neck nearly dislocated my vertebrae; I heard Liam shout and saw his sudden movement as he loomed over the pair of us, then felt the press of Sil's mouth as he brought my head down level with his, so that his words blew into my ear with the minimum of intervening space. 'It was you …'

My spine was bent uncomfortably double, and I had to put my hands on his chest to prevent myself from sprawling on top of him, but his hand gripped me so tightly around the base of my skull that I couldn't move back without either breaking his arm or my neck. 'Me? What was me? Sil, please …'

'Memory. Yes, that's it. Memory. Looking for … for you, no, not you … mother. Down there, in the dark, all papers and files and … couldn't find my pen. And a girl, laughing …'

The ice crystal that had sat in my heart while he'd been lost reformed around my core. 'Girl? You were with a girl?'

'I'm getting it all.' I saw Liam holding up his tablet, RECORD ENABLED flashing across its screen, and I'd never been so glad to see a mechanical device in my life.

'Sil. Concentrate. Where were you?'

His head whipped away from mine for a second and he took two shallow breaths. 'Quick. Metabolising.'

'Then talk fast. Where?'

'Records … Office. Looking for the file. Knew the right year, picked her up from census result … right year, right book but … not there. Numbers were right, just … no certificate. Oh. Then … shot.'

'Jesus.' That was Liam. 'This is bad, Jess.'

'Then … voices. Arguing about what to do … they wanted to kill me but I would be missed, then … starving. So … hungry. I called for you, but you weren't there, it was dark and … fear. Hunger.' Tears pooled in the corner of his eyes, against the closed lids. 'You weren't there …' A deep breath, almost a sob. 'You weren't *there*.' Then the words stopped coming, his grip loosened and his hand fell onto his chest. 'Losing it now.'

'What does that mean? Jess?' Liam pushed the tablet closer, almost between the vampire and me, as though he could capture the meaning of the words by proximity.

'He's working through the blood. He'll be back in the land of the living in a minute.' I glanced up and met Liam's worried stare. 'We're not going to get any more. That must be all he can remember.'

'Oh, shit, Jessie …' Liam grimaced. 'I don't like this.'

'I can't process this right now. We need to get away, back to the office or … somewhere.' I rubbed the back of my hand over my face, feeling the sweat of low blood pressure clammy against my forehead. 'We need to get where Zan can see us, so he doesn't suspect anything. I'll take the car back to the hospital, you come and pick me up there – he thinks I'm there anyway, so we can do that legitimately. Then …'

'Then we can panic.'

I flashed him a grin without humour. 'Yes, probably.' I found my hand inadvertently cupping itself around Sil's head, treasuring the feel of what was left of his hair. 'I'm going to get him back to the house first.'

'No.' Sil spoke quickly, decisively for someone who was still half-stoned. 'Let … let Liam take me. You need … get clear.'

'No. This is down to me. Liam, you get back to the office and I'll meet you there. If Zan calls then I'm … out on the streets somewhere. You don't know where I am.' Liam hesitated, but then held out a hand. 'What? I'm not going to tip you.'

'Car keys. I need to get your car under cover, just in case someone spots it. And don't hang around, Jess. I need you back at HQ; there are a lot of implications here.'

'Yes, boss.'

Liam closed his fist around the keys, screwing his fingers tight enough that he was going to have Volvo embossed on his palm. 'Be careful.'

'Just go.'

I waited until we heard the sound of the car moving into the lower yard before I tried to lift Sil to his feet. He staggered against me, the feel of his cool, firm body triggering the desire to coil myself around him, hide somewhere dark and pretend that none of this life-threatening stuff was really happening. To lie in his arms again with his cool body above me and his eyes fixing mine, to feel his whisper against my bare skin and that tremble at the edge of my soul that was my love for him.

But that was a weakness I couldn't afford. Not right now. There was simply too much at stake for me to give in and cry in the arms of my lover for a world we couldn't have.

'Jess.' Sil's voice was a breath in my ear that licked its way into my brain and short-circuited away all good sense and resolution. 'I did not betray you ... In London. There was no other. There can *be* no other for me now.'

I tried to keep him upright as we wobbled out of the barn and down the stony track to the farmhouse. 'It did cross my mind that you'd gone to ... well, to do vamp things. Without me knowing.'

'You believed I would do that?' He moved away from me slightly so that he could turn his head and look down on me. 'To *you?* But surely, Jessica, surely you must know ... how could I ever do something that would cause you such pain?' His eyes were oddly shaded, the various colours that usually gave them tone seemed to be twisting, undecided how to settle. 'That I would do that to *you* ...' he muttered, dropping his gaze to the cobblestones as we reached the back door. 'I would have to be insane.'

'What are we going to do, Sil?'

My question seemed to stop him in his tracks. He paused

in the hallway that led through to the living room, almost rocking to a standstill. 'Keep breathing. Keep hoping that there will be an answer to all this.'

'No.' I followed him as, motion restored, he stepped over a cat in the living room doorway. It flicked an ear, but didn't wake. 'I mean about us. You and me. This ... whatever it is that we've got going on. You're vampire, you're pretty much going to live forever and I'm human, well, human where it counts, and ...'

His mouth was on mine, stopping the words, swallowing them down into a place where they never existed. His hands pulled me so close to him that we could have worn the same trousers. '*Jessica*,' he whispered into my hair as his mouth slid along my jawline, 'however long my life may be, I cannot imagine one second of it without you. I do not *want* to imagine it without you. You are my all, do you understand? You are my purpose and my rationale – whenever I think of the times before you it is as though I am staring into the darkness.'

My heart seemed to climb up through my ribcage, trying to get even closer to his touch and I knew he could feel it, his fingers were cupped under my chin, trailing against my jugular. 'I ... don't know.' I stammered, but I did. I knew from the cool strength of his body against me, from the warm flicker of his eyes as they drilled into mine, as though the secret of the universe was printed on my pupils. The way he held me, half in supplication and half in protection, the utter, pounding *presence* of him. My blood raced itself to a standstill.

'Love.' He pushed me back half a step so that I could focus on his face. 'I am talking about love. And it is no longer a word to justify actions, it is a true *thing*. For the first time in a century, since my wife ... since *Christie*, since the children ...' Both hands moved to rest along my cheekbones, holding me so I couldn't look away. 'I have found my purpose. The reason I have this demon; my strength, my speed, it is all so I may better care for you.'

My inner cynic, the one that sat on my shoulder whenever I had to deal with the sheer splendour of vampires and whispered in my ear that they were only out for what they could get; the thing that protected me from their glamour and poked holes in their film-star sexiness, muttered, *Yeah, right*, but it was almost inaudible. Everything else inside me had hung out the bunting, put on the party music and was blowing vuvuzelas and whooping. 'I am capable of taking care of myself, actually,' I said, but my grin was growing as I said it. 'But thanks for the thought.'

He was grinning back. 'I know. It doesn't stop me from wanting to assist you though.' Then the grin fell away and he moved to hold me as though we were about to step into a rumba. His lips brushed my ear. 'You hold my entire long life in your hands, and my demon heart beats with yours. Without you, the thought of eternity is unbearable; I wish to fight with you, to love with you and to be by your side whenever the end may come.'

That cynical voice vanished.

When it returned, it was too late to have any input at all. I was wrapped in Sil's arms, my head on his chest, in a lazy blur of emotion. 'Wow,' was all I could say.

'Wow, indeed. This may not have been the time or the place, and yet ...'

He made love to me. Every action weighted with emotion, with an unspoken commitment and the kind of gentle promise of more to come. And I responded in kind, with a degree of feeling that almost frightened me. 'Love,' I whispered. 'So this is what it really feels like.'

'Generally it does not have quite so many cats associated with it.' Sil nodded his head at the audience of baffled felines ranged along the back of the sofa, various sizes and colours making it look as though we were being ogled by a patchwork quilt. 'But, whatever works.'

'Talking of work ...'

He sat up. 'Yes, I know. Back to the office.'

'I have to.'

'But it is different now. Now I know you are ... what are you doing?'

From my position, sprawled on top of him on the living room floor, I had seen something strange. 'Just help me move the rug, will you?'

'As post-copulatory activities go, I usually prefer to read, or possibly eat something. Not rearrange the furniture.' But he helped me to pull the heavy mat aside.

Our ... ahem ... somewhat vigorous activity had rumpled it and I'd seen a corner of stationery poking out. It was an envelope and, lying underneath it, a crumpled sheet of headed paper. 'What is it?'

I scanned the words and felt my heated skin chill. 'Sil ...' His demon rose, feeding off my panic. I could sense it in the speed of his movement as he took the letter from my numbing fingers. I closed my eyes.

He read the letter. Folded it carefully, meticulously, into a perfect square and placed it on the floor between us. Raised his eyes to mine and, very gently, laid his hand on my cheek. There were no words. Nothing either of us *could* say.

Chapter Thirty

Liam stared as I came in. 'You were gone a long time. And your shirt is inside out, by the way, so don't try telling me you had to go to the bank. Unless the manager has got *really* strict about your overdraft.'

I held out the perfectly folded piece of paper. 'We found this. In the house.'

Something in my expression or my tone made him straighten. 'Jess?'

'Just read it.'

He read it. Aloud, which didn't help my already frayed nerves.

'"Government Department of Human/Otherworld Affairs" – swish headed paper, this. D'you know, I think they've even got *embossing* … must be serious.

'Dear Mr Grant,

'We, at the Department, have been advised that, some thirty years ago, you were in contact with a woman named Rune Atrasia. Our records show that she was deceased in 2008; however, there is some confusion regarding her life prior to that date.

'To clarify. Rune Atrasia was a member of a Government Department, which she left under somewhat unpleasant circumstances in 1979. The Department lost contact with her around that time and now wish to establish details of her whereabouts and arrangements between this date and her decease – to whit, whether she formed any relationships and whether she gave birth to any children who may still be living.

'Our information shows that in 1980 Miss Atrasia

entered a programme to assist young women living on the streets during the Troubles, and that both you and your wife were connected with this scheme whilst you lived in Exeter. Therefore we feel you may be well placed to have knowledge of her life up to, and possibly beyond, this time. Any information you can give us regarding her known associates will be treated in the strictest confidence and will be subject to an Order of Government Dissemination.

'"Yours," – something illegible which certainly doesn't look like the James Doyle that's typed underneath it – "Under Secretary for the Department."'

'Jessie?'

'I think it's what caused my father's heart attack. He wasn't having a fit when my mother found him: he was trying to hide this. I found it shoved under the rug.' I took a deep breath. 'I think they're looking for me.'

Liam cupped his hands over his face. 'But they don't *know.* It sounds more like they're fishing for information, and your parents have always told everyone that you're theirs, haven't they?'

'But what if Malfaire told someone? What if it got out on that side? And'—I gestured towards his tablet, propped up on the desk and still playing the recording we'd made of Sil—'what about *this*? Where does it all fit in?'

Liam lowered his head to his folded arms. 'Shit,' he said, muffled.

I swivelled my chair from side to side, using the motion to burn off some of the bitterness that churned through my stomach. 'Sil went to London looking for my mother's records.'

'Sweet, really.' Liam's chin came up so that he could look at me. 'Sounds like he wanted to find her birth certificate.

Maybe he wanted to trace your family, draw you up a family tree or something? Perhaps you've got relatives still alive? On your mother's side, obviously, any rellies that your dad might have left alive aren't exactly going to be the type you invite over for Christmas, are they? Unless you have, like, really demonic Christmases, with blackened-soul pudding and roast eyeballs and stuff.'

'You have clearly never eaten my mother's sprouts.' I carried on spinning. 'Eyeballs would be an improvement.' I stared at the tablet. 'So. Sil went to the records office to trace my mother, he found the book she should have been in, and the birth certificate wasn't there, yes?'

'Yes, oh queen of the recap.'

'I'm trying to get it straight in my head. But, there's loads of reasons that the certificate wouldn't be there. I mean, she was born during the Troubles – maybe she didn't get registered?'

Liam shook his head. 'Not possible. Births were monitored, had to be. Humans needed accurate accounts of the numbers in case ... well, they just did, and you couldn't get aid or housing or pretty much *anything* without the official paperwork.' He stared hard at me and I realised I was frowning. 'I've got a degree in modern history. You did *read* my CV, didn't you?'

'There was a page from *Colour In Pirates*, I thought that was it.'

'Very funny. But the chances of a birth going unregistered ... well, that opens a whole can of worms that I'm not sure I want to have to shovel back in.' His stare hardened. 'You are understanding the implications here, aren't you?'

'Um.'

'It was a legal requirement – well, still is, that all births in a district be recorded, and those records be duplicated in a central location, in London. In case of enemy destruction of one or other location, you see.'

'Coffee. Now.'

'In a minute. This is the first chance I've had to use my degree since I wore the silly hat, and I am bloody well going to go on a bit. Besides, it looks like it might actually be *useful* for once, and some of those essays took *days* to write, so you are going to shut up and listen. Unless you're about to fire me for what I just said, in which case I apologise deeply and will go and get the mugs.'

'No.' I sighed. 'You're right. I am going to regret saying this but, do go on, Liam. Just, you know, not for too long or anything. I've got a healthy bladder and I'd like to keep it that way.'

'So the fact that there is no record of your mother is odd.'

'Could her record have been lost?'

Liam moved his head thoughtfully. 'There *was* an Otherworld movement to try to destabilise the human government by creating disorder ...' He glanced around the office. 'You're not working for them, are you?'

'I'm going to stop listening—'

'But it never really succeeded. Humans are too good at paperwork. Well'—another quick glance around—'*some* of us are. Besides, Sil said something about "numbers" being right. All birth certificates are numbered; I'm presuming he meant that the numbers were consecutive, so that rules out a certificate being torn out or mislaid.'

I kept swivelling. Motion made it easier to think. 'Possibilities, then? One, she wasn't human, in which case her records would be somewhere else ...'

'But remember when they did the blood test on Malfaire, to try to find out what kind of creature he was? We used your blood as the control, and it showed you as half-human. So we know that much.'

'Two, then, she wasn't registered. And that's the scary one.'

Liam just made a motion with his head, like a half-nod. 'She "left the programme" in 1979. When she would have been ... how old?'

'I was born in 1981, when she was seventeen, I think Mum said. So, fifteen. Unlikely she'd have been employed that young; she should still have been in school.' I stopped the chair's rotation. 'What the hell kind of programme *was* it? And then Sil finds out that there was no record of my mother and, suddenly and amazingly coincidentally, he gets shot and put somewhere until he was starving.'

'And let out near a crowded shopping street when he must have been so hungry that his demon just took over.' Liam pulled a face. 'Woah. Like I said, can of worms.'

I found that I was swallowing hard and continuously, almost as though something was rising in my throat. Sil. Trying to surprise me, to give me the gift of knowledge, something, anything about my birth mother and now having to hide in fear of his life. He could die and it wasn't his fault ... 'We need to talk to Zan. Once he knows that it wasn't Sil going off the rails ...' To my surprise, Liam bent forwards with his hands on his knees, almost as though he was trying to stop himself from fainting. He blew a series of long, deep breaths. 'You're not about to give birth, are you?'

'I'm thinking. This is my "thinking" pose. Also my "not shrieking like a girlie" pose and my "oh God, help help help" pose. You might want to adopt it too.'

'Why?'

He straightened up. 'I know it's Sil, and I know how much he means to you. But where the hell is your paranoia? Because, just for once, I think it might come in useful.'

I stared at him. Various thoughts were dashing through my mind like a sprint final, in first place was, *It wasn't Sil's fault. We can tell everyone what happened and Zan can let him off* ... followed by, *He loves me enough to try to find my mother's family*. Trailing in a dim, distant third was, *So what really happened in the Records Office*? 'Paranoia?'

'We need to keep quiet! Sil wasn't drugged just so that they could move him somewhere – they could have just tranqued him ... Somebody has tried very hard to make sure he wouldn't remember what he went there for – they couldn't know that you'd make a frankly quite fantastical leap of logic and try using your blood. And whoever it was knew that killing him, having him disappear completely, would throw up more questions, so they starved him and then let him out among humans so that he would condemn *himself* to death. Just a heads-up, this is where an "oh God, help help help" pose comes in useful.'

I stood up and yanked my jacket down from its peg. 'I need to get out on the streets.'

'So, what? We pretend that none of it happened? We keep calm and carry on? You realise that's just a slogan, you're not supposed to actually *do* it.'

'But I *have* to, don't you see? We can't afford to start flapping about. Any hint that we know something weird is going on will make people sit up and notice us. We've got the best cover of all at the moment – the fact that York Council barely bothers to acknowledge we exist.'

'Yeah, we're like the Avengers, if the Avengers were invisible and underpaid. I get the picture. Keep functioning, keep up the pretence of normality so no-one suspects we know anything.'

'*All* our normality is a pretence,' I said. 'We're pretending that I'm completely human, for one thing.' I pulled on my jacket, pocketed the tranq gun and headed for the door. 'And we're pretending that you've got a full complement of testosterone, for another!'

I heard the thump of whatever he'd thrown at me hitting the door as I closed it behind me.

Chapter Thirty-One

I went to the warehouse where Richard worked. Almost the entire workforce was made up of zombies; it was like watching a computer game seeing them driving the forklifts and stacking crates, all with the slightly jerky, imprecise movements that a rotted nervous system and a careless hand with the Bostik gave. The supervisor – human, of course, which gave me a tiny prickle down my spine – stopped the shift to let me talk.

'So, how are things? Any more problems with the bully boys?'

The zombies looked around among themselves for someone to speak, and Richard shuffled forward. 'There's threats,' he said. 'They keep saying they're going to burn us out.'

My hand travelled to the gun. I hadn't even realised I was touching it until the chill of the barrel hit my fingers. 'It's just talk; they're always mouthing off that lot. They daren't do anything. You've got rights.'

'But we haven't, not really.' Richard said. He'd assumed the sunken attitude that zombies tended towards, as though their necks had collapsed under the weight of their heads, a kind of prolonged shrug. 'We don't come under human laws because we're ... well, we're dead, aren't we? It's not our fault we got that Otherworld infection and everything just keeps going ... And the Otherworld lot won't touch us either. So we kind of fall in the middle, well, slouch anyway, there's nobody backing us up. 'Cept you, Jess.'

'Maybe I could talk to Zan?' I glanced around at Richard's crewmates. Lacking the need to drink coffee or go for a smoke or a loo break, they were standing around the factory floor looking purposeless and a bit lost, rather like a bunch of mushrooms that had just broken surface. 'All your friends, all of you, could be in danger. There must be somebody who's interested in stopping it.'

'We tried. But we're practically indestructible, so they don't take us seriously; they just mutter something about keeping away from naked flames. It's the glue, y'see,' Richard said, somewhat sadly. 'Goes up like a firework.'

'But, *someone* has to do *something*. These bullies can't be allowed to carry on treating you as though you're just ... just ...' I whirled my hands as I tried to search for an appropriate word.

'Things? We're treated like that by pretty much everyone, Jess.' Richard creaked his head around at the warehouse. 'Don't need sleep, don't eat ... we're machines that just happen to be shaped like people.' There was a tired resignation in his voice that really annoyed me.

'Do you want to stay that way? Maybe you don't have rights at the moment, but you need to make some and then stand up for them! Without anything falling off, obviously.'

He looked around again. 'But how would we do that, Jess? We're the grunts, doing all the grubby, dangerous jobs that nobody else wants to. We're, like, invisible. All over the world, loads of us, laying undersea cables, getting rid of explosives left over from the Troubles and all that stuff.'

I sighed. 'I'll have a think, all right? Just stay together – they won't tackle you if you're with your mates – and I'll get back to you.'

Another zombie, one I only vaguely recognised, came forward. 'We can't even revolt,' he said. 'That's what they don't realise. We haven't got the glands. Can't do anger or anything. All we can do is moan, and no-one takes any notice of the moaning.'

In my pocket my phone vibrated. Rachel.

Why not pop round for a cuppa?

I looked from the screen to the slightly doddery people in front of me and had the merest flicker of an idea. 'I think I might know someone who could help you do something about your situation, but it might take a few days ... I don't suppose that zombies have a pension scheme, do they?'

Chapter Thirty-Two

A few days passed with nothing more terrible than the occasional picture and snidey side-bar remark in the paper. I went on a shopping trip with Rachel that netted me three pairs of cut-price slingbacks and some sturdy underwear; visited the hospital, where my Dad was being threatened with discharge, but was fighting a rearguard action to stay in, since, apparently, the food was far better than my mother's cooking. I even managed some risqué e-mail exchanges with Sil. Things were, if not looking up, then managing to keep a steady horizon-gaze.

After another long day sitting in front of the Tracker program while Liam made unwise eBay purchases and terrible coffee, I headed back to the place I still couldn't think of as home. The house was its normal dimly lit and hushed self, but there was a marked absence of dimly lit and hushed vampire about the place, even when I checked in all his usual haunts – hallway, under-stairs cupboard, cellar …

'Zan?'

I went into the kitchen. As with all the rooms in Vamp Central it was well, if a little sparsely, furnished with ornate pieces that Zan seemed to have bought from a French medieval house-clearance. Some of the chairs were so elaborately carved that it was like sitting on very hard crochet work. But it was difficult for any room that contained a kettle and fruitcake to ever be really unwelcoming, so this was the place I was most comfortable. The sensation of not having to pretend to understand what was happening, or have a plan, or have to keep my life partitioned, came with me, and stayed for as long as it took to make a mug of tea and collapse in the only chair that wasn't more fretwork than substance. Once I sat though, with my hands around the warm, if rather floral, china, the cold terror came creeping back, filling my mind with 'what ifs' and a scenario that seemed to have been pulled from a horror film, if any horror films had Liam padding around in the background saying 'I told you so'.

What am I doing? Hiding a Treaty-breaker? The confusion and the stress and my longing for Sil crashed over my head again, accompanied by that drag in my lower abdomen, as though my soul was trying to escape and get to him. My head hunched forward until my chin nearly rested on my mug, and tears sprang into my eyes. *My beautiful Sil. Risking ... no, not even risking, he had no reason to suspect any of this would ever happen, just undertaking something that he thought would make me happy. Wanting to give me that little gift of knowledge, a glimpse into the person who had been my mother – to know where she'd been born, her own mother's name, anything.*

I sniffed, and realised that guilt was rising up inside me and pushing the tears out of my eyes. *Why* had I made such a big thing of never having known my mother? Why hadn't I just shut up, accepted that I'd been brought up by two loving, if occasionally overly grammatically correct, parents? Did it really, truly matter who my mother had been? A girl, adrift in a time when nothing was safe, with humans and Otherworlders at war and the future seeming to hold nothing but darkness? Or something else, something darker, something that the government of the day had wanted to keep hidden, to the extent of wiping out her birth records? Whoever she'd been, she'd made one stupid mistake, got tangled up with a demon and ... here I was. End of story. Did it really matter so much that I didn't know which part of me came from her and which from my ghyst father – my chest which strived for an independent life of its own; my dark hair that, come to think of it, was also a life-form in its own right; my complete lack of adherence to the normal rules of filing? Why did it matter?

I sniffed again and tried to mop my eyes on my wrist, feeling Sil's absence stinging on my skin. *I wish you were here. To hold me. To let me cry, to tell me stories of your childhood to distract me, tales of your absent parents and the string of nannies and tutors passing through your life, until I feel better about only being lectured on my English grammar and not having to worry about Latin and Greek. To hold me ...* I stifled the sob that hovered like a demon inside my chest. *And this is why it matters. Because I want to know who I am. What I might become, or whether I have already become it – I want to know why my mother was so afraid of the child she carried that she handed her over to people she barely knew and then never visited, never tried to make contact.*

'Jessica?' Zan's voice came from the doorway. 'Has something happened?'

I tried to rein in the tears, to perform some kind of misery-suckage that would recall all these feelings into the neat little box I'd kept them in so far. I couldn't *afford* emotion, not when I had so much to hide. I relaxed the white-knuckled grip on my mug. 'No. I was just ...' I sniffed hard, blinked and tried to pretend that the tears rapidly stiffening my cheeks were nothing. 'Just thinking.'

'Hmm. I suggest you stop: it appears to distress you.' He strode into the kitchen, as unconcerned and poised as a cat, and sat elegantly in one of the more semi-transparent of the chairs, the sleeves of his impeccable jacket along the arms and trouser-leg creases lined up with the spindly white-painted wooden ones.

I stood up so as not to have to face him, not while my skin was still salty and my eyes were still red. I felt awkward, caught out, as though crying had been declared illegal and

Zan was some kind of Tear Police. 'It's nothing. Just ... life, I suppose.'

When I looked at him over my shoulder he had one eyebrow raised. 'How very *human* of you. To be distressed by a life which, to all intents and purposes, will last a mere blink of an eye.'

I stared at him. He seemed relaxed, or as relaxed as Zan ever was, like a cat that's just seen a strange dog walk into the room. 'I don't think you can even spell "sympathy", can you?' I refilled the kettle and carefully counted the tiles behind the sink to give my eyes a chance to dry up and my mouth to not come out with anything more sarcastic.

'I am afraid that sympathy would be misplaced. The Otherworld does not give space for such emotions; they are a waste of personal resources that are better spent in action.'

'I am not going to start this argument again, Zan. I'm human. I was brought up human and I have human values, whatever my bloodline might indicate, and I choose to stay this side of the line, so you can keep all your Otherworld observations to yourself.' The kettle pinged and I poured water onto another teabag. I didn't really want any more tea – I was on the verge of tannin poisoning – but it was useful to have something to do.

'I don't wish to argue with you.'

'But you are going to, aren't you? I know that tone of voice, my mother used to use it all the time when I was growing up.'

'But what were you growing *into*?' Zan dropped the words so heavily that the surface of my tea rippled under them. 'Your behaviour is not that of a human, Jessica, surely you can see that? You keep yourself aloof from contact, you refuse to allow memories in that may distress you – I am using your current state as an exception that proves the rule, incidentally, before you try to cite it in evidence.'

My tea slopped as I spun around to face him. He looked perfectly at ease, hair so precisely parted that it looked as though he'd done it with a set-square, skin smooth as a pebble and his classical profile was so impassive it could have been carved. Yet his words had been incendiary, and he knew it. 'What do you think Liam and Rachel are, imaginary friends?'

A gracious inclination of his head dragged his hair down to his collar. 'You have an Otherworld attitude to friendship; you encourage those who can be of assistance, and any others you dismiss.' He leaned forward a little, and his demon was rising behind his eyes. 'Can you truly say that you are there for them in their times of trouble? Or do you forget them when they are no longer in your line of sight?'

'I ...' I put the mug down on the table. 'That's bollocks, Zan, and you know it!' But deep inside me a little prickle of doubt was needling my gut. *Did I?* 'Besides, being stuck here with you hovering around like the Dark Angel is not exactly conducive to having dinner parties, and my job ... I can't go out on the piss in case I'm needed.'

'Needed by whom? By your council, of which you purport to be entirely dismissive? By your filing and your paperwork, which you maintain comprises your job?' Zan's voice was stronger now; he was assuming the personality of the York City Vamp, the one he rarely needed to slip into. Was he trying to impress me? And if so, why? I knew Zan too well; he was like an ironing board – there, but I wasn't entirely sure what his purpose was. And now ... he was doing the whole alpha thing again, powerful and commanding. And really, *really* annoying.

'Well, I suppose by your reasoning I don't come under either heading. Half-human, half-demon, you can't just claim me for your side when it suits you, Zan. I'm choosing for myself, and I choose to be human and to regard myself as bound by human laws and the human council. If that means I'm condemned to a lifetime of getting excited about new stationery products and the shoe sales, then so be it.' I whirled around and prepared for a showy exit.

'Your mother agrees with me.'

And I stopped, dead, with my hand on the door. Every millilitre of my blood had solidified; my heart had slowed under the weight of it. '*What?*'

Zan stood up – I heard the chair squeal across the tiled floor but stayed where I was, unable to coax my muscles into action. 'Your mother. We spoke at the hospital. She agrees that you are becoming more Otherworlder with each passing year.' I only knew he was moving because his voice was coming closer, otherwise he made no sound. 'We conversed at some length, in fact.' And now he was right behind my shoulder, a cold presence. Standing so close, in fact, that when I spun round I nearly headbutted him.

'Did you glamour her?' Her vagueness, not knowing what they'd talked about ... The bastard had got inside her head ... poked about in her psyche to find out about me; it was the only explanation. 'Because, if you did, I have to warn you that I shall go straight round to your office with one of Liam's "special" programs, and every time you switch on your computer you will be faced with more weird-shit porn coming at you than even the average teenage boy could handle. Right?'

A pause, as though he was thinking this through. 'So,' he said slowly, 'why should you expect me to confess that I had glamoured your mother?'

'Oh, I don't know. Basic human decency and the desire for truth? Oh, wait a minute ...'

'I did not. We merely conversed, and I ... put some options before her. Options that do not concern you at present.'

'And why wouldn't they?' I turned slowly and must have

had my 'vampire hunter' face on, because Zan raised his head and took a steady step back.

'Because they are between your mother and me. Or are you assuming that any decision made without your permission is to be disallowed? That is a very Otherworld mindset, Jessica.'

Well, at least I'd stopped crying and wondering about Sil. My teeth were so tightly gritted that expressing anything other than a snarl was not an option right now. 'You ...'—I groped for words—'you ... *vampire*!'

But every word he said was heading, with the screaming noise of a pin-point accurate bullet, straight into my heart. *He's right. Oh God, he's right ... I'm one of Them.*

A tilted eyebrow. 'You say "vampire" as though it is a bad thing.' Zan smiled, or rather he twitched his lips in an expression that never even made it as far as his cheeks. 'You may want to think about that.'

It was leave the room or burst into tears again. I chose the 'leaving' option.

Chapter Thirty-Three

I looked in through the door. Mum was sprawled untidily on the pull-out chair, covered with a fleecy blanket and emitting occasional lady-like snores. She'd unpinned her hair from its usual careful coiffure, and it coiled in a greying, careless mass around her head and neck, as though an unhealthy wind had passed through the room. Dad lay surrounded by machines that beeped and ticked, and his eyes were open.

'It's late, love.'

'I know.' Careful not to wake my mother, I crept around to the other side of his bed and perched on the plastic chair, my eyes tracing the rise and fall of his heartbeat, measured in green waves on a small screen. 'I couldn't sleep.'

'You should try having these things fitted.' He raised an arm to indicate the various drip attachments and wires that issued forth. 'If I turn over, it sounds like an Xbox game.' The lifted hand found mine. 'What's the matter, Jessie?'

'Nothing, I ...'

'Come on now.' My father patted my hand. 'You didn't come all the way over here just to steal my grapes.'

What could I say? That I'd come to the hospital in the middle of the night to reassure myself of my humanity? That I needed to know that, out in the real world, people were going about their usual business without vampires and zombies and demons being part of it? 'Mum's been talking to Zan. Or, more likely, he's been lecturing her and she's been too polite to knee him in the— Well, to tell him to go away.'

'I haven't seen him. They must have chatted down at the coffee shop.'

I opened my mouth to say that Zan didn't 'chat', the vampire didn't have a casual bone in his body, but realised it was pointless. My father didn't know anything, and my mother hadn't seen fit to confide in him. 'Tell me about my birth mother,' I said, leaning forward so that I could see the expression in those autumnal eyes. 'Rune. What was she like?'

A twitch of the fingers over my hand. 'Why do you want to know?'

'I found the letter. From the government.'

The fingers curled for a second, as though in pain, and then flattened. There was a tone from the machine, and then the reassuring 'bip bip' noise resumed, and my father sighed. 'It was a bad moment when that arrived. I wanted to keep it from … from you all.'

'Dad …'

'I just want to keep you safe … to keep you away from them.' A breath that sounded difficult. 'We didn't know, Jess, love. You have to believe that. She was a nice girl, nervy, but that was to be expected under the circumstances … Pretty little thing though.' A sideways smile. 'You look very much like her.'

'Nice try, Dad. But … what was she *like*?'

He sighed. 'I'm sorry, love. Yes. We should have told you all this before. She was …' He seemed to search for the words. 'Rune was afraid. Of everything. She never talked about her background, about her upbringing, parents or anything, just … fear. Always looking over her shoulder, always … like that old collie we had, the one that we got from the dogs' home, you remember?'

'Ziggy? The one that used to bite anyone who came to the door?'

'He'd been ill treated as a pup, y'see, love. Never forgot it, poor lad, but he was a good worker, great with the sheep. It was just people he hated. And Rune – she had something of the same about her, like she was just waiting for it all to happen again, but then, I suppose, with your father being …

what he was, she was right. But I always thought there was more to it than that, almost as though ... sounds a bit silly really, but I remember, when I was teaching, some of the students ... almost as though she'd been *born* afraid.'

'Like paranoid, you mean?'

He made a face, drawing his mouth down at the corners. 'Like she wasn't quite right. That's the best I can describe it, as though she'd never been right. That's why ... that's what I put it down to, her not wanting to keep you. Not because of who your father was, but because of *herself*, because she was afraid of who she was.' Another pat of my hand. 'She never spoke about it, but we suspected there was something in her past, some kind of abuse ... but we never thought ... not the *government*. Well, you wouldn't, would you?'

'So what do you think happened to her? Before, I mean?'

Beside the bed my mother stirred under her blanket. 'Brian?'

'I'm fine, Jen. Go back to sleep.' Then, dropping his voice to a faint whisper, he said, 'She gets upset when you ask. About Rune. Takes it badly. Doesn't want you to know but ... she thinks we did something wrong, taking you in, pretending you were ours. Something bad.'

I couldn't answer. Couldn't reassure him. My throat strained and ached with words I couldn't say and tears I dared not release. 'No.' The words echoed off the hollowness. 'You did what you thought was right.'

A quick glance at my mother, who'd half-turned over, one crumpled hand clutching the blanket to her shoulders. 'That's all anyone ever does, love. What they think is right. And now I think'—he lowered his voice even more—'maybe they took Rune when she was very young or something. Can't even guess why, but it won't have been good.' He moistened his lips with a dry-looking tongue. 'I wish I was out of here, wish I could *do* something.'

I tried to smile, but my mouth wouldn't co-operate, and only went as far as a straight-lipped grimace. 'With the best will in the world, Dad, I don't think filling in farm subsidy forms is going to be any kind of preparation for this sort of thing.'

'No, but I could …' He stopped speaking so suddenly that I glanced over to the monitor. The trace was irregular, though at least it was there. But he'd closed his eyes as if he wanted to avoid looking at my face. 'I should protect you.' A whisper so faint that it barely registered over the beeps and clicks and whirrs, and a tear slid from the corner of one closed eye. 'I should be *there*.'

The machines steadied, the peaks and troughs ironed by approaching sleep into a smoother line. 'It'll be okay.' I willed the words to sound strong, and raised his bruised-looking hand to my lips. 'I've pretty much got a team on my side, after all. I mean, I know it's Team Obsessive-Compulsive, but it's still a team.'

'Be careful, Jessie.'

I kissed his cheek as he started to slide towards sleep, and watched the machines settle into another, slower rhythm. 'Thanks, Dad. I will.'

A mumble and he was asleep, his hand slack in mine and his face oddly younger. I tiptoed from the room and went back to the only place I could think that I might be welcome right now.

The computer beeped at me in a parody of Dad's monitors. The mugs sat on my desk positively begging for me to call Liam, even the pencil sharpener glared at me with its bladed eye of disdain and I wavered over the phone for a few seconds. My fingers did a little dance, miming the digits of Liam's number, but I balled them into fists and refused to give in. It was barely seven a.m. and Sarah was, if I was not reading completely the wrong script between Liam's fairly widely spaced lines, getting a little bit annoyed with him being called in at all hours – I didn't want to spark any relationship discord. Liam was so level-headed you could practically use him as a cup-holder and he had to stay that way. With me slowly turning into a walking psychological disorder – *Like my mother,* whispered that treacherous bit of my brain that refused me sleep, had forced me to sit in the office almost overnight and was currently warning me away from the barely-hidden HobNobs – one of us had to stay sane.

I flicked the Tracker program up. Nothing flashed, no warnings. When I hovered over the little dots that represented our Otherworlders all I got was the little 'Permitted' icon. It would have been nice, right now, to get a call out, to go and take some of my frustration and confusion out on a wandering vampire or out-of-area were-creature, but there weren't any. In the end I decided to go and see Rachel and raise the subject I'd been putting off for a while.

'You want to know about *what*?' Rachel carried on folding laundry. Apparently Jasper was unwell and had been sick all over her duvet, although from his smug expression I suspected he'd coughed up hairballs in a bizarre revenge attack. 'Sounds like you're starting to take life seriously, Jessie, and it's about time too!'

'Well, no, actually I'm not, or I am, but not like this. And it's not me who needs to know, Rach. It's ... some ... err ... friends of mine.'

She slowly brought two edges of a sheet together and thoughtfully smoothed out the creases. 'I suppose I could. Is it vampires?'

Rachel has a really weird penchant for vamps, despite losing her entire family to them during the Troubles. She just has this whole image of them as deeply troubled, emotional creatures who only need the love of a good woman to get over the whole blood, sex and death thing. I do keep pointing out that what she's thinking of is a goth band front man, but she still keeps mooning around whenever I mention Sil or Zan.

'Not exactly.'

'I wish I had your job, Jessie. Honestly, I'm sick of boxing up perm lotion! Do you know, the most dangerous thing I get to do is sometimes turn a blind eye to someone buying more than one box of Nurofen at a time! Can I apply for a place in your office? Would you put in a word for me?'

I wondered what she'd say if she knew, *really* knew, about my job. About the ulcer-invoking anxiety, the perpetual armpit-drenching terror of *getting it wrong*. I tugged again at my collar, thanking any of the Powers That Be that I'd got Sil to bite me low down on my neck. 'The pay is terrible,' I said. 'Really bad. I get through tights like nobody's business, and the hours are shocking.'

'Maybe not, then. I mean, I have to be there for Jasper; I couldn't do difficult hours.'

I sat down and took another sip of my herbal tea. There I'd been, assuming that I missed the flat, the secret chocolate supply, the freedom to come and go as I'd pleased, when I'd really missed the chats, the vegan-orientated magazine-reading evenings, the gossip. And Rachel herself, with her biased acceptance of my job and my affiliations. The *normality.* It just highlighted how weird my life had become now that I was thinking of a fridge full of bean curd and a vet on speed dial as normal.

A sudden grin broke out above the duvet-folding. 'I've missed you, Jessie. Honestly, if you ever want to come back to the flat, I'd love to have you.' A small pause. 'I might have to put the rent up a bit, though, what with the demons burning holes in the carpet thing.'

I carefully didn't remark on this. I had a feeling, just a

small, needling kind of worry, that Zan was keeping me at Vampire Central simply so that he could watch my comings and goings, and wouldn't take kindly to me decamping back to my old stomping grounds. He wouldn't be able to criticise my laundry proceedings or my predilection for *Top Gear* repeats if I moved out, and I was beginning to suspect that passing judgement on my pastimes was the nearest he got to a hobby. It said something about life *chez* Vegan that this was *still* preferable to coming back to the flat.

'Thanks, Rach. That's nice to know. That I can come back, I mean, not the bit about the putting up the rent.'

'That's okay. Now, when would you like me to come and talk to your friends? Only I ought to be off to work now, it's my day for opening up. I don't want to hurry your tea though.'

I looked down into the cup. The liquid was the colour of healthy wee. 'I think everything that can happen to this tea has already happened. Which pretty much sums up my friends too. How about tomorrow?'

Chapter Thirty-Four

'But'—Rach gripped my sleeve as we walked across the yard—'they're *zombies*, Jess!' A sheaf of papers slipped from under her arm and she attempted to retrieve them without taking her eyes off the group who stood watching us. The fact that they were all wearing their warehouse coats made them look a bit like an army of the undead, if that army had uniforms with little logos of bicycles on the pockets, and 'Hurson Brothers' Bikes' embroidered on the back.

'Yeah, so?' I gave her a small shove and she stumbled a couple more steps.

'But ... they're *dead*! You said it was vampires ...' Which went some way to explaining why she was wearing so much make-up. You would have had to poke her face quite hard with a long stick to reach the real Rachel underneath. 'I'm sure you did.'

'Rachel, are you or are you not a union rep, newly appointed to do your best for the under-represented section of the community working in exactly this sort of job?' I looked across to where Richard stood waiting. There had either been more trouble lately or he'd had some kind of industrial accident, because one arm hung lower than the other, as though an elbow had detached. 'Because these guys, dead or not, need your help to get themselves organised.'

Rachel hesitated. 'Seriously? I mean, you didn't just bring me here to get my brains eaten, or anything?'

'Er, no. *Dawn of the Dead* wasn't a documentary, you know.'

I was proud of the way she straightened her back and set her jaw, then stepped forward to meet Richard, who was lurching towards us, even though she did hold the paperwork out in front of her, as though a massed zombie attack could be held off with lists of workplace codes and bank authorisation forms. 'Organisation is my *raisin detrer*, Jessie. I shall do my best.'

'I know, Rach.' I stood back to watch the unlikely scenario of a warehouse yard full of zombies listening to my mostly-built-of-bosom friend giving her All Brothers Together speech. It was surprisingly effective and I found myself rethinking Rachel, who'd been my best friend through school and my flat-share partner for some time after that. I hadn't realised that she had a core of steel, although, since most of the rest of her was built of Quorn and tofu, I should have known that there must have been something holding her up from within. Her lecture on the Rights of Man was emotionally given, and I could see the zombies collectively drawing themselves up as she talked about equal rights for all (even though her voice did waver a bit when someone's leg fell off, and I was sure she added the bit about 'championing the rights of all members, *living or deceased*, to exist without fear of discrimination').

When she finished talking and waved a bunch of membership forms, a small and somewhat uneven cheer went up and a queue began to form. I even caught Rachel batting her eyelashes in a slightly uncertain way at Ryan, the good-looking zombie I'd helped by the riverside. Prejudice and Rachel obviously went together about as temporarily as ice cream and flamethrowers, luckily, and just as well, otherwise her future as a union representative would have been very short.

Richard was the first to sign the forms; then he came over to talk to me. 'I think this is just what we needed, Jess,' he said.

'Unionisation? It's only a start, Richard, you know that. The union can only protect you in the workplace. I just thought it might help.'

He waved a careful hand to where Rach was writing down the details for a zombie whose ability with a pen had been compromised by having a hand on backwards. 'It's not just that. It's the fact that we're being taken seriously. The fact that now we've got somewhere to turn for help, despite the fact that we're not ... Well, there's a box on the form that says, "Do you identify as gay, lesbian, bisexual, transgender or Differently Vital".' He nodded. 'It's a sign,' he said again.

'Anything that helps, Richard. Anything that helps. And I'll do what I can, you know, to get the Zombie Rights up and running; being part of a union is just the first step to being recognised properly.' I patted his shoulder. It felt a little bit lumpier than it should have, but who was I to judge? 'You just have to stand together, all right? It's going to take time, but you'll get there.'

We watched the queue get shorter, and those zombies who'd already signed grouped together talking animatedly, well, animatedly for zombies. There was a decidedly militant feel in the air now, a collective straightening of a spine that had previously become bent under the weight of human dismissal. 'Thank you, Jessica,' Richard said at last.

'It's Rachel you should thank. She's the one with the forms and the tidy handwriting. And the desire to organise everyone. She'll have you all marching with banners soon for better tea breaks. In height order, probably, knowing Rach. Although I don't think you're going to be getting a pension plan any time soon.'

'But you thought of it. You brought us together.' Richard gave me what I think was a grin. 'We owe you one, Jess. Even if this doesn't help us fight the thugs on the street it gives us hope that we can stand together. Thank you.'

I'd better bank that gratitude, I thought, waiting for Rach to give me a lift back to the office. It might be the only time I ever got any.

Chapter Thirty-Five

Sil stared at the pictures, and then around the room. Jessica's parents' bedroom was like a shrine to normality; there was even a tube of denture-fixative on the bedside table and a bookcase full of farming handbooks and veterinary pamphlets which seemed to indicate that sheep had an alphabetical death wish.

He paused for a moment and used his thumb to ease the knot of worry that he could feel forming between his eyes. *All those words, all I spouted about decency, about killing myself if I proved to be untrustworthy ... And I never believed any of it. Never believed that it was truly I who was responsible for all that happened down in London.* He dug both hands into the ruin of his hair and let his head fall forwards. *I thought I had been magicked, glamoured somehow to behave the way I did. Yet it seems I went to London of my own volition.* A snatch of recovered memory, a room, high-ceilinged and dark with books; a girl sitting by him and smiling, laying a soft hand on his sleeve as though to hint at an intimacy recently past. *No mistake. No glamour. Just memories that I have locked away and can no longer retrieve.* Another faint whisper from the back of his mind, words uttered under the influence, memory fetched with the help of Jess's narcotic blood. *You, Jess. I went to London for you.*

He raised his head and pushed the thoughts away, went to the small cupboard in the corner of the room and, with a quick whispered plea for forgiveness, opened the first drawer and began scanning through the paperwork it contained.

Somewhere here ... somewhere, there must be a clue, he thought, trawling the farm subsidy payment records, the animal movement book, using vampire speed to read notes and sidebar headings. *Somewhere … These are organised people, people who need to keep their lives recorded. How Jessica could ever have thought she was related to people who maintain an orderly series on sheep diseases I cannot imagine.* He slammed the drawer shut and pulled out the second, but his eye was caught by a small picture half-hidden underneath a carefully-folded copy of *Classic Tractor*. He drew it free, forgetting his search as his breath stopped. *Jess.* A more recent picture than those he'd found in her bedroom. Jess and her sister standing in a garden, possibly the garden to this house. Abigail staring at the camera with a heavy, serious expression, while Jess seemed to have been captured in movement: her limbs were blurred with arrested energy and her lips were parted as though she'd either been photographed mid-sentence or about to eat a sandwich. *Knowing Jessie, it could have been either,* he thought, and found himself stroking a finger over her image before he jerked himself back and began stacking the documents onto the bed. *Somewhere here there is an answer. Or, if not an answer, something that will make the questions a little more focused.*

Chapter Thirty-Six

'Jess?'

I jerked upright and tried to pretend that I'd been looking for something under my desk. 'Urgh? Oh, morning, Liam.'

'You were asleep, weren't you?'

'No, no, I was just …'

'Licking the desk? You've got dribble round your mouth.' He hung up his jacket and came over to collect the mugs. 'Okay, so what occasioned today's early-morning start? Has Zan finally thrown you out of the House of Doom for leaving molecules scattered around?'

'I was googling.'

A sceptical eyebrow raised. 'Okay, and Zan has outlawed the use of all search engines under his roof? No, it's fine, Jessie, if you'd rather be here than anywhere else … I understand. I mean, I don't, because, let's face it, this place is only one step away from being a teenager's bedroom.' He looked around at the half-open filing cabinets with corners poking out like extras in a stationery-based Beau Geste film, and the dark orbits of long-dead mugs of coffee on the desks. 'Irresistible. If you're fifteen. You can't even see fifteen in the rear-view mirror, so what makes you want to hang around here in the depths of the night, and don't say work because … seriously?' He looked into the depths of my mug. 'You didn't even make coffee, and if you've learned to work without the stuff then I think you've moved up the ladder on the twelve-step programme. You probably get a badge.'

'If I learn to work without coffee, you are out of a job.' I rubbed the back of my hand across my eyes, trying to smear away sleep. 'No, I woke up early and thought I'd come in. It's better than trying to eat toast with Zan lurking behind the teapot. All that stalking around – seriously, would it kill him to slouch once in a while? He's like Death without the personal touch. So I came here. I *was* going to do something useful but …' I propped my elbows on the desk and rested my chin in my hands. 'I couldn't think of anything.'

'Figures.' Pointedly Liam took a letter off my desk, glanced at it, pulled open a filing drawer and slid the paper inside. 'You put the filing fairies off their nightly chores.'

'You are one small step away from mincing, Liam. I tell you this for your own good, obviously. Just go and do what you're best at, don't hold back on the biscuits, and then come back in here. I need someone to think at.'

He hesitated and, just for a second, I saw an expression cross his face that I didn't think I'd ever seen there before. It tightened his eyes like fear. 'Jess …' His voice was similarly unfamiliar. 'I need to talk to you.'

'It's not to declare undying love, is it?' His strange manner and odd body language made me flippant. 'Because I've told you before, I couldn't take the shame of being associated with a man who buys second-hand cybermen suits, I mean, think of the sweat!'

Liam still hadn't moved. 'I had a phone call. From Head Office.'

'Seriously? Head Office think you're five! They think you came in on a Bring a Schoolchild To Work day and just never left. Why would they ring you, unless it's to try to source illegal Pokémon cards?' His lack of movement was making me nervous now. Liam knew his main duty was to make me coffee and keep the paperwork from sliding down the stairs and onto the street, and his reluctance to carry this out was worrying.

The slam as Liam hit the desk made me jump. 'No! Stop it!' He used his fist, punching at the flimsy MDF in a way guaranteed to make the whole office rock. 'Jessica. This is serious.'

'It must be,' I said, staring at him. 'You haven't been this butch since Sarah did the pregnancy test.'

'Stop it!' To my surprise, and slight horror, Liam moved away from his desk and stood in front of mine, hands bunched almost as though he wanted to hit me as hard as he'd hit the furniture. 'You're always doing this, treating me as though I'm some kind of idiot foil for your brains ... and I'm not, Jess. Seriously, I'm *not*.' His voice rose to something nearer a shout, and he scattered the paperwork off the surface of my desk with the side of his hand so that he could lean over towards me.

'Liam, I ...' This was slightly scary. A bit like being attacked by a tea-cosy.

'No. Shut up for once and listen to me.' His breathing was quick, his shoulders hunching up as though the words he had to say were heavy and weighing on him. 'Head Office want me to take over from you. They think you've been compromised by Sil and Zan; that Sil going rogue has affected your ability to do your job, so they've approached me with a view to getting you to step down.'

Half of me wanted to laugh, a little hysterically perhaps, but still ... the image of Liam out on the streets with a tranq gun was so incongruous that it made my lips twitch. But the other half of me felt a cold, creeping dread. 'They're going to *fire* me?'

A brief nod.

'And you're going to take over?'

'Thinking about it. I want ... I *need* to be getting on.' And now his voice was a little more normal, nearer to the Liam I relied on. 'Sarah ... she's getting sick of me being dragged out of bed or away when I've promised I'll be home; she ...' A quick shake of his head, as though to dismiss painful conversations. 'I could lose them, Jess. Sarah and Charlotte. They'll go if I don't start getting regular hours, some actual money and fewer phone calls in the middle of the night.' His tone was sad. 'And I'm not prepared to throw it all away. Much as I ... you and me, what we've got here, it's great and I ... *you're* great. But Sarah is mine and I love her and my daughter, and I will do *anything* I can to keep us together. Do you understand?'

Now it all made sense. Liam's tension, the half-heard muttered conversations during the late phone calls. I'd dragged him into this, a world of uncertainty and low-paid stress, and I hadn't even noticed what was happening to him. Zan's words about my only needing people when I was using them came back to me, with a little twinge of guilt. Now, with what I felt for Sil ... I'd do anything, *was* doing anything, to keep him safe, and Liam just wanted the same for himself. How could I deny him that? But if I was no longer employed at Liaison, then how could I use the system, my network, to help Sil? 'How long have I got? Before they throw me out?' I tried not to look at him, remorse was needling at me, just underneath my heart.

'I haven't given them an answer yet. Well, unless you count whooping down the phone, but they want that in writing.' Liam sounded a little bit sheepish now. 'I didn't know what to do. I don't want you kicked out, but I need ... I have to think of the future. And a future without my daughter, without Charlotte and Sarah, well, it's not the future I want.'

'You'd do it? You'd seriously do my job?'

A tentative grin lightened those strained eyes a bit. 'I don't really want ... Well, it is mostly drinking coffee, eating Kit Kats and swearing, and I think I've got a handle on all those.' The smile became sad. 'I told them I needed a few days to think about it. So I guess you've got that long. They don't want the office unmanned, and I'm pretty sure they're not going to go to some temp agency to try and find someone willing to get eaten by werewolves in the line of duty, so ...'

'So I stay here until you decide to tell them you'll take over.'

Liam leaned in closer. There were small lines of tension creasing the sides of his mouth and his eyes were shadowed. I knew that this whole conversation had cost him dearly, and that he knew our relationship would never be the same again after this. Our easy 'boss and sidekick' roles were gone, blown out for an uncertain future and my palms were clammy at the emptiness that lay ahead. 'I can hold off until you sort something for Sil,' he almost whispered. 'When we know he's safe ... then maybe you can negotiate with the council, get posted somewhere else? Maybe go work for Laurie across the river.'

I suddenly felt tired. As though my sleepless night had rebounded and hit me in the back of the head. 'I don't have much choice, do I?'

He reached out. Took my hand where it lay limply on my desk and gripped it. 'I don't want to do this to you. Seriously, I don't. Liaison isn't *me*: I'm born to be a second in command, and I'm never happier than when I'm hiding the emergency biscuits from you – gods, woman, you've got a nose like a bloodhound for HobNobs – and I *love* being your backroom guy. But I need ... I need *more*. More money, more resources, better tech, shorter hours ...'

'That's less, then.'

'A proper contract. Health and Safety protocols, an R&D budget, overtime that isn't paid in garden centre vouchers, overtime that's paid at all, actually. All that. A *real* job. And this'—the hand not holding mine waved to take in the concentrated chaos of our office—'is *not* a real job.'

But it's all I've got, I wanted to say. But didn't. 'Okay then,' I said with a careful confidence I didn't feel. 'We both want to get the Sil business sorted as fast as possible. You so that you can get this place arranged and colour-coded, and me so that I can ... well. Whatever.'

'Jess ...'

I shook my head. Business as usual, at least for now. 'Until then, I am still your boss and I rather think that I need coffee more at this minute than I have ever done before. Unless you're going to come over all Bond Villain on me; although I think I actually still have the power to fire you, which could cause an interesting case of recursion to ripple through Head Office. If I fire my replacement before he even becomes my replacement, well, we all might disappear up some anomaly ... any chance of a coffee?'

Liam gave me a mild raised eyebrow. 'Of course. And then you said you wanted to think at me?'

When he reappeared, two mugs braced out in front of him, like the world's most domestic knuckleduster, I said. 'I need to go up to the farm. I think I need to talk to Sil again.'

A coaster appeared to cushion my paperwork from the mug. 'Not such a great idea, Jess. The more often you go up there, the more likely it is that Zan will get suspicious. Actually, no, he's already suspicious, got to be, with a walk like that. But, seriously, can't you just phone?'

'He doesn't have his mobile and he wouldn't answer the house phone.' I took my first, life-saving, mouthful of coffee. 'Besides, I might need to ...' I wasn't even aware that I'd done it, but my finger must have touched the now-healed bite under my shirt, because Liam slammed his mug down on his desk.

'No. No. Not again. I've still got the bruises from last time.'

'Well, obviously, let's get our priorities right here.'

'You can't keep giving him blood every time he gets a bit forgetful! What's going to happen if he goes senile – you walk around next to him like a human Snack Bucket?'

'This isn't *a bit forgetful*, Liam, it's something that's been done to him that my blood can partially reverse, even if only temporarily. And we need to know more.'

Liam picked up his mug and stared into it, shaking his head again. 'Crazy. It's all getting political here; I never signed up for political. I signed up for making the world a better place, equality and fraternity and not staking blokes just because they're wearing eyeliner! Not some deep shit in London with non-existent birth certificates and your boyfriend getting a death sentence. This is way, way beyond my brief.'

'Well, it won't be worrying you for much longer, will it?' I hadn't meant to sound quite so sarcastic and tried to mitigate my words. 'Once this place is all yours you can make the job as unpolitical as you like, can't you?'

Dark eyebrows flicked at me over his mug. 'I might complain about them, but one thing I do know about politics is that they generate a *phenomenal* amount of paperwork. Best bit of the job, paperwork.'

'And, incidentally, great for starting fires.' My gaze went back to my computer screen and an itchy little ache set up between my heart and my lungs. 'Something is wrong.'

'With Sil?'

'With this whole thing. Sil went to London to look for records relating to my mother, okay, so far, fine. Next thing he knows he's shot; then he wakes up starving and ... well, his demon took over.'

'Yes,' Liam said gently. 'I know. I was there when he told you.'

'Right.' Then, aware that hadn't sounded very butch. 'Right! Get on that machine and find whatever census result it was that Sil got up. We might as well be working from the same parameters. Oh, and keep that security level up high; we don't want Zan hacking in and finding out what we're doing.'

'Bloody hell, when did you come over all MI5?' Liam said.

'And I am going up to the farm. It's all right, I'll take a cover story in case Zan is watching. Can I borrow your car?'

'Don't let him bite. Not without someone else there. I saw him the other day and he wasn't in control, not really. If I hadn't hit him …' Liam clenched his fist reflexively. 'Well, anything could have happened.'

'I have to trust him.' Ignoring my body's screams for a good night's sleep in a proper bed, I pulled on my jacket. 'Because otherwise there's nothing between us.'

'Well, all right.' His keys, with the flashing TARDIS keyring, flew across the desk. 'But take care, kemo sabe.'

'I've always thought of you more as Robin to my Batman. Only without you in tights, obviously, because, ugh.'

'Just go.'

Chapter Thirty-Seven

My cover story involved going via my parents' neighbours and picking up the old Labrador they'd been minding. All right, as cover stories went it was fairly flimsy. I mean, what was I going to say, that the dog had to pop home to pick up the post? But it was all I had, and Gem was pleased to see me, at least. He leaned against me from the passenger seat all the way up the lane in a lovely familiar way.

'Sil?' I pushed open the front door and the dog waddled past me towards the kitchen, in an ever-hopeful search for dropped food. 'Where are you?'

Silence. But he knew I was here. I could *feel* it, somehow, like an expectant pulling near my navel, as though we were being zipped together slowly. And then I saw him, standing on the staircase. Dark. Shadowed.

'Jess.'

Even his tone was dark and, for a second, I wondered if Liam had talked to him, told him that the job I'd done since I was eighteen, the only job I'd ever had (if you didn't count being a very bad waitress or helping at a Pony Club rally) and the only one I was qualified to do, was being taken away from me because of him. But the deepness of his eyes held words his mouth didn't seem to want to say, and being fired by York Council was more of an 'Oh well, there's always McDonald's' occasion. 'What is it? Sil?'

He came down two more stairs but still stood above me. 'I've ... there are things.' Still dark. Still shadowed. His slashed hair left his bone structure bare, made his eyes look bigger and his mouth less friendly. 'I know it was wrong but I thought ... I am sorry.' He was holding something out to me, a blue folder of the kind that Liam insisted we should use to keep call-out records in. I thought Post-its and the odd paperclip were perfectly sufficient. 'But it is important.'

The tiredness was back, now accompanied by a black Labrador licking my ankle. 'Can we just pretend it isn't?' I said. 'Please, just for a few minutes can we imagine that none of this is happening?' My hands came up and covered my face; I could feel the welling heat of tears trying to break out from my chest. 'I've already had as much as I can handle for one day.'

The folder was withdrawn and Sil descended the final stairs. 'This is not going away,' he said softly. 'And this may be no time to weaken.'

'This isn't weakening.' I squeezed the words out between my teeth, trying not to let any tears go with them. 'It's lack of sleep; it's losing my job; worry about stopping zombies getting torched; having to contend with your, quite frankly, weird boss stalking around outside my bedroom at all hours; and it's ...' I lost my battle and a few uncorralled drops fell from my eyes. 'It's just *everything*.'

Sil took my hand and pulled it away from its attempts to prevent emotion leaking out. 'Come,' he said softly. 'Sit with me. Time is not important at this moment.' One hand guided my shoulders into the living room and over to the couch.

I sat down next to him, feeling my skin prickle at having him close, the firm press of his body against mine and his scent in my nostrils. There was a comfort to it, like coming home after a long journey to a cup of tea and warm slippers, and I snaked my fingers through his as we rested our heads against the sofa, eyes closed.

'How's the zombie thing coming along?' he asked, eyes still closed, fingers still cupped against mine.

'It's ... well, they've made a start. Actually, I pity anyone who takes on a unionised zombie. They've got the chanting down now, even if it is something like "What do we want?

Equality! When do we want it? Whenever is convenient for you!"'

'That's good.' A pause. 'Liam sent me a message about Liaison.'

'Ah.' I didn't have the energy to open my eyes, but I knew he was looking at my face. 'Okay.'

'This is my fault. All of it. If I hadn't …' A sigh. 'If only I had *known* …'

A chilly, damp pressure on my cheek made me open my eyes, to see the dog had put two front paws onto the sofa arm and was staring into my face with a slightly accusatory look on his saggy old jowls. I hauled myself to my feet, disengaging my hand from Sil's. 'We need help, Sil. This is beyond me; hell, it's even beyond Liam, and he's practically beyond in his own right. I think we should tell Zan.'

Sil's eyes snapped open. 'He'll turn me over to Enforcement.'

I opened the door to let the dog potter out of the front, to cock his leg against a stone bootscraper. 'Dad's going to be allowed home soon, and what am I supposed to do, shunt you around the country under a dog blanket for the next ten years? And when Zan was talking about you he almost seemed to have some kind of emotion going on, supposing it wasn't a nasty case of haemorrhoids. It might be worth a shot. And …' I hesitated, a momentary uncertainty creeping in. 'I want you to bite me again.'

Sil hissed, his breath so loud that Gem let out a bark, lips wobbling. When I turned to look at Sil his eyes were alight and his fangs showed on his lower lip just a touch. 'Dangerous. I like your blood way too much.'

'We need to know if there's anything else you can remember about the Records Office. They did something to you to wipe your memory for a reason.'

'Oh, good. So much better than them just deciding to clear my mind of several days on a whim.'

'Shut up.' The dog pottered between my legs again, claws clacking on the tiles, nose snuffling for any so-far-undiscovered crumbs. 'And I trust you.'

His eyes moved from the vein in the side of my neck up to meet my gaze. I didn't know whether he knew it but his tongue had come out and run over his lower lip, almost as though he were salivating at the thought of my blood. 'Knowing what you know about me?'

'*Because* of what I know about you.'

'Oh Jess ...' He raised a finger and ran it down my throat, around my neck. Traced the tip around, I presume he was following the lines of blood vessels under the skin, his eyes an almost-hypnotic dark, like water of unknown depth. '*Jess.*'

'Do it. Quickly, before I lose my nerve.'

And then there was space between us and his hand had fallen from my skin. 'There is no need.'

'What?'

Sil turned his back on me, almost as though he was afraid he wouldn't be able to control himself if he had to look at me. 'I have other information,' he said, and his voice was deeper, heavier, with a kind of longing. 'I do not need to bite you.' Then he turned and I was slightly scared by the blackness of his eyes and the fact that his fangs hadn't retracted. He looked ready to take every drop of blood I had in me. 'But I'm not sure of my control at this minute, so please don't ask me again.'

'What information do you have?' And then, when he didn't answer straight away, 'Sil?'

He sighed so deeply that it must have sent his demon scuttling lower within him, for cover. 'I was searching the house.'

'*This* house? My parents' place? But what for? What kind of information could you possibly hope to find here?'

Another sigh and he held out the blue folder again. 'This. Oh gods, Jessie, *this*.'

I couldn't take it from him. My hands were shaking so much that he had to push me back to the sofa and place it on the seat beside me, and, as soon as I saw the familiar writing on the outside, carefully lettered in black felt tip, I felt the cold dread rising again. 'But this is my mother's writing. Jen, I mean, not Rune.'

'Open it.'

Not a suggestion, not a command. More of a tired statement of a fact that hadn't yet happened. I turned the folder around so that I could read the deliberate lettering. 'To my daughter Jessica Amelia. Only to be opened after my death.'

'But she's not dead! Well, she's drinking hospital coffee, but it doesn't immediately follow, you know.'

Sil sat beside me again and waved a hand at the file. 'You need to know,' he said. 'Please. I'll wait.'

I flipped back the cover and pulled out sheets of paper. Gave one a quick look, then another, and then flung them back onto the sofa, leaping to my feet as though the words were scorpions and cobras. 'These are ...'

'They are letters. To you. From Rune.'

'You've read them all?' I was staring down at the sheaf of carefully hand-printed stationery, scattered like spent bullets on the mocha fabric of the couch. 'Sil?'

'Yes. They hadn't been opened. Your mother ... Jen ... had instructions to keep them for you "until she felt you were ready". Most seem to have been written not long after you were born, or maybe even before that, while she waited for your arrival. There are a few later ones.'

I stared again. The loops and curls of the script seemed almost to hang in the air above the papers, and I found I was reaching out a hand as if I could somehow touch Rune if I could touch the space where she'd been. 'She wrote to me,' I said, wonderingly. 'My mother ... oh, this is confusing, my *other* mother said that they'd stayed in touch with Rune for a long time after they moved up here.'

'You need to read them.' Sil caught my hand as it floated, trying to touch atoms of Rune. 'Now.' And he pushed my fingers down until they hit the papers. 'I am here.'

So I did. I sat in the living room while the air darkened around me and read the letters. Sometimes through tears, sometimes I laughed, but all the time Sil stayed beside me, unmoving, until the implications hit me and I held onto him as though somehow we could unhappen the past.

'She was bred by the government to bring down vampires.'

'A succinct appraisal.' Sil's lips moved against my hair. 'Her mother was one of the Twelve brought in when the Otherworlders first came through.'

'And her mother was ... *mated* with another of the Twelve. My mother was born and then managed to get away after the Troubles.' I stroked the letters softly with a fingertip. 'It's funny, she goes into a lot of detail about her life up until the end of the Troubles, and then she glosses over things a bit, almost as though she's *ashamed*, but with nowhere to go and no experience of living outside the facility ... no wonder she ended up with Malfaire. After what the government had done, he probably looked like a good bet.' I riffled my fingers over the letters. 'To someone who'd never met a nice person, obviously.'

'It is unlawful, it is unethical ... no wonder the government don't want this to become public. No wonder they tried to prevent me from telling anyone that your mother had no birth certificate. They fear that someone, somewhere, may make connections.'

'If we'd only said something my mother may have given these to me. She had no way of knowing that Rune and you being starved would be connected.' I breathed carefully. 'She was going to make me wait until she was *dead* to know any of this.' My father's words came back to me, *Your mother thinks we did something wrong in keeping you.* 'She didn't want me to know about Rune.'

'The letters were sealed. Your parents didn't know either. That letter we found under the carpet, the government were fishing for information your parents didn't have. Rune never told them where she came from, what had happened to her, probably to spare them just this sort of thing happening.' Sil stood up. 'Your bloodline must be very, very important to them. I wonder what they think is going to happen; why they need to bring in all those who may be immune to vampires.'

We looked at one another for a very long moment. 'And now we fetch Zan,' I said. 'On so many counts.'

A long, slow nod. 'But you realise that he may still call for my end?'

'I hate to say it, but we need him. I *think* I may be able to persuade him to scale back on the hunting you down and killing you thing.' Without looking at him I reached out and touched his face. 'But we can't do anything without him. If we're going up against the human government ... if word gets out about me being Rune's daughter ... I hate to say it, but he might be the only thing that can protect any of us.'

'Of course.' Sil nodded. He had his back to me, and there was something very defeated about the dip of his head and the roundness of his shoulders. Of course, the shrunken sweater and low-rise chain-store jeans were also the epitome of subjugation for a vampire. 'May I keep the dog? It is lonely here, and I long for ...' He turned his head; his hacked hair mostly concealed his face, but what I could see looked haggard and vulnerable. 'You, Jess.'

'If an elderly, overweight dog can stand in for me then you had better be prepared to apologise profusely when this is all over.' I didn't dare touch him or kiss him farewell: he looked as though he might break completely. 'I'll message you when there's more news.'

A quiet moment, then he turned. There was still grace in him; he still had the gorgeous, sculpted face and the poise, but there was also an acid-stain of defeat blurring his features. 'Thank you for assuming there will be an end,' he said quietly. 'Because I feel that this is my entire life now. Hiding.' His voice tailed off and he shook the rag-tag ends of his hair. 'Tell Zan I …' Another shake of the head. 'Just tell Zan: if he ends me, then so be it. I cannot live like this.'

I searched for something meaningful to say, but couldn't find it. 'Oh, shut up. If there's any "ending" of you to be done, then it will be me doing it because I don't want any doubts about you getting up again afterwards, all right?'

There was a tiny puckering of his lips that was either a smile or his fangs. 'I would expect no less.'

'Right. And you'd better look after the dog, because my anger is nothing compared to my mother's if she finds puddles on the good rug.'

'Understood.'

I couldn't look back. I had to walk out and squeeze myself into Liam's little car, drive away with an insouciant wave from the window, because if I'd caught Sil's eye, or even seen him move towards me, I would never have left. I would have wrapped myself around him and never let go.

Chapter Thirty-Eight

Zan was sitting alone at a bare desk. The chrome of the computer gleamed at me and my shoes made little squeaky sounds against the carefully polished wooden floor, it couldn't have been further from the Liaison office if it had unicorns as coat hangers. 'Jessica?'

'That's Sil's desk.'

'I know. I work here.'

The computer wasn't switched on. Zan had just been sitting, apparently staring at the empty screen and the neatly stacked papers that Sil had left. When I went over I saw that there was also a picture of me, newly framed, beside the keyboard – me standing alone at a party. One of the ones the newspapers were so fond of printing alongside made-up tales of my misdemeanours. Somehow it looked better here: I looked heroic and strong. *He keeps a picture of me on his desk.* The little ball of screwed-tight emotion that I was barely restraining made another bid for escape, but, in view of Zan's opinions on crying women, I forced it down. There was another picture too, pushed slightly towards the back of the desk and framed in wood, a posed family group in sepia tones. 'Is that Christina and the children?'

'Unless he has taken to placing random photographs within his line of sight, I would assume so.'

The woman was sitting in a chair, her son on one side and her daughter on the other, all immaculately dressed and precisely placed. Their features were mostly washed-out with age, but the rounded cheeks and carefully styled hair spoke of affluence; their steady, serious stares of determination. 'She looks nice.'

'Yes. He clearly decided to downgrade.' Zan's eyes were very green. 'Why are you here, Jessica?'

I looked at him, trying to decide what to do. He looked, as usual, precise and contained. I'd often wondered what would make Zan fall apart, but suspected that, if he did, gearwheels would have my eye out. 'I think I need your help.'

He went very still. He was always fairly still, but now he seemed to shut down every function except for listening, even his blinking stopped. 'Sil,' was all he said.

'Yes.'

And now Zan actually slumped. I'd never seen him do it before, at least not while he was conscious, but his shoulders rounded and his head dropped. 'He's alive?' A whisper.

'Yes.'

'And you know where he is?'

'Look, let's stop playing twenty questions, shall we?' I must have sounded fierce because Zan's head snapped up and his demon moved, a fleeting presence behind Zan's eyes for a second, making his fangs slide into place.

'Do not attempt to order me, Jessica.' He laid his hands flat on the desktop and stood up, using the smooth vampire glide that was so alien. 'You have kept things from me.' Alpha-vamp had come to the party again.

'Indoor voice, Zan, please. I'm not impressed by you pulling the whole "I am Vampire, hear me gnash" you know, and I'm not scared of you either.' It was a bit of a lie; I wasn't *exactly* scared, but Zan was an unknown quantity when it came to actual aggression, so I was cautious at the very least. I wasn't going to let him know, though: it would only make him even smugger, and Liam had used up York's smugness quotient already. 'I want some assurances from you before I say anything else.'

'Assurances.' Zan moved out from behind the desk. 'From *me*? And what bargaining power do you have, if I may ask?'

He ran his hands down the lapels of his Neru-collared jacket, like a nineteenth-century businessman who'd just been asked for a discount. 'Because I rather think I do not have to assure you of anything, other than that I can, and will, kill you if you do not reveal what you know.'

Bugger. I really should have gone back for the tranq gun. But I kept my voice steady. Not showing fear was the key to making Zan listen to me; if I broke and started to whimper he would have the upper hand over me forever. And that would be like being ruled over by a Praying Mantis, so, no, not going to happen. 'First. I want you to tell me that you will not send the boys in to do away with Sil. Second, I want your promise that he will be pardoned of all crimes against Humans. Thirdly, oh, sod, there was a third thing ... damn!'

'Presumably it involved assurances of safety for yourself, Jessica? I cannot promise anything. I must hold the city to the Treaty that Sil has so wantonly broken.'

'I think what happened to Sil has something to do with the human government,' I said quickly, before I could chicken out, back down and pretend that I knew nothing. The words were incendiary, and I knew that once they were said things would never be the same again; the way Zan's face set as soon as I let them out told me I was right. His long fingers curled, dragging splinters from the mahogany desktop and leaving score marks in the wood; his shoulders straightened as though he was prepared for a huge weight to settle on them.

'I think ...'—there was a new gentleness to his voice, but a gentleness that sounded as though it was wrapped around an iron bar—'that we should go home and discuss this.'

'But I ...' I was desperate to explain but had no time to get any more words out before Zan was in front of me, pushing a hand across my mouth, the fingers that had scratched those parallel lines into the hard wood leaving me with no uncertainty about what they could do to my face if I protested. I restrained the urge to bite him because I could feel his usual cool façade trembling – it was a bit like being silenced by a rockface when you can feel the earthquake coming.

'We will go home,' he said, into my eyes. 'Yes?'

He wasn't trying to glamour me; he knew that wouldn't work. He was using his eyes to convey some other message, but Zan was too alien to me, with his OCD and his fussiness. I'd never tried to forge any kind of bond with him, even friendship would have been like trying to befriend a plank, so I had no idea what was going on behind that moss-green stare. However, he'd overcome his hatred of personal contact far enough to risk my spittle, and that told me how serious he was without any eye woo-woo; so I nodded, and felt his fingers relax away from my face.

'Just one question.'

He gave me a cautious look as he took a handkerchief from his pocket and used it to wipe his palm. 'Perhaps.'

'Are you driving the Bugatti?'

Zan sighed and looked at the ceiling. 'Even *now*? Seriously?'

'Appearances are important,' I said, sulkily.

'Yes. We will go in the car.' He opened the door to the office and another vampire, not *quite* as top-rank sexy and classy as Sil and Zan but only one film-star notch down, handed him his keys. I'd never asked, but always assumed that some low-level kind of telepathic thing went on between vamps, and this seemed to prove it, unless Zan just had his staff *really* well trained.

Almost bundling me, but without actually making any physical contact, Zan got us out of the office and down to their (underground, guarded) car park, where the Bugatti sat amid a series of other show-stoppers. It was like a *Top Gear* wet dream down there. Once we were in the car, he turned to me.

'Do you understand why we must leave the office to talk? I ask only because I do not want you to start thinking that I am abducting you again.'

'Are you worried that we may be overheard?'

'I am worried all the time. I have ceased to remember how it felt *not* to be worried.' He started the engine and steered the car expertly through the tight turns of the parking system and out onto the main road, while I sat silent.

Zan was telling me how he felt? I wouldn't have been more surprised if the car had piped up and asked us to ease off the throttle because it felt a bit peaky.

'Is it safe here?' Something in this general background level of paranoia must be catching.

'I think so, yes.' Zan fiddled with something on the dashboard and a little 3D image of the car sprang up with points of light dotted around it. 'Yes. The car is clear.'

I leaned back, closed my eyes and told Zan about Sil going to London and about the letter my father had received. It took the drive home and most of a pot of tea (me) and a large bottle of O negative (Zan), and when I'd finished we both looked a bit bloated.

'Why did you not come to me?' Zan tipped some more blood into his glass. He'd loosened up a bit, and had actually put his elbows on the table, but not to the evidently disgusting level of drinking from the bottle.

'Because you kept telling me that he'd gone rogue and had to die. Several times, if I remember rightly.' This was odd. I always hated it when Zan treated me as an equal, and now here we were, practically doing one another's hair.

'But, if I had known that he was shut away … starved …' Zan shook his head. 'I would not have called for his end.'

I poured another cup. What I'd really wanted was a

sturdy mug of builder's tea, or one of Liam's 'proper coffees', so thick that the spoon bent and biscuits bounced off the surface, but I'd thought Earl Grey was a little more Zan-friendly, so I was quietly perfuming myself to death. 'There's something else, Zan.'

'Regarding Sil?'

'It's more about me, actually.' I told him about the letters from Rune. I left out some of the more emotional stuff, but laid it all out about her having come from a government breeding programme, about her mother having been selected for being resistant to vampires.

And then Zan dropped the bottle.

It smashed against the ornamental quarry tiles of the kitchen floor with a noise that made my head sing, and when I looked at him his eyes were glowing the kind of red that really imaginative artists used when they drew hell. He was looking at me, but almost as though my skin had become invisible and he could see my bones moving beneath. 'No,' he said. 'No.' Then he stood up and started pacing the floor, and what frightened me more than anything was the fact that he left the broken bottle beneath the table, ignoring the glass fragments and the remains of the blood that spiralled out from the impact and dotted the tiles with darkness. 'No,' he said again, reaching the doorway and jerking the door open with such force that the handle split and the carefully waxed solid wood panel tore away from the frame.

'All right, that's got that out of your system,' I said carefully, putting the cup down. 'Now, can we carry on our conversation? I understand your need to pull City Vamp out from under the bed every now and then, but I need to know what the hell is going on because my lover is sitting up on the moors with nothing but a deaf Labrador between him and any shit that is going to come down on his head because of this.'

Zan made an obvious effort to pull himself together. 'Eloquent as always, Jessica.' He laced his fingers together and cupped them in front of his mouth, thinking. 'We need to go to him,' he said, as though coming to a huge decision.

'Sil?'

'No, the Labrador. You do understand what is happening here, don't you?'

'Not really, but I know you're scared, and that is *terrifying* me, so, yes, whatever, let's go.'

Chapter Thirty-Nine

Sil walked back from the barn. The dog had given him a serious staring-at until he'd opened the door, and then the freedom of the air had called to him and he'd decided to stretch his legs as far as the property perimeter. No further, because the sole was becoming detached from one trainer and scraping the ground with every step, making him lift his knees like a trotting pony, although he hardly even noticed it now. *I can go no lower.*

The tug came, jerking at his midriff and making him flex uncertainly, a fish hooked but not yet flapping on the bank. *Jess?* Then the dog was barking and running stiffly towards the track and Sil saw the Veyron slithering like a metal ghost into the gravel circle in front of the house. His heart and demon jumped in a ballet of synchronised movement when he saw Jess get out of the passenger seat, and then died to a muted crawl through his chest as Zan climbed out next to her. *Zan. My friend through all these years … now I find out where you stand.*

Gathering his courage, he walked down the hill towards the house. *If I am going to die, at least I can tell Jess what she means to me before I go. I can look into those lovely amber eyes and tell her how loving her has been the only thing that has kept my humanity in place.*

Zan and Jess, looking surprisingly sociable, were in the kitchen, sitting on opposite sides of the scrubbed table. When he walked through the door they both stood up, and then looked at one another in a slightly awkward way, as though they had formed an orderly queue to throw themselves into his arms and weren't sure which one was at the front. But Jess, as he had known she would, won and crossed the floor in two strides to encircle him with her arms and bury her face against his chest.

He closed his eyes and breathed the lovely scent of her. She smelled of faded light, of coffee on a breeze, of sweet things underlined in metal. Her hair rioted, so when he looked down all he could see was a mass of silken black threads.

'It's going to be all right,' she said, her words brushing his skin. 'It has to be.'

Zan was standing, impassive. 'Jessica has told me everything. I fear she does not understand the implications, but that is Jessica in a nutshell, is it not?'

'We need to work out what we do next.' Jess pushed lightly at him until he stepped back and enabled her to turn around. He kept a hand on her shoulder, needing the contact. She was excited, he could feel the adrenaline running through her blood like sugar, and under his touch her skin gathered into bumps. 'How we can save Sil.'

'It is not Sil who concerns me at this moment.' Zan's words made her still under his touch. 'It is you, Jessica. You have suddenly become a very dangerous person with whom to be connected.'

'How the hell can *I* be dangerous? Zan, I practically define safety and moral rectitude. Well, all right, not moral rectitude, but safety, certainly. I'm not allowed anything more dangerous than a gun that puts you to sleep for twenty minutes – it's like having an arsenal entirely made up of Kalms tablets! The worst you're going to get from me is nightmares, or a date with an Enforcement officer who, on present evidence, is going to be Harry Leonard, the world's biggest pushover.'

'Jessica.' Sil tried to intervene, to calm her. He could tell Zan was walking a tightrope of emotion, although almost none seeped out. Any onlooker would have thought the old vampire was calmly watching and listening, but Sil could sense the cocktail of hormones that Zan's demon was currently feeding from as eagerly as a starving man at the remains of a feast. 'What makes her suddenly so dangerous, Zan?'

A moment. Sil would remember that moment as the one on which time pivoted, when the world swung from its superficial Treaty-led organised state into one with layers of threat and treachery so deep that none of them knew how far entrenched they were. Then Zan spoke. 'I believe ... that if the government are trying to regroup the Twelve, then they may have plans for ending the Treaty.'

Meaning upon meaning slammed into Sil with such force that it drove him back from Jess, made his eyes ache and his skin burn. 'No,' he said, finding himself covering his mouth with his hands as though to deny the words. 'No. Surely, we would know? After all this time?'

A pause. And then Zan looked at Jess. 'Perhaps they have discovered the ultimate weapon,' he said.

Now Sil looked at Jess too. *The Twelve were never proven to be anything more than tales to terrify, rumours to force us to peace.* But if Zan was right – *If,* he reminded himself – then this woman, who kept him from becoming the animal he despised in himself, was created by an evil that made her demon father look like a kitten in a snowstorm.

Chapter Forty

The two vamps were staring at me as though I was about to detonate. 'What?' I asked. I hadn't missed the way Sil had pulled away from me either. 'For God's sake, *what?*'

Zan shook his head. 'You must do this, Sil,' he said, and he'd got that gentle tone in his voice again – he usually only sounded like that if he was talking to a cat. 'You must tell her.'

'I can't.' Sil sounded broken. 'Zan, please.'

'If one of you doesn't come up with the goods in the next ten seconds I am going to take those car keys, wrap that bloody Veyron round the nearest tree, and then, never mind explaining things to me, you are going to have to talk to your insurance company and, trust me, I am a *much* better listener!' They were starting to spook me, what with all the staring and the weird quiet voices. I much preferred vamps when they ran around all toothy and bitey, this was just *strange*.

'You need to sit down,' Sil pushed me until I perched on the edge of the nearest chair. 'It's not good.'

I sighed. 'Since when has anything ever been good? And can we hurry this up, only I have to go back to York and help my best friend sort out some very wobbly subscription forms.'

'Listen to me. This is important. So, *so* important.' Sil reached out a hand and touched my wrist. His gesture was cautious, as though he feared my skin was about to peel back and reveal knives. 'The stories at the time said that the government took the Twelve. There was an incident, back in the eighties, where a whole load of vamps got slaughtered. They'd been part of an invading force down in Sussex, all bound for London to try to take out what remained of the human wartime Cabinet and …' He shook his head. 'We never found out what happened, but they were all killed, and the word went out that the Twelve had been involved. Our fear hastened the signing of the Treaty.'

I stood up. My spine felt as though it was braced with jelly. 'And that has what to do with me?'

'The Twelve were bred. Engineered. And their offspring were more powerful still.' Sil stopped and shook his head, as though the words refused to be spoken.

'And one of those truly powerful offspring mated with a demon. An almost immortal demon,' Zan said.

'And nowhere, Jess, nowhere in those letters does Rune mention how she met your father, does she?' Sil's voice was soft. 'She came to your parents already pregnant.'

'But they said that she left the programme in 1979! She didn't have me for another two years …' Both vampires were looking at me as though I were on the verge of discovering something they already knew but didn't want to push me into. 'Hang on, hang on … what are you trying to tell me with your big moody silences and your meaningful glances … you think Rune was *deliberately* given to Malfaire? That she escaped when she was pregnant …'

'The government lied in that letter to your father,' Zan said. 'Hoping, perhaps, that he would get in touch and give them Rune's version of events.'

'I really hate this kitchen,' I said. 'Every time I come in here someone wants to tell me something that makes me just that *little bit* less human. Next time I'm going to sell tickets.' My head had started to hurt. This was just … too much, too fast. I wiped my hands across my face to let my expression crumble without having to see the look in the vampires' eyes when it did. 'So my blood being vampire drugs is part of what they did?'

'It would make sense.' Zan's voice was still calm. 'Breeding humans with disabling blood would allow them to kill the vampire while he or she was knocked out.'

Shock was pinwheeling about in my chest; whenever I tried to think about what I'd just been told my brain refused to grip the words. *Your whole life, Jess. Blown out of the water once, and now* ... Tears pushed behind my eyes, burned at my throat, and I fought my body's demand that I lie down on the floor and howl with everything I had. 'None of this is helping!' I gulped. 'All very interesting – the family history people are probably baying at the door – but it's not going to get Sil out of here without him being killed, is it? Zan, there must be something you can do.'

'Must there?' Zan said. 'If there is, I am afraid it eludes me. We cannot reveal what Sil was doing in London without exposing your history to the world, Jessica. And I am not willing to do that.'

'Please.' I clearly surprised all three of us with my tone. 'Please, Zan. Come up with something, I don't care what it is ... What's the point of you being about two hundred years old and all Master Vampire and stuff if you can't help him now?'

Zan gave me a considering look. 'If I assist Sil to escape death ... what price would you consider to be too great, Jessica? Your freedom for his? Your *life* for his? Because I fear this situation will not end without there being some penalty, some trade, and it may be one you are not willing to make.'

Adrenaline had burned out in me. I could almost feel my body trying to squeeze the last drop of reaction out of glands that had long since been exhausted. 'Anything, Zan. If you get him out of this, I will owe you anything you care to claim from me.' I met the cold, clear green gaze; it was like looking into interstellar space. 'Only not sex, okay?'

Zan curled a lip in what could have been a smile or extreme distaste. 'I can promise that will not be a price either of us would be willing to extract.'

Sil put his hand on my arm. 'Don't, Jessie. He *will* hold you to any promise you make, we both know that.'

'But *someone* has to do *something*!' I covered my face with my hands and let some tears seep through, tears of sheer powerlessness. 'Otherwise you're dead and I'm ... without you.'

Sil leaned towards me, so close that his cool cheek touched mine. 'Maybe *that* will be the price,' he whispered. 'Had you thought of that?'

'I can't do this. I can't deal with this.' I dropped my hands from my face and watched Zan recoil. Zan regarded tears as nature's way of telling humans that they are prey. 'I've got a job to do, I've got people to see and stuff I can't ...' The words got sucked down into my chest and obscured by my breath. 'I can't.' I wanted to lie down, I wanted to cry, to melt against Sil and sob until nothing made sense any more. To have him hold me, tell me that nothing made a difference, that the world would continue to turn and I would continue to be a mere speck on its surface. But somewhere deep inside me something was telling me that I had to keep going. Some central core was turning out to be made, not as I had previously suspected, of chocolate and biscuits, but of something cold and hard. Something that braced me, pushed me forwards, away from Sil's comfort. 'I have to get back to York.'

'I will take Jessica,' Zan said, moving to the doorway. 'I must return to the office with this knowledge, to continue research into the human government's possible plans for bringing about the end of the Treaty.'

I turned to look at him. 'And my mother?'

'If there is relevant information, we shall share that with you, of course.'

Relevant to whom? I thought, but I was still too shocked and horrified to make an issue out of it. 'I must get back to the office. Liam will think I've decamped with the tea money.'

'Then I shall return you.' Zan gave another of those formal bows that looked as though he had Russian Cavalry officers in his genes, and left the kitchen, jingling the keys to the Bugatti, which left Sil and I staring at each other.

'I need you, Jess.' He breathed the words, moving closer so that his body touched mine, his hand slipping round to the back of my neck to bring me in still closer. 'It is not something that lies easily with me, needing another, but you ...' His other hand came around, his index finger brushing my lips until I looked up to meet clouded eyes. 'You are all.'

His mouth touched mine and I was filled with the desire to lose myself in him, to hide from the world in the arms of this strong, gorgeous man. To let him possess me, to take me away from everything.

'Jess?'

'I have to go.' I pushed one hand into his chest, forced him back the step I needed to be able to turn and run from the once-so-familiar room, which now held the ghosts of so many terrible secrets.

Chapter Forty-One

I'd lied about going back to the office. The thought of walking in to find Liam measuring up my chair and upgrading my computer into something more suitable for his needs – which were mostly browsing eBay and *Doctor Who* forums – was more than I could take. So I went to the only place where I could be completely human, without question.

'Oh good, you're here. Hold this end, will you? I want to check the spelling.' Rachel handed me a pole and stood back to examine the banner. 'They lose concentration a bit half way through.'

'I thought you might be at work,' I said feebly, holding the broom handle above my head to stretch the sheeting out, until I felt like someone making the kind of bed that fought back. 'I only popped in on the off chance.'

'I'm going on a march.' Rach gestured at me to let the banner drop. 'Well, I *say* march ... they can't keep in step, poor things, and I have to tie the statements on to some of them.'

I looked around the flat. Every surface was scattered with bits of paper, forms and notes and random newspaper cuttings. It was enough out of character for Rachel to make me nearly forget that the vampires considered me to be a walking time-bomb. 'What the hell is going on?'

Rachel stopped her perusal of the banner and stood back with her hands on her hips. 'You were so right about them,' she said. 'The way that they were being abused when they do work that is so vital ...'

'And by "they" you mean ...?'

'We've decided to stop using the "z" word: it's prejudicial. They're marching as the Ambulatory Deceased. ADs for short. Plus, the whole "zombie" thing ... it was just too far down the alphabet to be any use, and nothing rhymes with it, which is just *hopeless* when you need a slogan.'

'Oh.'

'Yes. Honestly, Jessie, getting them joined up to the union was the best thing ever. Now we're getting more and more on board, and we can threaten to close down loads of industries if they all come out on strike, you know. ADs do all the clearing out at power stations and running cables across pylons, all the stuff that results in almost certain death for people like us.'

'Right ...'

'Isn't it great?' Rach gave me a huge grin. 'I'm actually doing something *useful*. Getting people to realise how much we need the ADs, and if they're being threatened by horrible people they could use their union to go on strike and then we'd have no electricity!'

'Ah. A sort of blackmail.' I collapsed onto the sofa; there was so much paperwork underneath me it felt like sitting on origami. 'Rach?'

'Mmmm?' She turned around, filling a bag with tape and glue.

'Do you ever think about your parents?'

A small pause. 'No.' She resumed her busyness, as though a small, busty whirlwind was whipping through the flat. 'What good would it do?'

'They died in the Troubles? In a vampire attack?'

She sat, suddenly, causing a banner to crease and its poles to fly together like giant chopsticks. 'My mum and my dad and my brother were killed. I was upstairs asleep and the vampires didn't know I was there. Or they did and didn't care, they weren't hungry anymore.'

I imagined that little girl tiptoeing downstairs to find the corpses of her family, drained dry. 'And you don't hate them for doing that? Or hate your parents for dying and leaving you?'

Rachel sighed. 'What is this really about, Jessie? Only, the Troubles were a long time ago. It's exhausting, hating people for things they did so long ago that it might as well have been a different life, if vampires didn't live for, like, hundreds of years. It's life. You just get on with it.'

I declined a cup of whatever wee-flavour herbal tea was currently in the pot and let her get on with her march preparations. She was right. Of course she was. The past was dead and gone; the Troubles were over so long ago that a whole generation was growing up without ever having feared vampires, without the dread of nightfall that even I only vaguely remembered. Now the Troubles were the stuff of adventure films, of screwball comedies where designer-label-obsessed vampires and camp, ineffectual Shadows hunted in shopping centres and were brought down by teenagers and a talking dog.

Long gone. History. And yet … it could come back. Do we really live on such a knife-edge? I looked around at the solid reality of the flat that had once been my home. TV, slightly singed mat and a circle of cat-fluff that pointed out, to any interested onlookers, that Jasper had taken to sleeping on a basket of clean laundry. *And because of this, because of me, Sil could be killed on sight by any Hunter, any Enforcement agent.*

I thought of the nights we'd spent, his cool arms holding me while I slept, the dark, earthy scent of his skin and the way his demon reacted to my presence, coiling and writhing inside him like an affectionate snake. The way his nearness made me feel that anything was possible, the half-amused grey flicker of his eyes telling a whole story of humanity lost and regained. *And without him? What would I be? I've loved him so long that I can't even remember a time when he wasn't there, first as an irritating, self-absorbed, image-conscious assistant in the Otherworld office and then, increasingly, as the only thing worth fighting for. If he ... if anything happens to him then Liam can have the office, can have my job with its humiliations and its anxieties. I won't care. There will be nothing to care about ever again, just an empty hole where my soul used to be, and the ringing knowledge that it was all because of me.*

Chapter Forty-Two

Sil sat in the kitchen and let the homely atmosphere drape itself around his shoulders like an attempt at comfort. His demon sculled inside him, lazy after the surfeit of emotion, but he couldn't relax, even with the cosy kitchen, the smell of coffee and toast wafting, with just a hint of second-hand dog biscuits, courtesy of the sleepily exuding Labrador on the mat.

The tug of Jessica's connection was almost constant now, like a thread drawing ever tighter between them; he could almost feel her at the other end. *Gradually, so gradually, she is losing everything ... Her certainties are no longer sure, and yet she endures ...* He held out a hand, imagining her at the tips of his fingers; randomly impressionistic, like a synaesthetic Picasso after a night on magic mushrooms – energetic hair overlaid with her wicked smile and, beneath it all in a wild dance, that luscious body, curves and vanilla and excitement.

He sighed and ran his tongue over fangs that nipped at his lips. *Oh, Jessie. My predicament is purely physical; yours runs through your soul and your heart, and yet both of us are lost.* But he, at least, had hope. He had Zan. The vampire who had been with him through so much, whose analytical mind and steadfast nature would find a way out of a certain death sentence if anyone could. And Jess? She had only herself, a devoted but impractical for all useful purposes, family, and Liam. No magic, no glamour at her disposal, just paperclips and chaos. That crazy way she had of seeing hope and answers in the unfathomable depths, when all seemed lost. *Unionised zombies?* Sil let out a small laugh, which raised the dog's head for a moment. *Genius. Raise their profile and the majority of the human population will rush to their defence – no-one wants their sewers to clog or their electrical power to cease. They just needed a presence, to stop being the backroom boys that nobody takes any notice of.*

The idea rammed into his mind so quickly that he jumped to his feet to dispel the energy and prevent it from blowing his head off. Suddenly power was singing in his veins again; he shrugged off the despondency that had weighted him down like a metal jacket these past weeks, and the lightness of hope drove his demon into a whirling frenzy deep in his chest. *An idea.*

Chapter Forty-Three

A few days later and Dad wasn't exactly up and dancing, but he was showing signs of being stronger, and discharge was definitely imminent.

'Is *he* still at the farm?' my mother asked from the corner of her mouth, like a spymaster in training. 'I mean, he's welcome to stay, of course, but your father'—a quick glance over her shoulder—'there are going to be doctors and people coming and going and we can't ... it might not be safe.'

I gave her a tight smile. All I could see was that file of letters she'd held from me. All that knowledge about Rune, everything I was, and my mother had hidden it away and not intended me to find out until she was dead and gone and didn't have to deal with the fallout. 'I'll think of something.'

'Are you all right, dear?' A hand on my arm that I nearly shook off.

'I'm dealing with things,' I said. 'A lot of things.'

My mother knew me well. Better, probably, than I understood. Her eyes were shrewd and there was an unfamiliar element in her voice now. 'Jessica. Just remember, everything we did, your father and I, it was always to keep you safe. That's all we ever wanted, you to be safe.' Her hand travelled down until it rested on mine. 'And your Sil wants that too, I know it. Please, look after each other.'

I nodded. There was a strange heavy sensation near my heart and a tiny voice whispering in my ear that *this* was my real mother. Rune might have given birth to me, might have written me nice letters about her hopes and fears for me, might even have *cared*, but this woman had sat up at night with me while I cried myself to sleep over dying kittens and lost boyfriends.

My heart hurt suddenly at the thought of these two people worrying so much about me. 'If we ever get him out of your house, Mum, I promise that I will never let him out of my sight again.'

She smiled now, and I wasn't sure if it was because of what I'd said, or because I'd underlined it with her real title. 'Good. Love isn't always easy, dear.' A glance over at the bed. 'I should know: I married your father.'

We smiled a complicitous smile at the waywardness of men, although to my knowledge my father had never gone berserk and bitten his way through a crowd. He had, apparently, been a terror with thrown board rubbers though. I left the hospital and headed for the office.

'Who are you?' Liam didn't even turn around as I came in.

'The person with arcane knowledge of the workings of the petty cash system.' I sat at my desk. 'Anything happening?'

'Zan is coming over. He has, apparently, got "issues of concern", but then Zan can get concerned over the quality of the paper they print bus tickets on, so I shouldn't worry too much about that.'

'Oh good. Something I don't have to worry about, that's a first. Why haven't you made me a coffee?'

Liam sniffed and began gathering mugs. Mine, I noticed, had been rinsed out and had lost the patina of coffee-aging that had given anything contained in the mug a character all of its own. And a taste like Bovril. 'It's been a couple of days. I didn't think you were coming back. I was *this* close to getting a nice matching set of bone china, with birds on. And Belgian chocolate cookies, which are, quite frankly, wasted on you. You've got a palate like a blacksmith's apron.'

I ignored Liam's impression of an oppressed mass and sat down at my computer, where the familiarity of the Tracker program, the uneven stacks of paper threatening to overflow the desk and the smell of coffee only slightly undercut by the odour of damp carpet, soothed my frazzled nerves. Even the opposing neatness of Liam's corner of the room had its own kind of unchaotic reassurance to offer, and I felt a small pang, realising that this place was far more home to me than almost anywhere else, certainly more than the palatially chilly rooms of Zan's house.

And then, I couldn't not say it any longer. 'So, have you told them yet? At Head Office?'

The clattering in the kitchen paused. 'Told them what?' And then the disruption of the Emergency Biscuit bucket – he knew exactly what I meant and was dealing with it in his own, particular way. His head appeared back around the office door, followed shortly afterwards by a plate of chocolate digestives. 'No.'

'Liam ... I understand. Really, I do. And, quite honestly, you're welcome to it, although I would recommend that you get some cheap plastic overtrousers and a rather more robust approach to innards before you take over.' My face was stiff; I could feel my expression setting into what I was hoping was 'good-natured acceptance', although felt rather more like 'rigor mortis'. 'I've decided I'm going to go and work with the zom— err ... the Ambulatory Deceased.'

Liam plonked the plate down on the middle of my desk. 'As what? Professional Sticker-Onner?'

'I'll think of something. PR, that sort of thing.'

Liam snorted. 'Don't be – and I am probably going to regret saying this – bloody stupid. This job is *you*, Jess, the vamps and the politics and the apologising; you're hardly going to get much action working for a bunch of guys with thumbs so opposable they fight each other.'

Hope swooped on my heart like a falcon on a mouse. 'You need the job, Liam, you said so.'

He pursed his mouth around a biscuit. 'Not behind your back, Jessie. If I do it, I do it with your blessing. I wait until you're out before I download *Doctor Who,* I wouldn't wait until you were out and then take your job.'

A polite cough from the doorway. 'I do hope I am not intruding on what could be, despite its volume, a private conversation.'

'Hello, Zan.' I didn't look at him. 'To what do we owe what I am absolutely not going to call a pleasure?'

'I have an offer to make. From what I overheard, it may be considered apposite.'

Now I did look at him. There seemed to be something about him today, something almost *energetic,* which was not a word I'd normally associate with Zan. 'Unless you are about to offer me a lifetime's supply of chocolate biscuits, Zan, I really don't think you've got anything I want.'

Zan stepped forward. His clothes contrasted with Liam's chain-store specials, pale creamy colours that made his skin look even more bloodless than usual. 'On the contrary,' he said. 'Liam has told me about your ... difficulties with York Council, and his hopes for his own future. And you were just telling most of the neighbourhood your feelings on the subject.'

I looked from the vampire to Liam. 'Have you been indulging in casual chit chat with the opposition again? I am cutting your biscuit ration and you can say goodbye to me signing the petty cash receipts next time you buy more duct tape than *any* person can safely use to fix piping.'

'He's also told me that it's really him running York, which you have managed to keep to yourself for quite some time, so I think we should listen to him.' Liam perched on the edge of my desk. 'Go on, Zan.'

Zan was looking me straight in the eye. Since he seemed to regard making direct eye contact as only one step down from exchanging bodily fluids, I felt my heart speed up, and it wasn't with desire. 'What is it?'

Zan sat down at Liam's desk, although I did notice that he checked the chair before he did so. 'Jessica, I am going to ask something of you,' he said, turning those green-glass eyes on me again. 'You made a promise, when you asked me to help Sil. You promised that you would pay whatever price I asked, and here and now is where I need it to be paid, without question or prevarication. Although,' he added, with a more everyday tone to his voice, 'since I already know you, I am well prepared for a good deal of questioning and prevarication.'

My skin was prickling. 'But you haven't helped him.'

An inclination of the head. 'And yet, you must admit, I haven't killed him either.'

'That is *not* the same thing!'

'And there may ... and I stress that, just *may* be a way.'

I sat up very straight. 'How?'

An elegant eyebrow raised. 'I want you.'

Liam stared. 'No, sorry, if anyone's going to be making her life a misery, then that position is already taken by me.'

'What do you mean, you want me?' I said, groping behind me until I felt the edge of my desk, so that I could lean against it. 'Think very carefully before you answer this next question: *in what context*? Because I think I've had just about all the skank I can take for one lifetime, thank you very much.'

'I have interviewed your "mother" quite extensively.' Zan gave the inverted commas extra inversion. 'Her opinion of your character, your conduct during your school years, all lead me to think that, despite your rather'—he gazed around the office, clearly searching for a word that wouldn't prejudice me into beating him to death with the pencil sharpener—'*original* approach to working methods, you would be an asset to Otherworld Affairs. Or, at least, a fairly useful member of the team. You could continue in your Liaison activities, just ... from the other side, as it were.'

I opened and closed my mouth a few times.

'If you're going to do that, at least shove a biscuit in,' Liam said at last. 'What exactly are you trying to say, Zan? We're not good at long words here, although madam is cracking at anything with four letters in, as I think we might be about to find out.'

Zan sighed. 'You must forgive me, I mean, I would *request* that you come and work for Otherworld Affairs, Jessica. Liam has led me to believe that your council is no longer satisfied with your work.'

I bared my teeth at Liam, who actually looked excited. 'What he said. I mean, no pressure, Jess, but ... no, actually, this is real pressure. If I press any harder you'll have me engraved on your back.'

'And I believe your talents could be more efficiently used if you worked for us.'

'What?' Yes, all right, I was going to need a job; preferably with an employer that didn't believe Monopoly money was legal tender, but, seriously? Working for *Zan*?

There was a momentary silence, which Liam broke. 'There's logic to it, Jess,' he said. 'If you think about it. Come clean about your demon dad, no more hiding, proper working conditions with holidays – a real office ...'

'But what about Sil?' I finally managed to stammer out. 'What's going to happen to him?'

Zan gave a dismissive flick of his head.

'Oh no you don't, you bastard ...' I shot around my desk and put myself squarely in the vampire's eyeline so he couldn't avoid looking at me. 'What are you planning?'

Suddenly Zan was standing. The office had become smaller, darker and was tinged with a hint of red light from his eyes. 'I will not tell you.'

'You're going to kill him, aren't you? Have all this over, sweep him away as though he'd never been, and, wallop, shove a demon's daughter and – and this really hasn't escaped me however hard you've tried to gloss over it – your *potential nemesis* into your office.'

'*No*!' The vampire's voice wasn't loud, but the command it carried rippled through the office as though it tore holes in the air. 'Jessica. If everything goes according to plan, he will not die. But in order for this plan to be put into place, in order for your lover to be saved, I need to know that you will do as I ask.'

The three of us stood in silence for a moment. My heart was making my ears pulse and there was a skim of sweat along my neck and down my back. *Work for Zan? But ... a fully funded office, proper holidays, regular hours and the kind of technology that Silicon Valley could only dream of?*

'I'll do it,' I said. 'As long as Liam comes with me.'

Liam looked around the office and gave a dramatic sigh that barely covered his expression of relief and renewed hope. 'First, Jessie, we should ask for relocation expenses. Then we should ask for a flamethrower.'

Chapter Forty-Four

It took two days for it to sink it. Two days during which I spent most of my time staring into cooling coffee while Liam packed boxes of 'indispensable documents', which mostly looked like back copies of *Doctor Who* magazines, and sang.

'Come on, it'll be great!' He poked me with the corner of a pile of papers. 'Cheer up, Jess. We're going to get an office with a carpet that doesn't sound like gravel when you walk on it – hell, we might even get a proper coffee maker.'

'We've got one. It's you. Except you're so improper it's practically obscene.' I took a deep breath and a mouthful of almost cold coffee. 'Seriously, Liam. Am I doing the right thing?'

He stopped midway through emptying a desk drawer. 'Jessie. What part of "technology that works without being wound up and a proper pay structure" don't you get? Okay, technically they're the opposition, but you're going to be doing Liaison still, aren't you? Same job, better biscuits – look at it that way, if it helps.'

I smiled. 'Yeah, I guess. And Sarah …?'

'Is delighted.' Liam crouched back onto his haunches. 'And I know you partly did this for me, so, thanks.'

My attempts at rebuttal were shrugged off as he stood to answer the ringing telephone, for which I was glad, but Liam's sudden drop in expression made me stand up. 'What? What is it?'

'It's HQ. Someone has seen Sil at Whitby. They've sent the Hunters, Jess …'

'Whitby? What, Dracula, abbey, moonlit ruins Whitby?' What the hell would he be doing out there? Running? Trying to escape? But … Zan said he had a plan.'

'You need to get there. Now.'

I was just standing, arms by my sides, as though the suddenness of the news had paralysed me. 'But … seriously? Where's Zan? What's he doing about this?'

Liam pulled my jacket down from the back of the door and I had the sudden, stupid thought, *I'm going to miss that coat hook*. 'Zan will meet us there.' He bundled the jacket into my arms.

'Did HQ say that?'

'Yes. Yes, they did. Now, get in the car.'

We ran down the stairs and out to Liam's Fiat, all the while questions were storming through my brain like an invading troop: *Whitby? Why go there? Why is he running?* And the follow-up thought: *He's found out whatever Zan was planning and he's running away from it … I have to stop the Hunters, have to tell them what's going on, that he's not really guilty.*

Liam put his foot down, making the little engine grumble and the strange knocking sound from the back became an insistent thrum, especially as we climbed up over the moors. *Did Sil want to die? Was this his version of throwing himself on his sword?*

The car grumbled and rumbled along the narrow lane that led to the abbey car park. Luckily it was late evening and the lingering tourists and sightseers were being hustled away by a couple of uniformed Enforcement, Whitby contingent, who were trailing green and white chequered tape across the entrances to the abbey. I was weak with relief to see a large Bentley that had to be Zan's. *Zan can stop this; he can make something happen.* Liam yanked the car around with complete disregard for marked parking bays so I could rush over to where Zan was standing by the wall to the abbey. When I looked around I could see a press car with a couple of local journos leaning against it, chatting and smoking. An

Enforcement wagon was parked inconspicuously at the very far end of the car park next to a showy Range Rover Evoque with tinted windows, which just *had* to be the Hunters' vehicle. They'd never learned the art of secrecy, and I'm sure they thought that subtleties and subtitles were the same thing.

'What's happening?' There must have been panic on my face, because Zan regarded me with as much distaste as if it had been leftover soup on my upper lip.

'He is in there.' Zan looked over to the ruins of the abbey, hanging in the darkening sky, standing against the horizon like sunset's dentures. He and Liam exchanged a look. 'Hiding.'

There was a distant tug from that connection that lay between Sil and I. Faint and diminished, as though he'd cut any mental ties we might have had, and these were the death throes. 'But why the hell would he be here?' I scrambled up the wall, trying to gain enough purchase to get to the top, drop down on the far side, get in there, *do something*. Overhead the Hunter airborne division, an old helicopter that used to be used for spraying bracken, circled and illuminated random patches of grass.

'We do not know.' Zan gave a shrug. 'Attempting an escape?'

'And you're not doing anything to stop this?'

The back door of the Land Rover burst open and four Hunters jumped out, radios crackling, straightening their jackets and jutting their chins in case of telephoto lenses. They were all armed – rifles with night-sights – and wearing their usual York Hunter combat gear of structured suits and Converse trainers. After a quick word with the journalists, and a couple of photos, they moved off, talking to the helicopter team through their headsets, heading towards the entrance to the abbey. 'They're going to kill him. Zan, please, you must do something!' My voice rose in a shriek that drew the brief attention of the Hunters.

'Miss Grant?' One of the Hunters, Grant or Jez or something butch like that, lifted his rifle in a salute. 'Presume you're here to identify the target?'

I gave a low moan. 'No. I came ... This has to stop. We can talk about this, can't we? I mean, there are things you don't know about the situation, about how he came to attack ...'

Zan gave Liam A Look, and I found myself hustled away by one elbow. Liam dragged me away from the wall to the abbey and out onto the headland, where the fields slowly crumbled into the sea. 'Jess, you have to shut up,' he said urgently. 'You are going to get yourself into so much trouble if you even so much as *hint* at what Sil was up to in London. We don't know anything, right?'

'We have to stop them!' I caught at his sleeve, tugging his arm like a child. 'Why are we here, otherwise?'

'Zan is here to make sure they shoot the right man. You're here because Liaison has to be, and I'm here because I'm driving. And that's our story. Jess. Jess!' He grabbed at me and used his body to stop me moving. 'You have to let this happen.'

'He's there!' The shout went up, and I saw the Hunters run, swarming towards the stone walls, now highlighted in the dusk by the slightly lighter sky. They fanned out across the ruins as the helicopter hovered, blades slicing the night and its spotlight cruel on the ground. I could see a distant figure, his movements rendered staccato by the wind that beat at the headland and the downdraught from the helicopter blades. And then Liam had a hand on my shoulder, pushing me, forcing me to turn away from the sight of my lover trying to keep stonework between him and the Hunters.

'Don't look, Jess, it's better if you don't.' Liam forced himself in front of me, hands on my shoulders, moving to block my view. I wrenched at him to see past, to catch glimpses of the dark figure beginning to climb, jerkily, irrationally, heading for the tallest point of the abbey stonework, where it jutted into the sky in an attempt to pierce the moon. Liam placed his hands on my cheeks to prevent me turning my head.

I fought him with all my strength, screaming in his face until he had to force me to the ground, pinning me there as the words became noises, then sobs. I twisted my neck trying to see around him with a strength I never knew I had, but only got a montage of images: the flashes as photographers jostled; remnants of stonework standing high against a black sky; Sil, his dark coat flapping in the night-breeze, his hair whipped into length as it blew around the silhouette of his head, almost, for one second, looking like it had before that tragic hacking he'd given it. I struggled against Liam's hold, but it was surprisingly tight and efficient. 'No, Jess. Stay here.'

Anger and fear made me savage. I raked and bit and tried to kick. 'Sil!' The words were coming from a throat so dry that they came out cracked. '*Don't—*' But there was a shout from the Hunters, an answering, softer, call from Zan, and then a blast of rifle fire. Liam's grip relaxed just a fraction and I saw, in terrible detail, Sil, half way up the ruins of the tall west window, caught by the bullets. I started to scream again, wordless syllables and open-throated crying as the ammunition found its mark, and Sil's body jerked, lost its hold on the stonework and fell, crashing the sixty feet or so to the grassy floor beneath, to the accompaniment of more camera flashes.

Liam let me sit and the first thing I focused on was that Zan was there, by the body. I saw him look down at his friend, his colleague, the crumpled shape spread on the innocently soft-looking grass. He nodded to the Hunters, who shouldered their rifles and went off to do some interviews with the journalists, while Enforcement, after a quick conclave, began coiling up the green tape. Liam increased his hold again, moving up to grab me by the neck to stop me ducking out of his grasp. 'Hush, Jess, it's all over now,' he said. 'He's gone.'

I turned my head, collapsing down into the grass, away from the sad shape now being draped in Zan's long overcoat, almost tenderly, away from the smug Hunter brigade being asked about their favourite foods and their taste in music, and broke.

'What am I going to do?' The pain was so bad I couldn't breathe. Didn't want to breathe. Wanted the world to stop turning and go back, unmake this moment so that I could change it. 'He was everything to me, Liam, *everything*.' The fight had gone now, with the feeling in my hands. It felt as though every agony in the universe was inside me, like I'd taken all the pain from the world and eaten it down. If I'd been able to move my fingers I would have clawed out my own heart and thrown it to the moon. I had no use for it any more. Liam sat and cradled me on the tussocky grass; I could feel the muscles in his shoulder, tense against me, smell the blood that I'd drawn on his skin, and all I could think was that these would be the last sensations I ever felt, the last things I ever smelled, that would mean anything. Sil and I were over. Everything was over.

Liam stroked my head. 'Jessie ...' His voice was a little fractured too. 'It will all be for the best, trust me.' And his hold became more of an embrace. 'It will work out.'

I fought him again, trying to make his grip something that would hurt. Push the pain outside, take it from where it was eating its way through my heart, making my stomach retch into my throat. *Break my arm, break my neck, this pain may as well be all I am.*

'Let me die.' I was repeating the words over and over,

into the air and then, when Liam pulled me around, into his shoulder. 'Let me die, let me die …'

'Jessie.' Liam had my head tucked under his chin and I could see my name move in his throat. 'We need to move.'

No. I have to stay where I was when he died. Life cannot go on. But I was too numb to speak, and let Liam draw me to my feet, although he had to hold me up once I got there. As I leaned in, with his arm around my waist, I felt the familiar kick that was the connection between Sil and I, a tremble along its length, as though life still moved down it. 'I can still feel him, Liam.' The words whispered from dry lips. 'I can still *feel* him, like he's alive in here …' I touched the core of the connection, just below my ribcage. 'Moving. Here.'

'Yeah.' Liam tugged me a few steps closer to the ruins. A long, slow car was driving past the car park turning and into the abbey grounds, with one of Zan's vampire henchmen at the wheel and two more black-suited vamps in the back.

'They've come for the body.' The words had life of their own. 'They're going to take him away, Liam.'

It was fully dark now. Hunters and Enforcement, with the air of jobs efficiently, if not well, done were packing back into their vehicles. The journalists took a few more pithy sound bites and piled into their car, probably to head down the hill to the nearest pub. Zan was still standing by the body, while the three vamps readied the hearse to take the remains. I could hardly see through the swollen wrecks that my eyes had become, and when Liam tried to move me towards the car I fell to my knees again. It was all I wanted. To embrace the earth and lie here quietly in the cold air – the last thing Sil had felt, before the bullets.

The car blocked my view of the body, and the vamps didn't seem in any rush to load it. Zan was standing beside it; without his coat his loose jacket and pencil-slim trousers were tugged into fractals by the wind, but he didn't show any sign of feeling the cold. 'We need to go to Zan,' Liam said, dragging me to my feet. 'He needs you there.'

I was too numb to remark, too dead to care, feeling nothing but the hot wire sensation in my midriff as Liam led me over towards where Zan stood, surrounded by the three vampires who'd brought the car.

'Jessica.' Zan inclined his head towards me.

'You let them shoot him.' There was no inflection to my words. I couldn't have told you how I felt then. Whether I hated Zan, whether I understood what he'd done, anything. I didn't care. There was nothing left to care about.

'Well, yes.' Zan nodded to Liam. 'Is the field of play clear?'

Liam looked around us. 'We'll have to load up and take him down to Vamp HQ, just in case, but, yep, for now I think we're clear.' He tried to lead me around to the other side of the car, but I balked and shied like a horse scenting blood.

'No. I ... can't, not yet, Liam. I don't want to see—'

'Oh, butch up, Jess,' he said, and shoved me firmly around the back of the hearse to the body on the far side. But Sil wasn't lying blood-pooled and broken on the cold grass where I expected him, where my heart couldn't bear to let my eyes look. The patch of ground where I'd seen him shot down bore nothing but a slick of dew and some cast-off ice cream wrappers, and the corpse itself was sitting up with its back propped against the passenger door with Zan's coat draped over its knees, smoking a furtive cigarette.

'*Ryan*?' The shock made my knees buckle again and I stumbled against the car.

The zombie gave me a sheepish grin. His chest was peppered with holes from the rifle fire, totally ruining one of Sil's floppy-fronted shirts and his long, leather coat. The dark wig he'd been wearing was askew, giving him the look of a rakish scarecrow. 'Hi, Jess.'

Slowly, I turned on my heel to see Zan and Liam grinning at me. Well, Liam was grinning, Zan had mitigated his usual condescension to a slightly softer grimace. My mind was fragmented with confusion: I couldn't believe any of what I was seeing. Everything was filtered through the grey mist of shock and disbelief, a shock that had sent me so far down inside myself that I couldn't even muster anger at their amusement. 'What's happened?'

Liam looped an arm around my shoulders. 'You had to be believable. No-one cares what I think, and Zan was convincingly ... well, Zan-like. We just needed you to completely believe that it was Sil dying out here.'

Ryan finished his cigarette. 'And we owed you, Jess, so I didn't mind. Quite good fun, really. I haven't climbed so high since I got my finger stuck in that lift door on a service crane.' A few last puffs of smoke billowed out of his chest cavity and floated away on the breeze. The greyness in my head threatened to block everything for a moment. I wished I could pass out, just be away from this situation, whilst my mind grew so cold and still that I half-thought I was dying by degrees. My whole body was a solid pain.

'So ...' My voice broke again, but I collected it up. 'Where is Sil?' I was surprised at how like me my voice sounded.

And then the tug came again, low in my stomach, that silver chord playing into the night. 'Here, Jess.' A vamp stepped forward from where he'd been concealed by stonework and the bulk of the car. His hair had been shaved, he'd lost the three-day-stubble that always covered his chin and he was wearing a generic black suit and dark glasses. Surrounded by others in the same clothes, he was almost unrecognisable.

Thump. My pulse moved in my throat, I felt my skin kick with it. *Thump*. As though my heart had remembered how to beat again. As though he was all I needed to be alive. I stood and stared. And then came the feelings, flooding through me in a tide that rose and rose until it filled my eyes and nose and took the place of the air, blocked out that windy headland with sensation roaring in. Unstoppable.

I flung myself at him, feeling his strength, smelling that scent of spices and rare wood, knowing that he was safe, he was here, he was *mine*. I couldn't speak, there was nothing I could say that he couldn't tell from the way I held on to him, as though someone had taken my ground away and he was all the contact I had left with the earth.

'My love', he whispered. '*My love*. You should know that not even death would make me leave you.'

I couldn't let go. My hands returned to him over and over, as though even my fingers couldn't believe the touch of him. I felt as though all my internal organs had been displaced, everything shuffled around so that my heart was the only part of me that still worked. And it was so busy holding Sil in its depths that it almost forgot to do its job. Relief made my head sing and now the grey mist held a hot scarlet tint as all the emotions that had been on hold while I grieved began to fight their way forward.

'Whose idea was it?'

The three of them exchanged looks, as though no-one was willing to take the blame. Then Sil cleared his throat. 'It was mine. At least, the outline was mine; Zan filled in some of the detail and Liam suggested that, since the zombies appeared to owe you a favour, actually *seeing* me die may give our charade that ring of authenticity.'

My fingers were clenched in Sil's, not daring to let go for fear that he may be snatched from me; that this was all a hallucination, that grief and terror were attempting to protect me from the loss. But the feel of him, the taste of him on my tongue, these were real. The almost silken draw of the connection between us, that was real. The touch of his cool skin where his hand stroked the tender skin of my wrist, that was real. *He is real. He is safe.* In this moment only the knowledge that he was standing beside me kept me from hurling myself at Zan and Liam in a ball of howling fury.

'What happens now?' I became aware that my cheeks were smeared with snot and mud when Sil reached a gentle finger out and brushed at them.

'I am dead, Jess. You saw me die.'

'Yes, but …'

Zan interrupted. 'Sil had to be "disappeared". This seemed the most effective way for that to happen.'

As though it had gained a life of its own, the hand that wasn't clutching Sil's shot out at the end of my arm and smacked Zan hard and loudly across the face. 'You bastard. You utter and complete *turd*! How dare you do this to me?'

Zan gave me a level stare. He didn't even attempt to touch the reddening mark which stood livid on his skin, he just stared me down with a hellish glow smouldering deep in those green eyes. 'You had a better suggestion?' One hand raised and moved quickly, removing any atoms that I might carelessly have left on his surface. 'I thought not. Sometimes, Jessica, one must act upon the moment that presents itself, not enter a debate.' His demon slid behind his expression, ecstatic at the emotional response. 'If we had to save Sil by committee vote, he would still be hiding with his life in peril.'

I couldn't speak. His dismissal of the agony I had been through was, although understandable from Zan, so cold-blooded that it cancelled out the heat of my anger, and all I could do was shake my head.

'We need to move.' Liam broke in to our staring competition. 'Get off this cliff before souvenir hunters start raking around for bent bullets and blood.'

'And you are so not off the hook either,' I said, quietly but with a goodly amount of future ill-will injected into my tone.

'Hey, you bit me! And I've got scratches that look as

though I've had a passionate affair with a Siberian tiger, so I'm up for calling it quits.' Liam's hand rested, briefly, on my shoulder, a passing touch of empathy, if not apology. 'And, like Zan said, nothing better was coming up, so …'

'If I may speak, as the corpse in question.' Sil squeezed my fingers. 'I really think we should take Liam's suggestion and move somewhere a little less public. The office, perhaps? Because, trendy as my new hairstyle may be, it does leave a certain amount to be desired in the heat-retention line.'

I looked at him again and my heart wouldn't stand still, it was leaping like a circus act. The shaven head made his face look entirely different, more regal and ninety per cent eyes. 'What happens next?' The question was quiet. 'To you. To us.'

Zan answered, and I noticed he'd retreated beyond arm's length, clearly I still had a murderous look in my eye. 'Sil will continue to work in our office, but it will be strictly in a backroom capacity, and there will be certain … measures taken to ensure his appearance remains altered.'

Sil smiled. 'We may still be together. It must be only when nobody is looking, of course, but in the privacy of the house …' His dark look and the touch of his fingers made me shiver. 'We may be as we were.'

'Oh, get a room,' Liam said, cheerfully. 'One without windows, though.'

'Won't anyone notice?' I managed. My emotions were still sitting there on that knife edge between ecstasy and breaking down in irrevocable tears, as though my heart couldn't make up its mind which way to fall. Going with practicalities was pretty much the middle ground as far as it was concerned.

Zan gave a dark look. 'It will be a part of your new job, Jessica, to ensure that they don't. And, just to establish some ground rules, that does *not* mean by burying the entire office in biscuit wrappers and pieces of scribbled-upon paper.'

'Right. Back to Vamp Central?' Liam asked.

Ryan was, uncomplainingly, stretched out in the cheap coffin in the back of the hearse. Another of the advantages of zombies – they could really do 'waiting'. 'Not too many bumps, guys,' he said. 'These things are really flimsy.'

'Customers don't usually complain,' Sil said, closing the boot. And in a parody of a funeral cortege, we drove back to York with the hearse leading the way.

Chapter Forty-Five

Sil and I lay in the paddock-sized bed, wound around in sheets and sepia-toned in moonlight. I still couldn't stop myself from touching him, although now passion had burned down to a low-lit gas and a vibration running under my skin.

'Wow.'

'I have missed you. Missed this.' He half-sat against the galleon-sail pillows 'I never thought it could be so, but I missed this life we have made.' A cool, long-fingered hand tangled in my hair. 'I am to be known as Jonathan now. Sil died at the hands of a Hunter, and so I reclaim my old name, the name that means something.'

'*Jonathan*,' I tasted his name. In some ways it brought him closer to me, made him more human. But in others it drove a tiny wedge between us – Jonathan had been married to Christina. Had a son and a daughter. Marriage, a lifetime commitment, not something I could offer someone who would live three times as long as me; for all he said he would be with me until the end, could I trust that? He would grow slowly towards the grave with his demon-enhanced beauty intact to the end, whilst I would start to look more and more like Yoda. Would he still love me *then*? And children ... Did he want to attempt to fully regain the life he'd lost by having a family? How did I feel about that – after all, with my confused bloodline my offspring may turn out to be anywhere along the continuum from enhanced human to outright demon.

But all that was in a future we hadn't yet contemplated. Had barely even begun to acknowledge as existing for us. We were here. Now. Alive. Undercover, but alive.

'Are you ready to forgive us for our deception today?' Sil

tipped my chin with a finger. 'We really did think it was for the best to keep you in ignorance.' And now his lips were close. 'Forgive us.'

'Of course I do.' I brushed his mouth with mine. 'You, anyway. The others can await my wrath. Liam lives on his nerves anyway.'

A laugh. 'Very wise of him.' Fingers moved from my hair to stroke my neck. 'But can you truly forgive me? For all that I did?'

I laid my head against his chest. 'You did what you had to, to stay alive.' My mind still hadn't let go of that image from the London camera of Sil standing in that street, blood on his mouth. And his eyes … they had been so *animated*. A glimpse of the vampire within the man I loved, the creature that made him what he was. 'And I can live with that.' Now I half sat, to look in his face. 'But if you ever do anything like that again …'

His eyes darkened from the pale sky-grey they'd turned during our love-making to a blue-black. Was that regret? And for what? His actions, or lost opportunities? 'Our relationship must be one of trust,' he said quietly. 'Or it is nothing.'

'Er, lying in bed with you. No noticeable armoured clothing.' And then I dropped the slightly sarcastic tone. 'I trust you.'

But it cuts both ways, I thought, losing myself to the feeling of his fingers on my skin. *You have to trust me too. And, given the information that has turned up about me, I'm not entirely sure that* I *trust me.*

'And how do you feel about this new position of yours?' His voice was still quiet, but his body had grown more relaxed, as though a secret fear had evaporated.

'What, the one where you …'

'Working for Zan.' A gentle hand moved lower and my

back broke out in pleasurable goose-pimples at the cool surety of that touch. 'The human government will not dare to touch you whilst you are under his protection, but there is still the matter of the rumours surrounding a new uprising.'

'Mmmm. Uprising. I like the sound of that. *Uprising*.' I writhed closer to him. 'But you're right. We need to find out where that rumour is coming from. Make sure it gets firmly … ooh, yes, *firmly* handled.' I shivered as his fingers moved from my back and trailed around my shoulder, passed under the cover and drew lace on my skin with their tips. 'I just wish Mum and Dad were allowed to know that you're still alive.'

'I am sorry. But for the safety of all, I must remain dead.'

'Yes. Don't worry: Zan explained it to me. In great detail. I think he would have used pictures if I hadn't threatened to stake him.'

Fangs just beginning to descend, he kissed my arm. 'Zan is very pleased that you have come to work for us.' Lower … 'But then, so many things about you are pleasing, Jessica.'

'I suppose I'm your boss now?'

The fingers continued their descent. 'Yes. Zan is handling the press release.'

I started to giggle. 'That's going to put a stop to the *York Herald* doorstepping me – I can threaten to go round there and set the vamps on them. Oh, I wish I could see their faces …' The giggles stopped and I bit my lip. 'Hey, if I'm your boss, I can tell you what to do, can't I?'

'Mmmmm.'

So I bent and whispered my instructions into his ear. And Jonathan complied with all of them, until I fell into pieces beneath him.

About the Author

Jane was born in Devon and now lives in Yorkshire. She has five children, four cats and two dogs. She works in a local school and also teaches creative writing. Jane is a member of the Romantic Novelists' Association and has a first-class honours degree in creative writing.

Jane writes comedies which are often described as 'quirky'. *Falling Apart* is Jane's fifth Choc Lit novel and the sequel to *Vampire State of Mind*. Her UK debut, *Please don't stop the music*, won the 2012 Romantic Novel of the Year and the Romantic Comedy Novel of the Year Awards from the Romantic Novelists' Association. Her other novels published with Choc Lit are *Star Struck* and *Hubble Bubble*.

For more information on Jane visit
www.janelovering.co.uk
www.twitter.com/janelovering

More Choc Lit

From Jane Lovering

Please don't stop the music

Winner of the 2012 Best Romantic Comedy Novel of the Year

Winner of the 2012 Romantic Novel of the Year

How much can you hide?

Jemima Hutton is determined to build a successful new life and keep her past a dark secret. Trouble is, her jewellery business looks set to fail – until enigmatic Ben Davies offers to stock her handmade belt buckles in his guitar shop and things start looking up, on all fronts.

But Ben has secrets too. When Jemima finds out he used to be the front man of hugely successful Indie rock band Willow Down, she wants to know more. Why did he desert the band on their US tour? Why is he now a semi-recluse?

And the curiosity is mutual – which means that her own secret is no longer safe ...

Visit www.choc-lit.com for more details including the first two chapters and reviews, or simply scan barcode using your mobile phone QR reader.

Star Struck

Our memories define us – don't they?

And Skye Threppel lost most of hers in a car crash that stole the lives of her best friend and fiancé. It's left scars, inside and out, which have destroyed her career and her confidence.

Skye hopes a trip to the wide dusty landscapes of Nevada – and a TV convention offering the chance to meet the actor she idolises – will help her heal. But she bumps into mysterious sci-fi writer Jack Whitaker first. He's a handsome contradiction – cool and intense, with a wild past.

Jack has enough problems already. He isn't looking for a woman with self-esteem issues and a crush on one of his leading actors. Yet he's drawn to Skye.

An instant rapport soon becomes intense attraction, but Jack fears they can't have a future if Skye ever finds out about his past …

Will their memories tear them apart, or can they build new ones together?

Visit www.choc-lit.com for more details including the first two chapters and reviews, or simply scan barcode using your mobile phone QR reader.

Vampire State of Mind

Jessica Grant knows vampires only too well. She runs the York Council tracker programme making sure that Otherworlders are all where they should be, keeps the filing in order and drinks far too much coffee.

To Jess, vampires are annoying and arrogant and far too sexy for their own good, particularly her ex-colleague, Sil, who's now in charge of Otherworld York. When a demon turns up and threatens not just Jess but the whole world order, she and Sil are forced to work together.

But then Jess turns out to be the key to saving the world, which puts a very different slant on their relationship.

The stakes are high. They are also very, very pointy and Jess isn't afraid to use them – even on the vampire she's rather afraid she's falling in love with …

This is the prequel to Falling Apart.

Hubble Bubble

Be careful what you wish for …

Holly Grey only took up witchery to keep her friend out of trouble – and now she's knee-deep in hassle, in the form of apocalyptic weather, armed men, midwifery … and a sarcastic Welsh journalist.

Kai has been drawn to darkest Yorkshire by his desire to find out who he really is. What he hadn't bargained on was getting caught up in amateur magic and dealing with a bunch of women who are trying *really hard* to make their dreams come true.

Together they realise that getting what you wish for is sometimes just a matter of knowing what it is you want …

To be published in December 2014:

How I Wonder What You Are

Jane Lovering

"Maybe he wasn't here because of the lights – maybe they were here because of him ..."

It's been over eighteen months since Molly Gilchrist has had a man (as her best friend, Caro, is so fond of reminding her) so when she as good as stumbles upon one on the moors one bitterly cold morning, it seems like the Universe is having a laugh at her expense.

But Phinn Baxter (that's Doctor Phinneas Baxter) is no common drunkard, as Molly is soon to discover; with a PhD in astrophysics and a tortured past that is a match for Molly's own disastrous love life.

Finding mysterious men on the moors isn't the weirdest thing Molly has to contend with, however. There's also those strange lights she keeps seeing in the sky. The ones she's only started seeing since meeting Phinn ...

Visit www.choc-lit.com for more details, or simply scan barcode using your mobile phone QR reader.

CLAIM YOUR FREE EBOOK

of

You may wish to have a choice of how you read *Falling Apart*. Perhaps you'd like a digital version for when you're out and about, so that you can read it on your ereader, iPad or even a Smartphone. For a limited period, we're including a **FREE** ebook version along with this paperback.

To claim, simply visit ebooks.choc-lit.com or scan the QR Code.

You'll need to enter the following code:

Q251403

This offer will expire June 2015. Supported ebook formats listed at www.choc-lit.com. Only one copy per paperback/customer is permitted and must be claimed on the purchase of this paperback. This promotional code is not for resale and has no cash value; it will not be replaced if lost or stolen. We withhold the right to withdraw or amend this offer at any time. Further terms listed at www.choc-lit.com.

Introducing Choc Lit

Choc Lit Spread

Twitter

Facebook